When the Wildflowers Bloom

Rupa Bhullar is a US-based Indian author. Her debut novel, *The Indigo Sun*, featured in several bestseller lists.

She also serves as a Senior Corporate Executive in the fintech industry. In 2015, she co-founded a non-profit dedicated to the development of rural education and infrastructure in India.

Rupa spent her childhood in Chandigarh and now lives in New Jersey with her husband, two sons and a golden retriever named Junior.

Follow her on social media: @rupa_bhullar

When the Wildflowers Bloom

Rupa Bhullar

Published by
Rupa Publications India Pvt. Ltd 2021
7/16, Ansari Road, Daryaganj
New Delhi 110002

Sales centres:
Allahabad Bengaluru Chennai
Hyderabad Jaipur Kathmandu
Kolkata Mumbai

Copyright © Rupa Bhullar 2021

This is a work of fiction. Names, characters, places and incidents are either the product of the author's imagination or are used fictitiously and any resemblance to any actual person, living or dead, events or locales is entirely coincidental.

All rights reserved.
No part of this publication may be reproduced, transmitted, or stored in a retrieval system, in any form or by any means, electronic, mechanical, photocopying, recording or otherwise, without the prior permission of the publisher.

ISBN: 978-93-90547-54-8

First impression 2021

10 9 8 7 6 5 4 3 2 1

The moral right of the author has been asserted.

Printed at Thomson Press India Ltd., Faridabad

This book is sold subject to the condition that it shall not, by way of trade or otherwise, be lent, resold, hired out, or otherwise circulated, without the publisher's prior consent, in any form of binding or cover other than that in which it is published.

*To those who hold a mirror
And point towards the sky
The ones who offer wings
Who remind us to try,
To those who let go, yet never ever leave
Becoming as we soar...
...the wind beneath*

Prologue

There are days we remember and days we can't forget. This happened to be both…

'How enchanting is this set up, Tara! It feels less like your backyard and more like a backdrop to some exotic fairy tale. Just watch how the comments start popping up left, right and centre as soon as I post this on Instagram,' Geetu chuckled, her eyes reflecting the twinkling glow of fairy lights, as she busily snapped the ambient setting and detailed accents to compile her perfect story.

The string of Edison bulbs crisscrossed over the lawn, creating a sparkling canopy. Fresh flower arrangements enhanced the elegant cream and gold table settings, with patio heaters and firepits creating subtle warmth.

For a moment, I stepped outside of my dismal mind and observed this set up from a spectator's view. It looked pretty, indeed; only if the reality were nearly as perfect as the appearance.

'Thank you, Geetu. I guess it kind of worked out.'

'Kind of worked out? Fabulous would be an understatement here! Stop undermining yourself, Tara. You've got to admit your brilliance with this creative stuff.'

'And to my point, remember your Sweet Sixteen? That evening is still etched in my memory. First, obviously because Sweet Sixteens weren't even a thing in Chandigarh back then, but second and more importantly, that incredible setting you pulled off even there. I still recall every detail so vividly—from those tall lamps to that raging bonfire and colourful streamers woven through lit-up trees. Even 22 years ago, I'd suggested you pursue a career in the creative space. But nope, all you ever wanted was to be a "happy mom", which no doubt you are, but talk about ambitious life goals!' Geetu laughed, nodding her head affectionately.

'Gosh, that was so long ago; feels like it was another life,' I smiled nostalgically as I reached for the spicy cauliflower served on silver platters, accentuated by a white candle votive.

'Anyway, you know me. These big bashes aren't exactly my thing. But since both my sisters happened to be in India for my birthday this year, I gave in to Tej's suggestion. And I did try adding a few touches here and there. These small details go a long way in creating a memorable experience,' I admitted.

'What can I say? You're gifted,' Geetu remarked emphatically.

'Well, o' well!' Tej interrupted. 'Someone seems quite eager to steal the credit here.'

A sharp stab of panic knocked me in my stomach, nearly expelling what I'd barely swallowed.

'I tell you Geetu, it's her taste all right, and no doubt she has fine taste, but taste goes only so far,' he claimed arrogantly, inching his short frame higher.

'In the end, it's money, my money that brings everything to life. I had standing instructions for the event manager to spend it like water, without thinking twice,' he claimed, wrapping his arm around my shoulder. 'No expenses spared. Whatever she demands—anything she puts her finger on. But it's hard to teach someone how to spend.'

'Expensive tastes are not so commonplace, you see,' he remarked disparagingly.

'Tastes need not be expensive to be refined, and money

doesn't always equate to elegance, Tej. I think it all came together equally well in a fraction of the budget,' I countered, releasing his confining grip around my arm.

'Maybe it did, by your standards, but certainly not mine,' Tej responded in a peal of condescending laughter as he turned to Geetu.

'Your friend here believes in frugality, you see. She will spare all indulgences and cut every corner to squeeze the most value out of money. She had the poor event manager secure quotes from three caterers. And in the end, all she wanted were these cheap lights and some plain flowers. Liliums,' he scoffed.

'I picked the wine and the orchids. This wine that you're drinking,' Tej pointed, running his finger lightly along the rim of the glass, 'is really fine. Rs. 20,000 for a bottle. It's French.

And even the invitations, how they set the tone for what's to follow! People don't get such statement cards printed for weddings, but I did, for her birthday. I do it all for her, but not everyone has it in them to be grateful. She doesn't look quite pleased or thankful, does she Geetu? Huh?' he questioned, casting a cold, disagreeable stare that lingered on long after he'd walked away.

I took a deep breath and turned to look away, far beyond the glittering lights into a pervasive darkness that I understood better.

I should have refrained from arguing. It was the last thing needed to fuel Tej's temper, but somewhere, I had grown tired. Tired of swallowing this humiliation every minute of my existence. And a minuscule existence it was, filled with shame, fear, subordination and that dismal feeling of utter rejection.

'Hey Geetu, why don't you go ahead and catch up with others, let me check on the kids real quick. I'll be right back,' I offered, clearing my throat as I stepped away.

Thankfully Meeta, Mala and mom were engrossed in a lighthearted conversation and failed to notice this unpleasant exchange.

Meeta, the oldest of the three of us, had always nurtured me under her wings like a second mother. Most of my kindergarten was spent sitting beside her, while she attended 4th grade classes, and following her from the restroom to the canteen like Mary's little lamb. Back then, it was hard to tell me apart from her shadow.

She also introduced the art of creative adventures into our plain, ordinary lives. 'Just imagine,' she would lead us on, as we warmly nestled around her, ushering us into these magical worlds where everything was possible.

Mala, the middle one, was feisty and rebellious. Armed with a 'but why' philosophy, she questioned even the simplest of norms. She often 'favoured' me as the scapegoat of choice for her daredevil experiments, where the probability of me witnessing the next sunrise hinged tentatively on the successful execution of her half-baked plans.

Nonetheless, if anyone so much as pointed a finger at me, she would go raging in fury to defend me, above all else. Herself included. For everything Mala might have been, she was righteous and fair. Always.

'Tara,' I heard Meeta call my name. 'Agreed, the birthday girl is in high demand tonight, but come, sit with us for a while,' she smiled, the mole below her full lip accentuating her delicate features.

'I'll join you in a few minutes, just going to check on the kids,' I confirmed, forcing a bleak smile.

I stood still, looking silently through the glass double doors that opened into the lobby. Mehar, my 13-year-old, revealed her pearly white teeth peeking through the metal braces as she giggled heartily with her best friend.

And my 11-year-old appeared intensely immersed in the

complex construction of a Lego Imperial Star, diligently connecting the tiny pieces. Sidak's brown curls dangled lightly on his forehead as he leaned intently over his elaborate assembly.

Their world still was as it had always been, empty but intact. There was neither a ripple nor a cloud, nor the faintest glimmer of sunshine.

'What are you looking at, Tara?' Meeta questioned as she walked up behind me.

'Not much, just watching the kids,' I answered, looking over my shoulder. 'This is what keeps me going—their innocent smiles and a world still holding up.'

Meeta glanced at me with knowing eyes and shook her head, pausing for a moment before reaching for my hand. 'Come, let's cut the cake now. It's getting late.'

I stood there, observing the brilliant candles marking a striking contrast to my years of insignificant existence.

'Happy Birthday, Tara!' a voice called out.

There was something about this voice. I recognized it. Beyond doubt.

I quickly spun around and found Vinay, my closest friend from school, standing in front of me, holding a bunch of flowers.

'Still as beautiful as I remember you! Not one thing about you has changed. Sorry, let me take it back, everything about you has gotten better with time. Tara Grewal—the timeless, priceless masterpiece!' he smiled.

My eyes widened and my jaw dropped. 'Is this for real? What a surprise! Goodness gracious, it's so good to see you, Vinay! When did you arrive from London? Gosh, 18 years and we meet here!' I exclaimed, gripped in equal measure by delight and bewilderment as he stepped forward for a hug.

Tej promptly turned around, looking towards me in questioning disgust, 'Am I missing something here?' he demanded, shuttling his gaze between Vinay and me.

Vinay smiled, extending his hand, 'So you are the lucky man, I presume. Vinay, Tara's friend from school,' he introduced himself.

'I was just complimenting your wife. Look at her, who can say she is married, let alone the mother of two young children. You married perfection. As lucky as a man gets!'

'You're right. I am a lucky man, indeed,' Tej remarked as he poured himself another drink and turned towards me.

'Surprise, surprise! Took me all these years and one birthday bash to realize you have many friends and a few admirers. I never quite knew!' he impressed in a deliberately caustic tone.

'Well buddy,' Vinay offered, his eyes gleaming with earnest warmth, 'in that case, we need to catch up. Tara Grewal, Miss Stephen's, was better known by her codename "The Star". Boys fell left, right and centre in her wake. And, man! What any girl would give to be her for just one day! I hope you realize what a feat you've accomplished by winning her over,' exclaimed Vinay, genuinely enthused. 'You've married *the* heartthrob of the town. The kind of girl everyone wanted to take home to their mothers.'

'Did you want to take her home to your mother?' Tej interjected, turning an awkward spotlight on Vinay.

'Of course, I was no different,' Vinay admitted, 'but Tara was!' he quickly recovered.

'Totally beyond reach... Like a true star. Much too timid to speak with boys, advances were neither accepted nor acknowledged. I tell you, she coursed through life wrapped in a bubble. What a good girl!'

'And for you, Tara, too bad if you regret not living your life while you had the chance. Literally, you could've had any man you put your finger on,' Vinay laughed, 'but I'm sure you decided well.

Tej must be worth the wait,' he affirmed, raising another toast.

'Cheers, buddy.'

Geetu nudged him, noting the obvious displeasure written across Tej's furrowed brow and pursed lips, made many shades darker from the deposit of nicotine and tar over the years.

His expensive taste in clothing, however, did project an appearance of sophistication. But only so long as he didn't open his mouth or limited himself to talking about history, one of the only respect-worthy interests of his life.

'Champagne is served, come, we're ready to cut the cake,' Meeta announced, handing me a glass.

'Not just yet. The birthday toast is on me,' Tej insisted as he clutched my arm, arresting my steps in place.

His bloodshot eyes conveyed an impending storm, accentuated by the tiny beads of sweat diffused along his prominently square forehead.

'Among all the admirers present here. And many that I shall never know about,' Taj added after a calculated pause, 'I raise this toast to your beauty,' he announced, popping open a bottle of champagne.

'Here love, do the honors!' Tej indicated, shoving the bottle towards my face.

'Relax, Tej. I have a glass. I will use that.'

'Why the glass? Wouldn't a taste of your lips sweeten the champagne for many?' he smirked, offering me the bottle again.

'Tej, please. Don't be ridiculous,' I muttered nervously, 'I told you I will drink from my glass.'

'Oh, will you?' he derided, lifting his head and arching his eyebrows in a questioning look that demanded an immediate apology.

'Yes,' I answered, a little defiant and a little afraid as my knees started to buckle under me.

His raging breath rose and fell against my cheek as he drew closer and plucked the glass from my hand. 'So now you will tell me how you prefer it?' he questioned. 'Hope you realize that I make you who you are. Even the nail paint on that tiniest finger of yours—I provide for.

Do yourself a favour, remember your place and don't dare to question me again. Ever. Now, come, take a sip.'

'Please, Tej. There is no need to create a scene here,' I urged, trembling inside.

'Oh yes, sweetheart, there is,' he responded, downing his fifth glass of whiskey.

My heart raced, my face flushed and my throat choked with tears. I knew what was coming.

'There absolutely is,' he iterated, smashing the glass on the floor. 'Among your many friends, admirers and beloved sisters, let's see who is willing to take you home and pay for you for the rest of your life. Anyone?' he mocked, raising my hand.

'Vinay—you, would you take her home?' he ridiculed, now inebriate.

'What nonsense, Tej? Stop this right here!' Mala demanded, forcing her way past the frozen spectators.

'And there comes your tempestuous sister to your rescue.'

'Mala, stay back, he's drunk,' I implored, struggling to look past my tears as I scouted for the house help.

'Bala,' I mumbled, reaching for my voice, 'Please assist sir to his room.'

Bala, the family's stout and steadfast caretaker, bolstered his shoulder under Tej's arm.

Tej struggled like a wounded beast, pushing Bala aside and charged forward in indignation. 'How dare you! You think you will tell me what to do? Who are you? Nothing, if not for my money! Go try to earn a living on your own. With your degree, all you will end up earning is if you go begging on the streets. Bachelors in English Literature! What a joke!' Tej laughed with a maliciousness that made me shudder. With fear, grief or loss, I did not know.

Mala trembled with rage. I squeezed her hand, begging her not to react.

Mala's well-defined jawline grew increasingly prominent beneath her soft face. Her pounding heart and rushing blood were distinctly palpable, perhaps more so since my own heart seemed to have stopped beating and the blood seemed cemented in my veins. I was rooted to the spot, numb and lifeless.

'Tej, stop embarrassing yourself and your family. Please leave,' insisted Mala, trying hard to maintain her composure.

'How dare you ask me to leave my house?' he demanded, his face livid with rage as he shoved her back.

'Tej, please, don't make this ugly,' I pleaded in tears.

'You!' he yelled, pointing a quivering finger at me, 'You stay out of it. You're the one who started this. Now face the consequences,' he snapped, muttering profanities under his breath as he repeatedly pushed me.

'Stop it, Tej,' Mala grabbed his hand.

I tried to intervene. A scuffle ensued.

The deafening sound of 'Get away, bitch' resounded in my ears as a violent push knocked me over with a thud.

I hit my head on the floor.

Everything started to blur. The voices began to fade.

I faintly heard Mala call out my name.

I think I passed out.

One

DRIVING past Verka Milk Bar and Ropar Wetland, I recalled some fond childhood memories of travel breaks by the riverside, enjoying hot tea with pakoras, following hours spent in the car singing, talking and daydreaming.

I couldn't help contrasting it to the numerous trips down the same road, with Tej and I sharing one car but different spaces. Each viewing a separate world, while the kids created theirs in the realm of gadgets. These countless hours were spent in close proximity, yet great distance.

I looked out at the familiar road. It remained ever so the same, but how the journeys kept changing!

I wondered what was so special about our rather simplistic childhood.

We neither drove in ultra-luxury cars nor had fancy surround sound systems to keep us entertained. It certainly couldn't have been the travel experience, but perhaps, it might have been the journey itself. Looking out that window, connecting with new experiences, with one another and with uninhibited flights of imagination.

I'd like to think it was this pure emotion of loving the moment and feeling loved in return that stuck with me.

Although, as far as I recall, mom and dad never quite expressed their love for us in words. I don't remember 'We love you,' being explicitly stated. Ever. It was just understood. Beyond doubt, beyond questioning. Evident in all they did and in all that they did not do.

For love, I guess, is neither a conviction nor an assurance. It is an unquestionable knowledge. No one needs to tell you they love you. You just know it—their love is experienced within you.

Snuggled in the womb of tender memories and comforted by the warm sunlight, I soon drifted off to sleep.

'Tara babyji,' I woke up to the sound of my name. It was the driver, Balwinder's voice.

'Are we already here?' I asked, rubbing my eyes groggily.

'Not yet, but we are close. To Green Avenue first, babyji?'

'No, Balwinder, straight to the farmhouse.'

A queer glint of brightness appeared in the distance.

'What is that Balwinder? Haven't noticed it before.'

'Oh, that! It's the golden gate. The newly built entrance to the city.'

'See babyji, how much our Punjab is progressing,' remarked Balwinder with a deep pride lacing his speech.

'That's right, I do hear about some great strides they are making in tourism.'

'You belong to someplace close, right?'

'Yes, babyji. Batala, it's about an hour from here. But Amritsar remains my hometown.'

'Progress is always good, but for me, Balwinder, this city will always remain my Ambarsar. That chaotic vintage town I remember with tangas, rickshaws, scooters and occasional cows crowding the crossroads.'

'Babyji, what would you remember of tangas? That was a long time ago.'

'I do, Balwinder. One time, biji and I took a trip on one to the dispensary. Speaking of the dispensary, would you please make a quick stop at the next grocery store or supermarket? I want to pick up a few cleaning supplies.'

'With the family moving to the city, the farmhouse has not been lived in for years now. Not sure how much cleaning Premo would've managed after the short notice,' I added.

We stopped at a kirana store. A shop owner with a deeply content appearance was enjoying his morning tea out of a miniature-sized glass while reading Punjab Kesari, as Gurbani played on in the background. Flies buzzed. A woman with a dupatta tightly wrapped around her face, revealing only a pair of narrow busy eyes, was kicking up a storm of dust as she swept the entrance.

I entered the shop, devoid of doors and windows, with a single shutter rolled all the way to the ceiling. This place stood at least 20 years behind its modern convenience-store counterparts back in Chandigarh.

I browsed around, observing chunky slabs of brown-coloured desi soap and open buckets full of jaggery.

With no assistance or attention from well-dressed, eager-to-help associates, I proceeded at my own unhurried pace—bleach, disinfectants, hand soaps, sanitizer, mops, dusters and mosquito repellants.

Admittedly, I'd always been more than a little obsessive about hygiene and cleanliness. Beyond the point of annoyance, almost to the point of inconvenience. I attributed it to some significant form of OCD, that over the years, I had managed to make peace with, as with a lot of other things in my life.

'Babyji,' Balwinder inquired 'would you like me to carry any bags to the car?'

'Not yet, but I'm almost done. Do you think we might need anything else, Balwinder?' I asked, pointing to my line up of items along the wall.

'How about bottled water, babyji?'

'Not needed, Balwinder. Pump water is good.'

There was something about drinking water from those tall steel glasses. It lent a distinctly unique flavor—a strange mineral-earthy-richly satisfying flavor.

Back in the days when we were growing up, indulgence wasn't necessarily classified in terms of wearing branded clothes or carrying the latest iPhone, but rather in exploring the little joys of a simple life, filled with ordinary things that delivered extraordinary experiences. Drinking from exotic glasses, collecting colorful kites, experimenting with new flavors of gola and scrapbooking assorted candy wrappers.

The store owner scribbled the total on a receipt pad. 'That would be Rs. 2,394,' he said, sliding the pad towards me as he securely tucked the pen between his turban and his ear.

I handed him five bills of Rs. 500 each.

Holding the money in one hand, he briskly wetted his thumb and index finger on his tongue before counting the notes and placing them securely in the rutted wooden drawer, and without uttering another word, handed me a hundred-rupee bill and six Eclairs in return.

Candies, being more than fair change currency, I readily accepted and left the store rather pleased.

'To the farmhouse now. I can't wait to see what it looks like after all these years. I can barely remember when we came here last. I think it was the second year of my college, but even that was such a long time ago.

How long will it take from here, Balwinder?' I inquired.

'Babyji, with the new flyovers and expressway, we will get there in no time. Thirty minutes at the most.'

I looked at the Eclairs. Six, to be exact. Two for each of us... I missed my Mehar and Sid. I wished we could be together. I wished it hadn't turned out this way. I closed my eyes, leaning my head against the cold window, holding the Eclairs in my open palm.

The shrill horn of a scooter beeped past us, with an orange parna-wearing man waving a salutation.

I rolled down the window. The fragrance of eucalyptus trees mingled with the quiet sunlight as we turned onto a narrow dirt road lined with tall trees. These trees remained 'safedas' in our vocabulary because that's what biji referred to them as.

'Balwinder, why don't you go ahead and park? I'd like to walk up from here,' I suggested, closing the door behind me.

The fields were still. The day was warming up and an occasional rattling tractor passed by, leaving a storm of dust in its wake. The tall tree-lined eucalyptus driveway that once appeared like a tunnel to our tiny eyes, with a warm gray home awaiting us at the end of it, looked rather sparse now.

Dad would often pull his car right up to this corner and beep the horn thrice, signalling the start of a race that would have the three of us dashing down to reach biji first.

This patchy shade was a familiar place. We had spent many afternoons collecting cones, leaves and bark—our prized jewels—carefully stashed in treasure chests, to be traded someday for great value, or so we believed.

I strolled slowly behind these innocent memories that led my way.

The green welcome sign that my cousin had painted on the balcony was now weathered and washed out, reduced to a faint 'we come'.

My eyes turned towards the empty doorway. I missed nani in her elegant white suit with a wide chiffon dupatta gracefully covering her gray hair.

I stepped through the wooden door, which appeared more like a large window opening into a courtyard, enveloped by a thick brick wall. It was silent and still. Across the entrance was a step-up verandah leading to biji's bedroom. And on the other end was a detached home, with a few missing bricks along the commanding three-storey wall.

This void had been home to what everyone called a billbattori, which I much later discovered to my amusement, was not a unique species of birds, but just another name for a baby owl. Sadly, that was empty as well.

Premo came running from the open end of the kitchen, which housed the large wood-burning chulha and a tandoor. Thankfully, that too was intact. Really, the house had not aged much. It had only been abandoned. It seemed glad to see me, and so did Premo.

'Tara bhenji, look at you. You've grown up so much,' she exclaimed, holding me in an affectionate gaze.

I smiled, 'And look at you Premo, you haven't grown a day older.'

'Kitthe bhenji?' she laughed, pointing to her salt and pepper hair as she led me to the manja situated under the old baheda tree.

I observed the handpump and the open drain. It appeared as though a tiny sliver of time had managed to slip away from its fleet to a place where it could stand still for eternity.

'You must be tired from the journey.'

'A little,' I answered, feeling the weight of long-accumulated stress slowly lifting like the morning mist in the soft winter sun.

'Tea is almost ready,' Premo added, swiftly blowing into the pot to keep the tea from overflowing. I pretended not to notice, although she was quick to catch my pretense, and promptly switched to using a strainer to stir the boiling tea.

'That's a huge pot, Premo. You're not making tea for the entire village!' I joked.

'Not for the entire village, bhenji, but Darshi, Gagan, Meena, Rinku and a few others are on their way over.'

'Here? What for?' I blurted, taken off-guard at this prospect of unsolicited visitors.

Premo paused, strainer in hand and a horrified quizzical expression on her face, 'How else do you greet someone who has returned home after this long? In fact, these women are late. They should have been here well before you arrived,' she fussed, continuing to pour tea, 'no oil pouring, no welcoming…'

'But I don't even know these women, Premo.'

'They all know you, bhenji. You played stapu with them, and Darshi was the one who taught you how to sing. Remember how you two would spend hours swinging and practicing under that Pippal tree.'

'Oh her, the one with long hair who wore an oversized nose-pin? I think I vaguely remember. That's all fine, Premo, but I am not well.'

'Rab bhala kare! What happened to you, bhenji? You're still young.' She paused again, staring at me like she was looking at a ghost.

'Oh, nothing serious like that, just headaches and occasional fever. The doctor thinks I need rest.'

'Phew!' Premo heaved a sigh of relief. 'Then you've come to just the right place, bhenji. The water and soil of this land will cure you in no time. And if I may suggest, bhenji, this Gurudwara here is a place of great belief. People come from far and wide to have their wishes granted. And I have seen miracles happen with my own eyes. Pray for Waheguru's grace. He alone knows his ways.'

'Premo,' Balwinder interrupted, 'Where should I put these?'

he asked holding up the bags of supplies.

'What's in these bags?' Premo inquired.

'Some cleaning supplies that Tara babyji picked up on her way here.'

'Oh!' Premo let out a wise chuckle, 'Leave them right here. I'll take care of it.'

'Bhenji,' she giggled, 'this hasn't changed about you.'

'What hasn't changed, Premo?' I asked in earnest.

'This!' she repeated, pointing to the bags.

'Oh, the fight you would put up over using the "the dark, smelly and slippery" bathroom. After three days of trying to convince you in vain, we finally had to create an outdoor curtain enclosure for your bath. And the toilet with "creepy lizards and cockroaches," as you called it, had to be scrubbed clean with scalding Dettol water each time before you'd set your foot in.'

'I know exactly what to do,' she laughed.

'Let these women arrive. The place will be up to your standards in no time.'

'It's okay, Premo. I'm not that fussy anymore. I'll manage it myself,' I offered, feeling a little embarrassed.

'Hai bhenji, what are you saying? Why will you manage? You will not lift a finger around here. In biji's absence, I have the precious responsibility of stepping into her shoes. Now, I may not be as deserving, but I know my job well,' she smiled, exuding maternal warmth.

'Does anyone use biji's room?' I asked.

'Not really, it remains mostly closed.'

I glanced at the room and wondered about biji's wooden almirah. The place that first greeted us with happy cheer. That distinct triangular knob that biji would slowly slide upwards, while we waited impatiently for the unlocking of the world's sweetest treasure—jars full of patase. Big round ones and small square ones lined up in inviting glass containers. Nostalgically sweet and deliciously welcoming.

'I go first.'

'No, I do.'

'Close your eyes and find me. Whoever touches me first gets it first.'

I could hear the room come alive with the giggles and chatter of happy memories.

The further back I went in time, the sweeter life appeared. Was it selective conditioning, I wondered, or had something gone drastically astray in this world of fast food, digital relationships, self-absorption and instant gratification?

My happy memories were suddenly interjected by the approaching sound of loud chatter, as a group of unfamiliar faces converged around me.

'Is this Tara? She was a little girl back then; how quickly she has grown up!' remarked an older woman, running a greasy palm over my hair.

'She finally looks like her mother now,' muttered another as she pivoted my face and inspected it carefully.

'Just like a porcelain doll. I'm afraid even to touch her!' chuckled a third.

Even though I felt reduced to a mere observation, their expression was earnest and well-intentioned, and their warmth genuinely palpable. I didn't mind it in the least and smiled in return.

'Bhenji is not well. Leave her alone,' Premo interrupted. 'Finish your tea and let's get to work. Her room upstairs needs a good cleaning.'

'No, don't worry about that. I'm actually feeling better,' I added politely, trying in small measure, to compensate for Premo's abruptness.

'And are you Darshi?' I turned to the coy woman with remarkably long hair who hadn't spoken a word yet. She smiled, nodding her head ever so slightly as she retreated behind a woman's back. Her bashful eyes seemed curious and warm. She still wore a nose pin, but it didn't appear as large or distinctive anymore.

'I still remember one of the songs you taught me.'

She beamed radiantly, burying her head even deeper before lifting it just enough to peek over the shoulder as she spoke in a barely audible voice, 'I can teach you more if you'd like.'

'Oh, we could also have gidda practices after dinner,' proposed another.

'All right. That's quite enough,' said Premo. 'Didn't I just tell you Tara bhenji needs rest? Save all this for when she is better. We have work to do.'

I was already beginning to feel better, even if it was a fleeting state of mind, among people who knew nothing of my compromised life.

'What brings you here, Tara beta, and how long do you plan to stay?' asked one of the elderly women as she picked up the bag of supplies with one hand, adjusting the dupatta on her head with the other.

I hesitated, 'Um...'

'What kind of question is that?' Premo intervened. 'It's her home. Why does she need a reason to visit? And she is welcome to stay as long as she pleases. Now come this way all of you,' instructed Premo, leading the group up the stairs to the terrace on the third floor while I followed.

The terrace was wide and open, enclosed by walls that appeared unusually high. The quiet green fields stretched as far as the eye could see. There was immense silence. A restful feeling that had eluded me for years paid a fleeting visit. I turned towards the tiny room situated in one corner of the veranda.

Biji and darji had constructed this one-bedroom studio for their guests. It came with an attached bathroom, which in those times, was quite the pinnacle of luxury. The room was spacious enough to comfortably accommodate a full-sized bed, a wooden desk and a writing chair.

A large window with wooden shutters overlooked the courtyard and directly across from it was the double door entrance to the room. As a result, the cross-ventilation and natural lighting were both aplenty.

The bathroom showed signs of attempted upgradation. The floors were tiled. A plastic towel ring and shower caddy to hold light supplies had been installed. It also had two skylights, or roshandaans as they would more appropriately be called, lending the tiny bathroom an airy feel.

Premo had done her best to tidy up the room, which already seemed quite ready to move in. The table lamp had been strategically relocated from my aunt's room to this one. The desk was well-appointed with fresh flowers, fruit and a knife wrapped in a cloth napkin. There was also a bottle of water and a container full of nuts on the end table.

The bed, a genuine antique, appeared more appealing in real life than what I had recalled. The fine carving, minute inlay work and a visibly aged mirror embedded in the headboard conveyed a charm of a tasteful bygone era.

Of the few good things about growing up, one is that we finally learn to appreciate things in their entirety—for their beauty, for their scars, and most of all, for the stories that they hold within.

'Premo, I don't think this room needs much. This is quite perfect as is.'

'Bhenji, don't worry, we will not keep you waiting too long.

I'll call you as soon as we're done here.'

I sat on the ledge, surrounded by the silent fields, waiting for the women to leave.

The question stabbed me again. 'What brings you here, Tara beta, and how long do you plan to stay?'

What brought me here? Life, destiny, misfortune or Tej?

I stared at the open expanse as my thoughts drifted back to that one evening, which changed everything.

Could it have been avoided? Could I have done something differently?

Was it that one evening, or was it simply the last nail in the coffin?

Two

THE deafening sound of 'Get away, bitch' resounded in my ears as a violent push knocked me over with a thud.

I hit my head on the floor.

Everything started to blur. The voices began to fade.

I faintly heard Mala call out my name.

I think I passed out.

Doctor Meghadri's comforting voice ushered me into wakefulness. 'Good, now gently try to open your eyes.'

I slowly parted my heavy eyelids. A blinding light pierced through, 'Mama, please draw the curtain, this light is hurting my eyes,' I moaned, turning over.

My head throbbed. My body ached. I flipped over and struggled to sit upright, straining hard to connect events from last night to this point of waking up at mom's house.

'Where are Mehar and Sid? Are they all right?' I inquired, a little flustered as it all started to come back.

'Yes, my dear. Everything is all right,' mom assured me in her ever-composed demeanour.

Two giggling voices chimed in and out of the room, finally halting by my bedside, 'Mommy had too much to drink on her birthday,' Mehar chuckled.

'How funny, mommy! Who trips and falls just walking?' they laughed, amusing themselves at the expense of an always proper mother, who they finally had a scoop on. This was going to be their great retort the next time I threatened them with 'proper behavior' protocol.

'Yes, we all get silly sometimes and end up having way too much fun,' I admitted.

Mehar drew in closer and softly stroked my cheek, looking closely at the shiny bruise. 'Does it hurt, mom?'

'A little,' I responded. 'But don't worry, there is nothing that doesn't get better with time.'

'And laughter,' Mehar added. 'They say laughter is the best medicine. Meghadri uncle, do you agree?'

'Of course! You are a wise little girl, Mehar. I often prescribe laughter therapy to my patients.'

'Done. You are hereby prescribed to watch something funny each morning with breakfast,' Mehar instructed, carefully planting a peck on my cheek. 'I don't like seeing you unwell, mommy. You are better when you nag us with, "Get in the shower, eat your fruit, chew with your mouth closed." I like having you as the background score in our life. Everything feels mute and boring today.'

I finally smiled. 'I'm fine, love. I will be pestering you again before you know it. Now it's almost time to leave for school. Brush, shower and pack up.'

'Done, done and done. Ask Mala maasi, she inspected everything.'

'Good girl! I'm proud of you.'

'So Mehar, Balwinder and Mala maasi will drive you both up to school since I don't look too pretty right now,' I smiled 'but I'll be there next week.'

'You are always pretty, mom.

'And Mala maasi already told me about the fun things she has planned for the way. I'm so excited to see my friends. We've been texting non-stop for the last two days. I can't wait to go back after this long break,' Mehar chirped.

'Okay, Ria is face-timing me now,' she exclaimed, running off into the other room.

'See, Tara,' said mom caressing my hair, 'everything works out. And sometimes the toughest decisions in life are the best ones for us. You were so opposed to the idea of sending your children to a boarding school. How much you fought, resisted and cried, but look at all the wonderful friendships they've developed there. This will be the highlight of the life they'll remember.'

'You're right, mom,' I sighed. 'Good for them, but not so good for me. I wanted to experience every moment, every phase of their precious growing years. I wanted to be as much a part of their memories, as you are of ours. It hurts me every day, to be a mother and walk into empty rooms filled with neatly stacked toys and untimely short memories,' I said, regretfully.

The throbbing returned. I slouched back and closed my eyes. 'I don't feel too good. My head is spinning.'

Scenes from the previous evening started flashing back in my mind, as warm tears streamed down my pale cheeks.

'Did this really happen? Did this happen to me? How could he do this? Why did he do this?'

Meeta stepped forward, 'Dr Meghadri, this is how it started last night. She began rambling and grew hysterical to the point where she wouldn't respond to anything. She kept crying inconsolably and eventually exhausted herself to sleep.'

'She is in shock, Meeta. It's been a lot for her to process. I am giving her a sedative now. It will help her rest. We might need to get her through the next few days in this manner. Let's hope she's stronger than this.'

'Dealing personally with abuse is painful, Meeta, but public humiliation cuts much deeper. That one moment snatches your pride and confers a lifelong stigma on how people remember you. Even if sympathetically. Psychologically, it can be deeply damaging.

'Well,' Dr Meghadri added, 'I do notice, she finds unusual courage in front of her children. You should harness that motivation of wanting to appear stronger in front of those that expect it of her, to steer her forward.

I'm not just your doctor, beta, your father was a dear friend to me. I have watched you grow over the years. As a family, you have navigated every crisis, riding on courage and love.

You have it in you, and you will need to bring it out again,' he added.

'We're doing our best, uncle. We're trying,' Meeta replied despondently, taking the empty cup from his hand.

'Unfortunately, trying won't be enough. We cannot let her sink in this quagmire while we helplessly watch. I'm not sure she is in a state to help herself. We must pull her out of it. How? I leave that up to the three of you. You are sensible women. I trust your judgment and will stand by whatever decision you make. But you must decide.

'Beta,' he continued, pausing briefly at the door, 'if family doesn't stand up against abuse, who will? Yes, we want marriages to work, but there must be a final price we are willing to pay. And that price cannot be her life. Keep me informed on her recovery.'

I felt mom's tender hand caressing my face as she whispered, 'Tara, as long as there is life, there are possibilities. We will try to find them. I promise.'

I slipped deeper into a long, restful sleep.

※

'Where's my phone?' I asked, feeling around the bed. 'Mehar and Sid must have sent pictures from school.'

'How are you feeling, Tara?' Meeta asked as she stood up from her chair and walked over.

'Better,' I answered meekly. 'Did you see my phone anywhere?'

'It's with me. I turned it off. Just rest it out for now.'

'I've been resting all day and I will return to it as soon as I am done with their updates. Promise. I can't wait to see what their new dorms look like.'

'All right, in that case, just the pictures, I will read the texts out for you. You shouldn't strain yourself.'

'Mama, Tara is up, could you bring her some tea please,' Meeta yelled, turning the phone back on.

It felt good to be surrounded by family in the comfort of mom's home. Something about the quality of sleep when you finally let your guard down.

'All right! So Mehar says, "Mama check out my dorm, all ready with new sheets and pillows you bought me. I told you purple would be the perfect choice. See, I was right! Everyone here loves them, and they've been sending pictures to their parents asking them to buy exactly the same ones! Honestly, I think I'm becoming somewhat of a trendsetter,"' Meeta smiled as she read Mehar's message.

'Here, take a look, Mehar surrounded by her gang. And don't forget to check out the snack stash on her table,' Meeta laughed. 'I knew Mala would indulge them with every item on their shopping list,' she added.

My eyes couldn't get enough of that joy and sparkle in Mehar's eyes. I smiled. But no sooner than it appeared, my smile was wiped out at the sight of Tej's name flashing across the screen.

Meeta took the phone from my hand and disconnected the call.

'Don't bother, Tara, such a shameless man. After what he

did, I thought he would never have the courage to show his face again. I can't imagine what's going through his thick head. He's been calling incessantly and has come over four times demanding to speak with you. What's left to talk now? Well, the world would have plenty to talk about, but for him? It beats me!' fumed Meeta, clearly infuriated.

'Meeta, I know him. He is not only persistent but compulsively obsessive. He will never stop if we keep hanging up on him. Perhaps it might be best to let him say what he has to say and be done with it.'

'One, I don't think it's advisable. Two, certainly not in this state of mind. You need time to recover. I trust your judgment Tara, but what I don't trust is your ability to see through his lies. You are very vulnerable right now.'

'Meeta, I do know he lies. I see through his façade,' I insisted.

'All right then, let me rephrase it, you see through his lies yet give in to that wishful silver lining to this dark cloud, that only exists in your imagination.

'Look,' she said, softening her tone, 'I know how strongly you feel about family and how desperately you have been hoping for a miracle. He knows this too. And that's his license to get away with progressively worse things. He believes he can always come back and make it up to you. You will give him a chance, and another, and yet another. Don't you see that your desperation for family stability is fueling his insanity. You've got to put a stop to this, Tara.'

'I hear you, Meeta. I hear you,' I sighed.

'Tara, you should take some time off and really think this through. Let him keep calling. Let him wear out his shoes, driving back and forth. You talk to him when you are ready to talk, not because he wouldn't stop calling. You talk when you have the answers, not because he wouldn't stop questioning. And read up on domestic abuse. It will hold a mirror to his repetitive behaviour patterns and your predictable responses.

Anyway, I should probably stop here,' Meeta quickly retracted, observing the defeated look on my face.

'Sorry, if I got carried away. I only mean well,' she offered, placing a comforting hand over mine.

'I never doubted that,' I replied in a small voice.

'Forget that. There are better things to talk about,' Meeta suggested, switching back to the messages. 'You've got to love Sid. He's such an artist at heart. Look, how he painted these flowers and bandaged the vase with "Feel better mommy" posted across it. How adorable is that! You kids are such a treasure! Honestly, Tara, more than anything you think they deserve—they deserve a happy mom. They really do!'

The phone rang again, followed by a WhatsApp notification, followed by a message, 'I'm sorry. Call me.'

A few minutes later, the doorbell rang.

'He's overstepping it now,' Meeta sprung up impatiently.

'Relax,' said mom, 'it's Mala, and Jeetu is getting the door.'

'Thank god,' Meeta let out an exasperated breath. 'This guy is bringing out the worst in me. I had forgotten I even had a temper.'

'Well, hello, ladies!' Mala entered the room with a dazzling smile, holding a colourful bunch of flowers and a bottle of freshly squeezed apple juice.

'For you! Specially sourced from HPMC-Live Life Fruitfully!' she jingled, her eyes spilling a contagious cheer.

The whole room lit up a few shades with the positivity Mala brought along.

'And where did you find these wildflowers? These are beautiful!' I remarked as a tiny smile struggled to escape my lips.

'Oh, just around a bend as we were driving back. I literally had Balwinder swerve off the highway onto some godforsaken dirt road. He was so utterly perplexed and kept asking me, "Babyji, why are you climbing the hill for these flowers when there are better ones you can buy in stores?"' Mala laughed.

'But I could so visualize you sitting daintily in a white dress, singing away to these flowers like you always did. I just had to bring these back.'

'You still remember?' I smiled.

'Why wouldn't I?'

'I don't know. Maybe I've been surrounded too long with people who neither notice nor care.'

'Well, you were an extra special case. Not that easy to forget—you talked to flowers—flowers for your friends and flowers for your students. More than a little cuckoo, in my opinion, but that's beside the point,' Mala giggled.

'So, how was it?' I questioned impatiently. 'The ride, the weather? Did you hit traffic at all?' I asked, bolstering myself against the headboard, eager to take the virtual trip through Mala's actual one.

'Could I freshen up first? Even my hair smells of diesel fumes,' Mala grumbled.

'You see, nostalgia isn't always your friend. I decided to relive the dreamy uphill drives, when feathery clouds infused with pine scent came wandering through the windows to greet us.'

'Only this time around, these were clouds of smog, laden with the pungent smell of diesel. Sticky, yucky, but still somewhat endearing,' she laughed. 'Nah, overall, this was fabulous. I had memories waiting at every corner!

And speaking of the most memorable corner—we had lunch at Kartar Dhaba.'

'Oh, Kartar Dhaba still exists?' asked Meeta.

'Still going strong! But more later, let me shower first.'

'Go quickly,' said Meeta. 'And that reminds me of a funny incident…'

'Hey! Not allowed. No stories until I come out.'

'What if I forget it by then?'

'Not my problem, it's yours.'

'Listen to this twittering! It feels like the old times have returned and the house has suddenly come alive,' smiled mom handing Mala a towel.

'Don't worry, take your time. It's been a long day. I'll make sure no one shares anything.

Besides, it's also good for Tara to rest a little. This excitement may not be too good for her recovery,' said mom as she walked up and placed her hand on my forehead.

I swiftly moved her hand aside, 'I'm fine, mom, not all ailments go away with medication or rest. I need this family time. For just a little while, I want to wipe out all else and laugh. I haven't laughed in so long that I miss it. You know mom, I often reasoned with myself that being a parent comes with so many responsibilities that one forgets to enjoy the process. But you weren't like that. You laughed, you smiled, you dressed in pretty sarees and watched us build houses. You even sang with us. I don't know if I'm enough as a mother,' I sighed.

'Beta, times were different back then. Lives were much simpler,' mom answered.

'I disagree, mom,' Meeta interjected. 'Lives weren't simpler, people were. Compare dad with Tej. If he was anything like him, you wouldn't nearly be half the person you are today. It's not about the times you live in but how you live in those times. Happiness is not a state of life but a state of mind which stems from affection, acceptance, freedom and an undeniable trust in one another.

Aren't we laughing right here, right now?'

A piercing silence pervaded the room.

'And just to set the record straight, a bad relationship is not some unprecedented accident in the history of mankind. It's up to us how long we choose to bear the pain of it. Laughter never abandons us. We abandon it by the big and small choices we make each day.'

I was suddenly gripped by mom's affectionate gaze, painfully evaluating the extent of hurt on my bruised cheek.

Walking out of the bathroom, Mala noticed it as well. 'Come on, people, she's been in this dull bed forever. Let's sit in the verandah. Some fresh air will do us good.'

'Jeetu bhaiya, could you set up the tea outdoors, please,' Mala requested.

Steaming tea and hot samosas perfectly complemented the pitter-patter of tiny raindrops.

Tall gray planters wore a fresh coat of shine. Lime green plants embraced the white wall, looking fresh and youthful. The sky was overcast, the breeze was fresh and the pretty tea cozy and dainty cups appeared to be rejoicing against the backdrop of a faint drizzle.

Mom brought out a few shawls and three pairs of overused, out-of-shape airline socks.

'Really, mom,' Mala laughed, 'you not only stock up on airline socks but actually use them?'

'Of course, I do, they are lightweight and very comfortable. You can't really find them in stores easily.'

'Sure, you can't!' we laughed.

'Ah!' muttered Mala, gazing at the dark overcast sky, 'I miss Chandigarh rains. Remember how the streets would flood in a matter of hours? And with pants rolled knee-high, we'd wade right into overflowing streams of mud-laden water, floating paper boats containing hidden messages for our friends down the street.'

'Yes, I remember,' Meeta chimed in. 'Everything would instantly shut down as people gathered and cheered in the rain, as if it were some big celebration,' she laughed. 'And I absolutely loved how the radio stations played "monsoon specials" on repeat while we sipped on cup after cup of steaming coffee. And that customary drive down the city streets, blasting music to waves of undrained water crashing on the windshield,' Meeta chuckled.

'Oh, I'd take that any day over the warrior experience of returning from college, navigating a Kinetic Honda down these flooded roads,' complained Mala. 'What an ordeal it was to steer through limited visibility with camel eyes, while sharp arrows of rain pounded your face harder than a game of paintball!' she laughed.

'But the arrival home was always predictable, with Jeetu running to the gate wearing a plastic bag on his head, while mom stood at the door holding a towel. And that distinctly warm post-rain-trauma aroma of haldi-elaichi-cinnamon milk simmering on the stove!' laughed Mala.

'You're awfully quiet, Tara. What is your favourite memory of rain?' prompted Meeta.

'Um... bhutta by the lake. Yeah, I think that was my rain thing,' I smiled.

'And your rain-washed 17th? Do you remember the chaos?'

'I do,' I responded meekly with a reminiscing smile.

'For all the stormy weather, it ended up being truly memorable!' Meeta recalled fondly.

'And the dare that Karan had to undertake,' Mala guffawed. 'Pretend to confess his love for the birthday girl. Well, in his case, it was more a dream than a dare. Poor guy, he did like you so much.'

'I don't know. He never said anything to me,' I shrugged.

'Stop pretending Ms. Goody-two-shoes, the whole school knew. You just loved feigning ignorance,' teased Meeta lovingly.

'At least she got to feign ignorance. I simply got ignored!' grumbled Mala with a sour face.

'And who's to blame here? I told you to grow your hair out and dress properly. But you wore ugly clothes, drove around in jeeps and spent your days at mechanic shops getting tires replaced and engines fixed. You were nothing like you are today,' Meeta reminded her as we laughed over it.

'Don't blame me, Meeta,' retorted Mala, 'you singlehandedly made up for everyone's share of dressing up. Tara and I shared one humble closet while you had two dedicated just to your collection of clothes, shoes and record labels.'

'Well, that's the reason each time my teacher asked to speak with "my sister", I made it a point to take Meeta in. I would have people talking about it for days,' I admitted.

'Seriously, Tara? You discriminated against me?' Mala questioned accusingly as we broke into rapturous laughter.

Just then, the doorbell rang. A questioning silence descended, gripping each one of us in the same unspoken apprehension.

Mala stood up confidently, pulling her cascading hair in a loose knot. 'Don't worry. I'll get the door,' she said, her brown, kohl-lined eyes becoming fiercely determined.

'I'll come with you,' offered Meeta, following quickly behind.

Mom tapped my arm lightly, 'It's all right, your sisters will handle it.'

My nerves tensed up. My heart raced. And my ears remained tuned in to the slightest movement and sound. I was prepared to hear a quibble any minute.

A moment of anxious silence ensued as mom and I sat uncomfortably at the edge of our seats.

'Thank you,' I finally heard Meeta's voice. I let out a sigh of relief at the sound of uneventfully retreating steps.

'Who was it?' I asked, looking curiously over my shoulder.

'Flower delivery,' Meeta replied.

'Flowers?'

'From Vinay. I'll place these in your bedroom. Here, you can read the note,' said Meeta, holding out a little card.

'Hope you're fine. If my words or presence inadvertently contributed to the situation last night, I'm truly sorry—your friend, Vinay.'

'What does the note say?' asked Mala.

I handed the note to her.

'Poor guy, he's blaming himself for no reason,' said Mala holding out the phone to me. 'I think you should send him a message of thanks as a bare minimum courtesy.'

I nodded as I took the phone and began to type. 'Thanks for the flowers. I'm doing fine. Don't worry. You were not the reason, only an excuse. Will connect soon.'

'I'll be right back,' I said as I stood up.

A sudden lightheadedness came over me. Everything turned a faint blue. Feeling disoriented, I sank right back into my chair.

'Are you okay, Tara?' everyone flocked to me.

'Yes, don't worry, I'm fine. I think I got up too fast. I'm not sure why, but I feel a little unsteady. I think I might want to go back to bed.'

'Yes, you should,' insisted mom. 'I knew you still needed the rest, but Mala and Meeta keep getting ahead of themselves. You can't bypass the recovery process. Yes, eventually, you will get better, but we must take it one day at a time. It won't happen overnight,' she reproved, clearly unhappy to witness my relapse.

Mom situated me comfortably in bed and the three of them sat gathered around me. It was quiet again. The laughter had vanished and the grim reality resurfaced, looking even bleaker in the dim glow of the fluorescent tubelight, occasionally flickering around its darkened edges.

'I'm fine guys, stop stressing. I just needed to get a little comfortable. Now that I have all the room to myself, I'm quite at ease,' I confirmed.

Mala turned on the TV. Mom brought me her special khichadi, laced with melted butter.

No one spoke anymore.

I felt pampered, sick and hugely burdensome—all at once. I ate my dinner quietly and turned over in bed. The worthless feeling hurt like a stab.

'Meeta, please give me the sleep meds Meghadri uncle has prescribed.'

Mom immediately turned around, a little concerned to hear me ask for it. 'Take it only if you need it. These can get addictive,' she cautioned.

'Don't worry, mama. I won't get addicted, not at this age, and not to sleep meds of all things. Just looking forward to a night of restful sleep for all of us. That's all,' I assured her.

'Of course,' mom conceded, trying hard to sound supportive despite her fears.

I lay in bed. The nightlight shone. I meditated to the sound of the blower as it ran, shut off, and turned back on again. The sleep meds weren't much help tonight. The door to the room across had been left open a crack. Open enough for them to hear me move and closed enough to keep the light and noise from disturbing me. I overheard their worried conversations about my life, my future and the choices I was inclined to make.

From relocating, to going back to school for a professional degree, to counseling, to social work. My future was up for debate.

And then I heard mom's voice, 'Let her heart lead her journey. We don't know enough to lay down the path for her. We can point out the various directions but let her choose which way she wants to go. If at all she wants to go,' mom added hesitantly after a pause.

'I mean, all we need to do at this point is to support her unconditionally and get her back on her feet. The rest, she will handle.'

'Mom, we all agree that's eventually the goal, but remember how Meghadri uncle said she can't think for herself at the moment, and as family, we need to decide for her,' Mala pressed.

'She's my daughter. I have complete faith in her abilities. I will stand by her decisions whether they prove right or wrong in the long run. But she will decide, we won't decide for her. Let her seek out her own answers, in her own time. Mala, it's a lot easier to live with one's own wrong decisions than someone else's right ones,' mom asserted.

Tears ran down my face, wetting the pillow as I lay quietly awake.

Over the hours, mom, Meeta and Mala took turns checking on me, planting gentle kisses and leaving tender wishes by my bedside.

Slowly, the last light turned out. The darkness around finally blended with the darkness within.

Three

'I'VE asked Amit to extend my return by a few weeks. It would be good to spend some more time with you,' Mala stated casually, sipping on her morning tea.

'Actually, I've been thinking along the same lines. Perhaps, I'll stay on until the end of the month as well,' Meeta added.

'Oh, that would be wonderful!' mom remarked. 'Tara could definitely use some company.'

'Meeta, Mala, you don't need to extend your stay. I have already put you through enough. I know how you were looking forward to travelling and meeting with family. And all your plans got wiped out because of me,' I conjectured in a small, contemplative voice.

'Silly girl. Stop blaming yourself, do you really think we'd rather be any other place than our childhood home?' questioned Mala impatiently.

'It's not about that, but honestly, I can't take any more disruption in anyone's life on my account. It's a crushing burden to bear. The kids are alone. And it's not fair on jiju to juggle kids, home and work all by himself. Trust me, I'll be fine.'

'It's not about trusting you. It's about being there,' affirmed Meeta with utmost sincerity.

'No Meeta, I insist. Let's talk about it. What is your most pressing concern at this time? That I don't slip into depression or slide back into that dreadful existence again, right?' I demanded, inching myself up against the bed.

'Well, yes and no. You are right. We are concerned about your emotional state and your ability to pull through this alone. But none of us will ever keep you from returning to your home or to Tej, if you so decide. We just want to make sure that wherever you end up being, it is by choice and not by the lack of it.

Look Tara, you must allow time and distance to lead you to a rational decision. You can't let desperation and insecurity drive it. If what you feel today is also what you feel a few months from now, then it's the right decision for you. Remember, it's far easier to return than it is to walk away. And you know who are the ones most afraid to walk away? Those who fear that once they leave, they might never return,' said Meeta, looking deep into my eyes.

I grew quiet, reflecting on her words.

'This road can be rough, Tara,' said Meeta, reaching for my hand. 'You will need people you can depend on.'

'And it's not a matter of a few weeks for us; it's a matter of a lifetime for you,' she insisted. 'We can't take any chances.'

I placed my hand over Meeta's, 'I hear you. And while I may not be as strong as either of you,' I sighed, lowering my gaze, 'I do want to attempt this journey—my journey, on my own. You can walk along as far as you'd like, but you can't walk forever. You can't be my crutches for the rest of my life. I must learn to walk alone now, or I never will. Let me fall, let me struggle, let me stand up, let me learn how it's done.'

As much as mom was protective of me, somewhere in her intuitive wisdom, she also understood my resilience.

'I stand by her decision. Let Tara handle it the way she wants,' mom interjected.

Mala and Meeta exchanged a worried look, 'But mom, a few weeks...'

'She can do it,' mom persisted. 'And I'm right here in case she needs someone. We must respect her choices.'

There was an uncomfortable silence in the room.

'That man will not leave her alone for a minute. You know he will keep pestering and harassing her until she caves in. How do we prevent that from happening?' Meeta reasoned, looking visibly anxious.

'Well, how about a retreat?' exclaimed Mala, her eyes brightening at the prospect of her own suggestion. 'I could book her a few weeks at Ananda. Meditation, massage, nature—all things good for her recovery, and she can leave her phone behind. He would never know where she is.'

'Excellent idea,' Meeta concurred.

'There is little that I own,' I offered sincerely. 'I neither have a bank account nor access to my locker, even if I had to think of selling my jewellery. I have one dependent credit card and a small saving from shagans. That's all I can say for my standing in life right now. At this age, Mala and Meeta, I would gladly accept the gift of your love. But it would be excruciatingly painful for my pride to be vacationing in luxury on expenses paid by my sisters. My conscience doesn't agree. Don't get me wrong, but I have no desire to indulge beyond my means. Little or much, I have what I have. Let me make peace with it.'

'Poor wife of a rich man, admirable indeed!' Mala remarked in a light-hearted vein.

Meeta added, 'You don't have to explain Tara, we are all cut from the same cloth. For all else, we are proud women who will hold their heads high and refuse to trade self-respect for convenience or comforts.

'So, in that case, what do you plan to do?', asked Meeta. 'Why don't you come with me to Canada for a few weeks? Or to the US with Mala? That's home.'

'No, I'm neither up for travel, nor do I want to be too far from Mehar and Sid. Strange as it sounds, for quite a while now, one place I've been longing to visit is nani's farmhouse in Amritsar,' I replied.

'Amritsar? But what will you do at the farm? Alone? The family moved to the city a while back. Only a handful of servants run the house, and that too, it isn't in the best condition. It must be quite run down and dirty,' mom resisted.

'Dirt is the last thing that will bother me at this point. Right now, it's the most restful place I can think of. I'll take some books with me. It would be nice to get back to my love of reading. I can't believe all that I've given up for him, only to end up here.

Coming back to it, there are some very special memories of our summers at nani's home. I'll enjoy the sunsets and the stars and the vast stretches of happy fields,' I added, feeling relaxed at the mere thought of it.

'I'm afraid this sounds like a perfect recipe for depression,' Meeta concluded skeptically.

'She's right. There's only so much you can read in a day, and sunset lasts all of 15 minutes. What about the rest? Twenty-four hours each day is a long time to spend alone,' warned Mala.

'I'll go to the city if I feel lonely. There's the Golden Temple and historical museums to visit and plenty of rich, delicious Punjabi food to indulge in. I know what I am up for at this point and what I can't handle. I need this downtime. In fact, I'm really looking forward to it,' I said earnestly, as a tiny smile settled on my lips.

'If you insist. In that case, take an alternate number with you and keep in close touch. Remember, we're not far,' said Mala, reaching for her cold cup of tea.

'That's a deal! I know I can call you anytime and you'll be there before I blink my eyes.'

'Good. So, when do you leave?' asked Meeta.

'Soon after you both are off. I will make a quick trip to Kasauli to meet the kids and head out from there. Perhaps I'll spend the night at Ashok uncle's house. I hear uncle finally got rid of his tenants and renovated the house. He now spends more time in Kasauli than he does at his house in Delhi.'

'That was a beautiful property with breathtaking 360-degree mountain views. I'm happy he's back. How we looked forward to those special Kasauli visits! Uncle never met us without chips and chocolates,' recalled Mala fondly.

'All right then, it seems like we have a plan. It's good. Tej will never expect to look for you at either of these places. And now you be a strong girl for us,' Mala asserted.

I smiled in affirmation.

The next few days were spent disconnecting calls, drinking wine and reliving our childhood memories.

And then Mala and Meeta left.

It felt as though a large part of my strength left with them. I wanted to cry, but I knew I had to put up a brave act—for mom, for them, but most of all, for myself. Being proven wrong by my own decisions wasn't something I would take kindly in my stride.

Besides, Meeta's words seemed etched in my heart. *'More than anything you think your kids deserve, they deserve a happy mom.'* I had to do it for them.

My minimal bag was packed, books occupying a significant part of it. Mom handed me an alternate number, and at the crack of dawn, Balwinder and I left for Kasauli.

Since our growing years, early mornings had remained our favourite time for travel. Primarily because cars didn't come equipped with air conditioning back then, and it was best to arrive at your destination before the day warmed up. But now, it was purely out of habit and preference.

I enjoyed leaving behind a world quietly asleep. I also reveled in that gradual transition from the somber night sky, to a hint of mysterious blue, to a playful burst of purple, pink and orange. As though a giant canvas got painted live each morning and I got to witness the beauty firsthand.

Slowly, the birds began to stir. Dogs barked, waking up sleepy neighbourhoods, and the first stream of a predictable community made its early appearance—newspaper vendors, committed joggers, fervent devotees and motorbikes laden with dolus of milk, doing their morning rounds. These almost pious visuals were so often missed by a sleep-deprived and responsibility-ridden world.

'Tara babyji, would you like to eat something?' asked Balwinder as he pulled up to a roadside dhaba.

'You go ahead, Balwinder. I will have breakfast with the kids once I get to Kasauli.'

I stepped out to get some fresh air.

I stood there soaking in the brisk air of those silent blue mountains. My phone beeped. It was a message from Meeta, 'Reached home. Hope you're doing good.'

I took a photo and sent it to her, 'With love from the mountains—the journey has started.'

'How's the journey been so far?' she replied.

'Uphill, but worth it!'

'Uphill, but worth it,' I repeated as I settled into the backseat of the car, wondering if people change or their feelings change. Or do they simply stop pretending after a while and allow themselves to show their true form? For the first time, I found myself questioning what I had come to accept as a fact of life, much like a dark night or cold winter.

Was it all a pretense, I thought, or was I simply a challenge for Tej? Did he ever love me? When and where did he turn into the man he is today?

I didn't have the answers, but I finally had the most relevant question. Did I love him? Why did I marry him despite my gut nudging me otherwise? I held on to that thought.

That answer, I demanded of myself.

We soon arrived at the school. I took one final look at my face and touched up the bruise on my cheek with some concealer. I drew in a deep breath, practiced a full-hearted smile and closed the door behind me.

The walk to the office was long and steep. My feet carried me as fast as they could.

Mehar and Sid were already at the office, swinging their legs impatiently, waiting to be picked up. They heard my voice and flew straight into my arms. As I got on my knees, holding them against my chest, I felt my heart expand two sizes. If only I could encapsulate this moment and carry it to eternity!

I extended my arms and retreated a step to take a good look, from head to toe.

'Of course, you couldn't wait to wear this dress, Mehar. You'd picked this for your friend's birthday. What happened?'

'I wanted you to see how I look in it. That day when you told me to try it on and show you, I was too lazy. I kept feeling bad about it later, so I decided to wear it today. It fits well, mom. See,' said Mehar, twirling a full circle around.

I gave her a tight hug, touched by a thoughtfulness that far exceeded her tender years.

'Your face is normal again,' Sid rejoiced.

'That's how it works. What did you think, mom would be walking around with a bruised face for the rest of her life? Duh!' Mehar snapped.

'I didn't mean that,' Sid rebutted.

'Oh, stop it you two. Come on, let's get some breakfast now.'

'I'll have Balwinder bring up the bags that nanima sent. They're filled with all your favourite snacks.'

'Nanima is the best,' they cheered with big, hearty smiles.

The drive into town was consumed with aimless banter, resolving inconsequential sibling arguments and soaking in the stunning vistas.

Tall chir pine trees lined the narrow roads that overlooked serene mountains and silent valleys. Its sharp needles and tiny cones skirted around its fissured bases. The place seemed seeped in an element of deep tranquility.

We drove through wispy clouds, feeling tiny, cold droplets on our faces. Yellow hydrangeas bloomed in red planters next to various security checkpoints of green-tinned army establishments. And the well-preserved colonial structures evoked a nostalgia for this town's rich history dating back to the early nineteenth century, when it was first colonized as a British Cantonment. It depicted a long journey of evolution, from an obscure little town to a magnificent destination boasting of stunning summer homes built by officers, to entertain their family and friends.

Balwinder dropped us off by the city center and went to park the car.

The crowds at the mall road were rather lean, just the right amount of quaint and busy. The air was crisp and a slight nip could be felt in the bones even through multiple layers of clothing.

We walked down the cobbled streets of Heritage Market, arriving at a modest sweet shop which, over its 45 years in existence, had evolved into an institution of sorts. Narinder Sweet House—an experience now synonymous with this town's identity. The few benches crammed inside the tiny space were already occupied. The sight and aroma of freshly frying jalebis was especially inviting in this cold weather. We sat on benches located across the narrow street, indulging in warm gulab jamuns, hot jalebis, and everyone's favourite, bun-tikkis.

And just like that, engaged in random conversations, the three of us strolled down the meandering roads, arriving finally at our last stop—the Tibetan Market. Mehar picked out some colourful handwoven bracelets while Sid bought his favorite tangy tomato Lays from the shop next door.

The evening was upon us. We drove back in silence towards the school, nestled deep in the heart of these majestic hills, now the better home to my children.

Hugs, sobs, smiles and parting notes—all were offered in copious amounts. I stood by the steps, waving out to them until Mehar and Sidak disappeared out of sight. I started to walk back, struck by a sudden emptiness. I looked over my shoulder occasionally, hoping to catch one last glimpse, but they were gone.

A few minutes later, I heard a pair of footsteps rushing towards me. I could tell it was Mehar even before I turned around.

'Mom, I forgot to tell you something,' Mehar said, gasping for air as she reached me.

'What is it, Mehar?'

'I wanted you to know,' she huffed, 'if I were you, I would have left Dad a long time ago. I love you. Take care of yourself and don't forget your laughter prescription,' she instructed as she inched up to kiss me quickly and ran back before I could ask her anything else.

Her words resounded in my ears. What prompted her to say that, I wondered. Did she find out about the incident? Was she happy that no one had screamed or yelled at them today? What could it be?

'Tara babyji, where to now?' Balwinder asked.

'Ashok uncle's house.'

'Okay, babyji,' said Balwinder. 'The children looked very happy today.'

'Hope it stays that way,' I added reluctantly.

'Babyji, don't worry. God is kind to good people. It is all a matter of time. Everything will be all right. Waheguru Mehar Kare!'

'Thank you, Balwinder. I don't see how, but I hope you're right,' I responded meekly.

'Kids send love and a million kisses for the goodies. Heading to Ashok uncle's home now. Will leave for Amritsar in the morning,' I texted mom.

'Okay, beta, keep me posted.'

We drove up the winding hill towards a well-lit house perched at the top, like a brilliant tiara resting on the head of some dark resplendent beauty. The house appeared sophisticated, contemporary and warmly inviting.

For a moment, I felt a pang of nostalgia for the modest white house that used to stand there, with its green tin roof, but soon, I was captivated by the awe-inspiring minimalistic design of the multi-level floor to ceiling windows and expansive wrap-around verandah.

What hadn't changed, however, were the three sections of outdoor seating scattered about the garden. Ashok uncle often remarked, 'I like having my tea in different areas of the property best suited to greet the morning light, enjoy the colourful sunsets and witness the brilliant spectacle of inky nights.'

What luxury, I thought, to be able to do the most mundane of activities in such indulgent comforts. He was a true nature lover who instilled in us, even as children, an eye for not necessarily what surrounds you, but for what you see, and how.

Balwinder beeped the horn as we stood at the gate. Bahadur,

the house help, came running, holding on to his cap with one hand while opening the gate with the other.

'Welcome, Memsahib, good to see you.'

'Good to see you too, Bahadur. How've you been?'

'God has been kind,' he answered in a cheerful voice, 'Sir is expecting you. He's in the backyard. You can go around the house,' he indicated with a motion of his hand.

'Come on over, Tara beta. We have been waiting for you,' I heard uncle's voice as I made my way along the sidewalk towards the back of the house.

On the wicker table next to his chair, lay a bag of chips and a bar of Cadbury's on top of his evening paper.

'Seriously, uncle?' I smiled.

'Why? Is there an age limit prescribed on these?' he questioned as we warmed up to the joke.

'Oh, by the way, meet Dev,' he introduced the man standing next to him.

'Hello, Dev,' I greeted with a nod.

'Hi, Tara, good to meet you,' he responded, extending his hand in a firm handshake. His tall frame was lean but well-built and his deep voice commanded a compelling presence.

'Uncle has been talking about you all afternoon,' he added courteously.

'I'm sorry you had to endure that. There's hardly anything interesting to share.'

'Not at all. On the contrary, it was fascinating to hear about you and your family. It was by far one of the most enjoyable conversations this afternoon.'

'See, I told you, she always underestimates herself,' said uncle, pulling out a chair for me.

'Allow me,' Dev offered, placing the chair next to uncle's.

'Oh, by the way, Dev is Dalbir uncle's grandson. Do you know about him?'

'Oh, yes. Papa always spoke very highly of his airplane adventures. Pleased to meet you,' I added in light of the new connection I'd just established.

'Dev moved back from New York last year and is now based in Chandigarh itself. Well, when he's not shuttling between his travels. So now Tara, anytime you need anything, you know who to call. And if he doesn't drop everything else to attend to it right away, just twist his ear and remind him how I got him to deliver when he was a little boy.

And what a naughty kid he was! But we will talk about that another time. Remind me, Tara,' uncle instructed.

'What goes around comes around. At least in uncle's company. So much for the enjoyable conversations on your account all afternoon!' Dev remarked, his expressive brown eyes exuding a genuine warmth.

I delivered a fleeting half-smile, a little apprehensive of what uncle might have shared with this complete stranger. That was another thing about uncle. He was unreservedly transparent. If it was on his mind, it made it to his mouth, perfectly intact.

'How's aunty? Is she here too?' I asked.

'She's well. Busy with her women's groups as usual. She doesn't like to travel much, keeps herself occupied with morchas and debates.'

'She's still the same!' I added.

'Very much so, beta. Times change, people rarely do. We just learn to accept them better.'

'Saab, your driver is back,' Bahadur announced.

'Okay, uncle,' Dev stood up, 'I will take your leave now. Tara, I'm back day after, hope to see you around.'

'Well, I won't be here. I'm leaving for Amritsar in the morning.'

'Amritsar? Visiting family?'

'Not really. I've just been longing to visit my nani's home, even though no one lives there anymore. Trying to carve out a few days with absolutely no structure and no agenda. To read, sleep and relax is all I'm looking forward to.'

'Sounds wonderful. I have been out that way a lot lately, will connect if something comes up, given you are in the mood for company,' he added.

'Please do. I can always use some company. Nice meeting you, Dev. Safe travels.'

Dev's chiselled features and impeccable demeanour exuded an air of refined upbringing. He was dressed tastefully, with the absence of any flashy brands screaming for attention. He wore a crisp polo t-shirt with khakis, impeccably polished oxfords and a utilitarian wristwatch, somewhat of a rarity in an era of apple watches and statement pieces.

He bent forward and touched uncle's feet. 'Kush raho, beta,' uncle blessed him. 'Aur janam din mubarak ho.'

'Happy Birthday, Dev!' I wished him.

'It's not until tomorrow, but thanks, Tara,' he added, scratching his slender nose as he glanced at his watch, almost attempting to avoid this conversation. I could clearly tell he preferred to keep things low-key.

'So, my boy, 37 tomorrow,' Ashok uncle laughed with a wink.

'That's right,' Dev affirmed.

'So, by that admission, Tara, he's still your junior. By one full year. Make sure your order him around and assert your seniority well,' uncle instructed.

Dev smiled. 'Well understood. Anytime Tara, with pleasure,' he added.

As we walked back from the gate after seeing Dev off, Ashok uncle turned to me. 'So now, Tara beta, come, let's relax and have a good cup of tea. Fill me in on everything. How're things going?'

'Not too good. Mom must have told you about the most recent incident. But I don't know what choice I have at this point. He's left me with none. I was putting up with everything. I had made my compromises and peace. I was holding it all together while it was in my hands.

But with what Tej did on my birthday, it's not between us anymore. I can't readily go back and I can't move forward, leaving it all behind. I don't know if there even is a way ahead for me, at this age, with two kids, with everything I've given 17 years of my life to. It's too late to think about starting my life over again.'

'You don't have to start your life over again, but also, don't make the mistake of assuming there are only two roads, forward and back. Keep your eyes open for new directions and your heart open for what it might bring your way. Beta, don't try to predict life, try to explore it instead. Even the roughest, most crooked trails can sometimes lead you to magnificent places.'

I reflected on his words and nodded in silent agreement. Although his suggestion was about as helpful as turning on the lights for a blind person, nonetheless, I appreciated his kind words. They were well-intentioned and reassuring in whatever little I could make of them.

'How are Meeta and Mala doing?' he asked.

'They are fine. I'm so grateful to have them in my life. If it wasn't for them, I wouldn't be here today. They were keen to extend their stay, but uncle, you know how it is. I must make my own decisions so I can live with them for the rest of my life.

And as they rightly suggested, for now, I just need to put time and distance between us to determine if I even have the strength to stand alone. Time alone will tell.'

'Beta, I don't have much to tell you here, but relationships take a lifetime of work and sometimes even at the end of that, they don't work out. And you are left questioning if you should have done it all differently.

By then it's too late to change anything, so life just becomes one big regret. I still question, at 73, if I really should be here with your aunty. We have never been real companions. She has different preferences, my likes are different, but we have successfully cohabitated and created a stable household. We care for each other even though I can't say we have loved.

Or let me put it this way, over time we have learned to tolerate each other better,' he laughed.

I shook my head, 'You are funny, uncle.'

'One has to be. You can't go through life taking everything so seriously. In the end, we all have our stories, we have decisions that worked right and those that went terribly wrong. We all have regrets, we all have memories and yet none of us could predict any of this. That's the beauty of life, Tara. Each one of us has undertaken an unknown journey. And for you, the journey is far from over. Anyway, care for a drink?'

'Just one glass of wine, uncle. I have to leave early tomorrow.'

'Sure! Bahadur beta, bring out the bottle of wine that Sonu got from Australia.'

'Also make us a bowl of masala peanuts with some green chilies and chaat masala,' he said, rubbing his hands in anticipation of a good time.

'You remind me of papa. How he loved his evening drinks! No wonder dad and you were such good friends.'

'Not surprising that, in fact, we first bonded over our drinks,' said Ashok uncle as he offered me a glass of wine, 'and that evening was another story!'

'But how did you become friends? I'm not sure I ever asked,' I said, taking a sip, 'It's good. Thank you.'

'Well, I was in Delhi, attending an event with, what do you children call it, the "who's who" of town. It was one of those sought-after events that most people attended for bragging rights. But for me, the reason was quite different. Finally, I had decided to confess my feelings to the woman I had secretly loved through my college years. She was going to be there.

I tell you Tara, she was extremely charming. Every man on campus coveted her. And I, a rather obscure, unimpressive fellow at that time, could never dare to approach her. Forget approaching her, I did not even have the guts to look at her. So, I stole her picture from the administrative office and placed it right up on the altar where I offered my daily prayers, next to Shiva and Ganesha. I had made up my mind that I would talk to her only when I'm so successful that she can't refuse me. And if my worship was sincere, she would wait until that day. And this was going to be that day!

You can say I had made it by then. I would've easily wasted my life goofing around with friends, but for her love, I had decided to prove my worth. She had singlehandedly transformed my life and did not have the slightest inkling of it.

Well, coming back to that evening—everything was perfectly planned—top of the line. Private dining room, live band, candles, flowers and an exquisite diamond ring sourced from Africa. Just about everything you can imagine in the most romantic proposal. Not one detail was overlooked. After all, I had lived this exact evening, every day for five years straight.

Actually, your generation doesn't understand romance. They don't love like we did. Our love was grand and it only happened once.'

'And then, uncle? What happened after that?' I interrupted, quickly pulling him back from his favourite diversion and debate— the sad plight of a generation that doesn't understand romance.

He continued wistfully, 'I followed her around for a while but couldn't pick the right moment to approach her. I still remember her black saree, paired with a string of white pearls and that white rose tucked loosely behind her ear. It appeared as though divinity had descended on earth.

I decided some liquid courage would help. I was at the bar getting myself a drink. And as luck would have it, she came and took a seat right next to me. I thought the gods wanted to make this easy for me.

And just as I was about to ask her to join me on the floor, a young man approached from behind and threw his arm casually around her. With breath reeking of alcohol, he flirtingly whispered, "You're smoking tonight, even hotter than last night," as he walked away with a wink.

I was stunned. I waited for a reaction, anything— annoyance, disapproval, something. But she only smiled, her cheeks warming with that blush.

I crushed the glass I held in my hand and didn't look back. I walked away. Forever.'

'What happened after that?' I questioned curiously.

'I somehow managed my way to the bar downstairs and drank so much that I fell asleep at the counter. Your dad happened to be there. Previously, he had known me as an acquaintance, but that night, he became my friend. He heard me talk about her all night. All night I cried, and all night he consoled me.

Suddenly, my goddess had deserted me. My life had no purpose. There was nothing to work towards. Nothing left to achieve. I felt betrayed by her. I felt betrayed by the gods. I felt betrayed by life itself. And just the way you feel about Mala and Meeta, if it wasn't for your father, I wouldn't be sitting here today.'

'What happened to that girl? Did you ever meet her again?'

'The more I wanted to hate her, the more I found myself in love. I guess you value what you can work towards and win, but when something becomes unachievable, it becomes priceless. What do they call it—unrequited love!

Turned out the boy was some Casanova, engaged to her friend. They had been at a party together the previous night, and he was only flirting about her looks, in her capacity as his fiancé's best friend.'

'What! That's not good. Why didn't you pursue her after that?'

'It was too late. By the time I realized my mistake, she was already engaged to someone in London. She was gone.

Our minds can be quite the tormentor sometimes. I thought it knew better than my heart.

And that is why I often repeat that it's not what surrounds you; it's what you see, and how. Learn to see with your heart, not with your eyes. And when you do, this world will become a different place.'

'And then, uncle?'

'And then I moved on, perhaps too soon,' said uncle, narrowing his eyes, as though penetrating the depths of that garnet wine. 'And that will remain my greatest regret. I often question if giving up that love was even worth it? Say my fears were true, say they had been together the previous night. If I were a man enough, I should have had the confidence to win her over and the courage to accept her unconditionally. My love was unsure. It was conditional.

But again, who knows what would have happened if we did end up together. Regret has a way of weaving every story with the best possibilities.

Pour me another drink, beta. And the most important advice I want you to take along with you is this—neither trust your fears nor your regrets. Only trust the moment that's unfolding before you. Pay close attention to the choices of the moment.

Choose wisely and choose while you have the chance. Choices don't remain ours forever and time may not always be on our side.'

'I get what you're saying, uncle. Thanks for sharing this.'

'Beta, I want you to know we all have decisions that we hope to someday make peace with, although I don't know if it's really possible.

Not a day goes by when I'm not reminded of her. I think the act of moving on was only of my mind. To this day, my heart is beating at that bar, waiting for her.'

'Have you tried looking for her?'

'Yes, sometimes, just out of habit. I can't find her on Facebook. Maybe she's using a different last name.

Well, I think it's a good thing. Knowing your aunty, if she found out I have been searching for her, I would have a women's group doing a dharna outside my own house,' he laughed.

'Cheers, to lost love, new choices and unknown possibilities!' uncle toasted.

'Cheers!' I said, raising my glass.

Four

THE hills wore a cloak of darkness, standing still like an austere monk in deep contemplation. A few twinkling lights bore a precursor to the day that was just beginning to unfold. The sleepy hills slowly transitioned into busy urban plains, finally giving way to small towns and occasional farmlands.

An overpopulated concrete jungle dominated the landscape, interspersed with few patches of vibrant green fields, bathing leisurely in the soft morning light.

Balwinder and I were Amritsar bound.

Driving past Verka Milk Bar and Ropar Wetland, I recalled some fond childhood memories of travel breaks by the riverside...

'Bhenji!'

I was startled out of reminiscing by the sound of my name.

It took me a few seconds to reorient myself. I looked around. The sun was high. The fields were still. And I sat on the ledge, waiting for my room to finish getting cleaned.

'Bhenji,' Premo tapped me on my shoulder, bearing a worried look. 'Are you feeling all right? I've been calling for a while, but you haven't answered.'

'Sorry, Premo, I was just uh...a little tired from the drive this morning.'

'I hope you're not thinking about going back. Is everything comfortable for you?'

'Of course, it is. I was actually...just thinking about my

journey, where it began and how I am here now. A lot can change in a day!' I remarked, a little unsettled from the sudden cognizance.

'Bhenji, what can I tell you? Around here, nothing ever changes. Some days are warmer than others, some a little colder, occasionally someone dies or someone gets married, but mostly it's the same day every day.

But I came to tell you that we're finished cleaning. You should rest now.'

The smell of freshly mopped floors was inviting, even on this glistening, fractured stone.

'And here's the bell,' she pointed towards the antique-looking, handheld brass service bell.

'Just ring it in case you need anything or call out from the window. I'll come right over,' Premo offered, closing the door shut.

Finally, I was alone.

My aloneness crept towards me like a parasite, wrapping its tentacles around me little by little, thought by thought—one of anger, one of fear, one of regrets and another of despair.

I protested defiantly, shrugging off its dark aura. I opened my bag, hung up the clothes and began arranging my books on the table.

The sweet smell of paper offered me a familiar comfort. 'And soon, you will have plenty of company,' I whispered as I set the last book down, pleased at the inviting lineup.

And then I did again what I have done most of my life.

I reached for a book and flipped open a random page, knowing its words would speak to me. An advice, a clue or an answer, whatever it might be—but pages never failed to speak to me. And they always seemed to know. Perhaps, there's a greater order to randomness than we comprehend.

The passage read, '*And forget not that the earth delights to feel your bare feet and the winds long to play with your hair.'*

Resting the book on my chest, I lay back, staring at the ceiling as the words touched upon my empty heart, striking a forgotten chord. I swallowed a tear, feeling consoled by the promise of life these words seemed to convey.

I was barely a chapter into my book when a pair of bright headlights emerged in the distance. Before long, a vehicle came charging through the eucalyptus tunnel to a grinding halt by the main entrance.

'Premo,' I rushed down the stairs. 'There's a car in our driveway. Who could it be at this time?'

'It's Bittu,' said Premo glancing out the window. 'Doctor saab's son. Remember that 4-year-old with dishevelled hair and a perpetually running nose who wouldn't leave you alone?

He probably heard of your arrival and came to see you. But don't worry, I'll tell him to come back another day. News spreads like wildfire around here, I tell you,' Premo muttered to herself as she fixed her dupatta and hurried out the door

'Premo, wait! I'm feeling better. I'd like to see him. He must've grown up quite a bit.'

'Grown up? He shot up like a wild weed. He's 6'2", bhenji, but his brain is still stuck in his ankles. So immature,' she scowled, nodding her head.

I stepped through the narrow mesh doors of the baithak. A tall, well-built man clad in a black Pathani suit, sporting aviator glasses and a black turban stood texting on his phone. I observed his formidably thick kadha, a gleaming Ekonkaar pendant suspended from a heavy linked gold chain and a distinctly twisted mustache, pointed firmly up at the edges.

I stood still, a little intimidated and utterly unfamiliar with this somewhat daunting man in front of me.

'Tara bhenji,' spoke a deep masculine voice as he turned around, 'Sat Sri Akal,' he greeted, reaching swiftly for my feet.

I jumped back, 'Oh no, Bittu, that's not needed.'

He smiled disarmingly, removing his aviators. 'Why not? No blessing is too big or small, too young or old. I live by collecting these. Welcome home, bhenji! Mummyji has sent your favorite besan ladoos,' he said, holding out a blue plastic container. 'And she asked me to bring you home for dinner.'

Relieved to find an innocent familiarity behind the misleading appearance, I smiled, 'I must say you've grown up into a fine young man, Bittu. How time flies!'

A subtle blush and a hidden dimple appeared behind his coarse beard, 'It's been more than 20 years since you last visited. I hope you will stay for a few days this time,' he remarked.

'Hopefully, Bittu. And tell aunty, I still love my besan ladoos, but I don't feel too well today. I shall join you for dinner another time.'

'Not well? Shall I call daddy?'

'Oh, no! Nothing serious, just a little tired from the drive. But sit, we'll have some tea.'

'No, bhenji, you rest. I am right here, *tea-shea* can happen later. Premo, look after bhenji and call Mummyji if you need anything,' Bittu instructed.

Six hours and one decision had suddenly stretched my world. Familiar faces, familiar places and precious memories, it was all right there, but I hadn't been looking. Or maybe I'd been too busy looking for that which didn't exist.

I sat on the pidhi, as Premo served hot rotis right off the chulha. The smoke rose up towards the mesmerizing canopy of twinkling stars.

After small talks and pleasant conversations, I retired for the night. I proceeded to the terrace. Crickets chirped, stars twinkled and a cool breeze brushed against the crops in peaceful moonlight. I stood by the ledge for a while before heading to my room.

Sleep eluded me despite my long day of travel. I lay awake and stared at the ceiling.

My search for sleep was soon replaced by my search for answers. Why did I marry Tej? The question nudged me again. I had spent 17 years with him, not knowing why I had married him in the first place.

I had long come to accept this as a part of some fate that wasn't too kind to me. But today, for the first time, I wasn't willing to bury my head in the sand and wish the problem away. I sought hard, honest answers so I could make the right decisions, not necessarily the easiest ones.

I turned over and looked at the flowers on the desk.

Flowers, these beautiful, silent messengers sometimes come in hope, sometimes in sorrow and sometimes to contradict the reasoning of our hearts. Even then, I knew. Somewhere deep inside me, I knew…

※

It was her fifth frantic call in the past hour.

'Please, Tara. They only allow one single per two couples. We don't have any way of managing Ketan's friends' entry into the club. You can leave as soon as we get in. Oh, please, please come, Tara, otherwise we'll have to cancel our plans,' Shelly pleaded.

'Fine, Shelly. I'll come, but I won't stay long,' I begrudgingly conceded.

It was 7 p.m. on a Saturday evening when I pulled my car into an unpaved parking lot behind the club.

Shelly and her boyfriend Ketan stood waiting for me. Next to them, seated casually on the hood of a car, were two guys drinking imported beer out of cans.

'Thanks for coming, Tara!' Shelly ran up to greet me. 'We were hoping…'

'Tej. Nice to meet you,' our conversation was rudely interrupted by an unwarranted self-introduction.

'Tara,' I replied by way of a one-word reply, clearly unimpressed.

We proceeded to join a painfully slow-moving line on this sultry, breezeless summer evening.

Finally, after slapping a few mosquitoes dead and getting my wrist stamped for 'couple,' with Tej, I turned to Shelly. 'Happy? Now the guys are in. And I'm getting out. Enjoy.'

'Stay for a while,' Ketan insisted.

'Sorry, I have to go, but you all have a good time,' I replied even as my words drowned in blaring music.

As we headed towards the exit, I suddenly noticed a crowd converging around something, cheering in a wild frenzy. I looked back over my shoulder, and sure enough, it was Tej, climbing on top of a table. The next instance, he was grooving with full abandon, while crowds thumped and whistled around him.

Shelly and I gasped in horror. 'You sure have an interesting night ahead of you. Good luck,' I chuckled, bidding her goodbye.

I had barely turned on the headlights and was fumbling inside my bag for the parking ticket when I heard a knock on the window.

Startled, I looked up. It was Tej.

'Everything all right?' I asked, rolling the window down.

'You won't drive back alone,' he insisted.

'I always drive alone.'

'Not today. Not while I stand here,' he maintained.

'My driver will follow you in my car and make sure you get home safe.'

I looked in the rear-view mirror at the blinking Mercedes inching up behind me.

Suspecting he was drunk, and with no desire to extend the conversation any further, I shook my head.

'Nice meeting you, babe,' he waved his hand. 'Adios!'

'Goodnight,' I responded, rolling my window back up as I let out a deep breath.

'Babe?' Strangely brattish, I thought to myself.

The next morning, I received a flower delivery at home.

Flowers showed up again at my doorstep the next day, and the following day, and the following, with messages ranging from 'good morning' to 'have a pleasant day' and from 'just because' to 'someone will wait forever'. It went on every single day for 18 months straight until I finally conceded to their beauty and my interpretation of what they might be telling me.

But flowers are just flowers. They don't speak, and flowers can be bought. They can be manipulated to colour the sentiments of our heart. Eighteen months of colouring the sentiment until I could no longer recognize what I knew in the first place.

'Why did I marry him?' I questioned myself again.

On the face of it, I would like to think it was because he had persisted in pursuing me to a point where few could reach. Most suitors would've given up within a few weeks, or at most, few months of denial. He had repeatedly asked me the same question and unflinchingly accepted my stubborn refusal, day after day.

The nature of his proposal wasn't frivolous either. Unlike most harmless offers around coffee or movies, he had outrightly asked me to marry him. Startling and bold as this proposition might have been, it had for its basis, it appeared, a deep clarity and absolute conviction of his feelings towards me.

While on the surface, a lot could be ascribed to his unyielding persistence, but beneath the calm seas, there was another powerful current drifting me into an endless storm. A strange, hard to describe, tiny emotion that had over time assumed behemoth proportions.

It had nothing to do with love. In fact, it had little to do with him, a little more to do with his actions, but the most to do with my own responses to them.

All that he had invested in me—his time, his effort and his unsolicited gestures—had left a burden on my conscience. A foolish conscience which seemed to be keeping an account of all he'd done for me and what I somehow owed him in return.

I felt indebted, a little at first, but slowly his investment started to loom so heavy on the scale of my conscience that it tripped. I felt compelled to balance it out.

His commitments became my liability. His choices, my responsibility.

Like somehow, it would be unfair if I let this effort of 18 months of his life count for nothing. Sure, I owed him something— but my self was a big price I decided to pay.

Yes, a life-sized picture of mine, already adorned his bedroom wall. But in the end, it was that Sunday night phone call from his friend that sealed my fate.

At a party Tej had been attending, someone made an inappropriate comment about me. What started with a demand for an apology, ended with Tej in the hospital nursing a fractured arm and a broken nose.

Consumed with an overriding sense of guilt and responsibility, I went to visit him. That was the first step down the slippery road of no return.

Did I love him? Not really. But I did find myself wanting to like him.

With a heavily skewed perception, I started bending reality

to conform to my ideals. Everything good, I projected onto him, while the alarming red flags were conveniently attributed to all else, from an imperfect upbringing to a possessive temperament, to his extreme moodiness, perhaps even his company—anything that I could blame it on. Anything, but him.

But I will admit that for all his follies, back then, there still was an innocence lingering behind his brashness. An underlying colour of devotion that I could see and hold on to. It was there, until suddenly one day, it wasn't, not even a trace.

There were days when I desperately wanted to run back. While my steps inched me forward, my heart pulled me away. I was completely torn.

But to my 21-year-old naïve mind, it was already too late after I had visited him at the hospital. There was no turning back after that first dinner. An engagement certainly couldn't be reversed, and marriage—wasn't that a forever thing?

And finally, the kids came along and it was really too late.

Or so I believed!

I kept walking further along this 17-year-long road, only to realize that with each milestone, the burdens grew heavier, the distance farther and the pain deeper. This glittery path had been paved with shattered glass and led nowhere but a desolate dead end.

I tossed and turned. I took a sip of water and stared out the window at biji's room. It was dark and empty, much like my life. At some indeterminate point between glancing at the clock and staring at the ceiling, I fell asleep.

The soft sound of Gurbani soon eased me into wakefulness. I opened my eyes in a state of cozy slumber. It was pitch dark. I rolled over and pulled the blanket over my head, hoping to catch some more sleep. I could hear the faint whisking sound of the courtyard being swept. I inched up to look out. A group of busy women went quietly about their work in this peaceful hour.

It was chilly and foggy. Yet, the nip felt warmly inviting.

'Premo, how early do you start your day? It's 4:30 in the morning,' I said, walking groggily to the stove as I pulled my hair up in a knot.

'Bhenji, the kettle starts brewing at 4 a.m. each morning for our farm-workers. Biji had two simple mandates—that there be plenty for all and that no one should have to wait. The tradition continues to this day.'

'No wonder, it was right here that I first discovered my love of tea,' I said, wrapping the shawl snugly around myself as I pulled closer to the chulha.

Premo poured steaming tea from an aluminum kettle with a curved spout, straight into a steel glass.

'You still use these aluminum kettles and steel glasses, how lovely!'

'Bhenji, that's what everyone uses around here. If you prefer a cup instead, we have a whole tea-set in bhabiji's drawing-room cabinet.'

'No Premo, this is perfect, keeps me warm,' I said, gripping the glass with both my hands as I carefully blew into it before sipping.

The sky was still dark, but a faint orange light was beginning to break through, sweeping away the dark shadows cast by the previous night. I walked across the freshly swept courtyard, as the soothing chants of the morning prayer permeated the air, as though purifying the cosmos itself.

There was something about this Gurbani. A strange, inexplicable pull that I'd never experienced before. I was one of those people who visited Gurudwaras only on special occasions—birthdays, bhogs and weddings. And while I didn't quite fit into the neat category of religious believers, I did acknowledge some greater power. Perhaps, a distant, kind God who watches over us. I hadn't ever connected with him in a personal sense, but we had maintained a cordial, respectful arm's-length association throughout.

I hesitated for a moment, then stepped over the threshold of the Gurudwara, bowing my head in complete surrender. I stood still for a while. Soon, tears began to flow, as though I was baring my soul in front of someone who had already seen it all.

While I had nothing to say, this gentle presence seemed to know it all.

Gradually, a calm assurance settled over me. I started to blabber, 'Waheguru ji, I have no idea where I am and why? I also do not know which way I'm going, or if I should be going at all? I stand at these crossroads looking for a direction while darkness fills my life and my heart. I am utterly lost.

Show me a path. Show me the way. Show me how. Please.'

As I approached the stairwell, I heard the faint sound of my phone ringing upstairs.

'Hi, mom. Everything okay? How come you're calling this early?' I enquired, answering the phone.

'Beta, Meeta and Mala are also on the line,' she added.

'What's going on, mom? Is everything all right?' I snapped with worry.

'Relax, Tara. It's nothing critical,' Mala answered, 'but still important enough that you should know.'

'Go on, I'm listening,' I added apprehensively.

'Well, initially Tej came by a few times demanding your whereabouts, going so far as to threaten to file a police complaint.

When that didn't yield any results, he came back regretting his conduct and even apologized. And then he returned yet again, completely drunk, crying about how sorry he was for his misbehaviour and how he wants you back. All with the assurance that he was willing to do whatever it takes to keep his family together.'

'I knew he couldn't handle this,' I rattled breathlessly. 'Sooner or later, he was bound to realize his mistake. He has no ability to control his temper. It's only when he returns to his senses, that he recognizes the blunder he has committed.'

'Well again, don't jump to any happy conclusions that you think would put an end to all your problems, just yet. There's more to this story.'

'What more?' I questioned reluctantly.

'Bala came over yesterday,' Mala continued.

'Bala? What for?'

'I'm sending you the pictures Bala shared with mom. You can see for yourself,' Mala added.

I tapped the message. There Tej was, walking down the stairs of our house, his arm wrapped around the waist of a 20-something girl.

My heart felt numb.

'Either that was a quick transition, or two weeks is an incredibly long time!' I exhaled, trying hard to conceal my anguish.

I wasn't sure what hurt me more, looking at what I'd seen often enough in open chat windows and carelessly managed photo libraries, or the fact that now, finally, my family had seen it too.

And while that pained me, it was the next picture that pierced right through my heart, shattering this 17-year-long myth that was my marriage. Strangers strewn across couches and corners, empty beer bottles rolling across the floor and half-finished glasses of spilled vodka decorating the mantel. Sid's artwork hung silently on the wall behind and Mehar's desolate board games stood abandoned among the chaos. I did not recognize this place.

Was this the same place I had brought my children home for the first time? That sofa where I had rocked Mehar to sleep, the floor where Sid had painted, the mantle which proudly displayed our reception photo in a silver frame. How did all that get replaced so quickly by something so ugly? Was that an illusion, or was this a horrible nightmare? Or were these parallel realities that had finally converged? A questioning silence lingered over the phone.

'Tara, are you still there?' asked Meeta.

'Yes. And I finally see it. A house that I kept wanting to turn into a home. It neither was nor will ever be. I just found my answer.'

'What a two-faced pathological liar!' muttered Mala. 'Really! Where did he find the guts to come begging for redemption while doing this behind our backs? Like he couldn't wait for Tara to be gone so he could live his life up.'

Mom interrupted, 'Tara, would you like to come home?'

'Which home, mom?' I questioned bleakly.

Mom hesitated, 'The home you grew up in—it will always remain yours.'

'What's mine? I do not know anymore. I'm just about finding out,' I said before hanging up.

I sat down on the edge of the bed and stared at the phone in my hand.

Contrary to what I expected, I felt nothing.

Neither anger nor pain. I wasn't wounded, nor was my heart ripping to shreds. I remained surprisingly unaffected.

If anything, in a strange sense, I experienced relief—a reconciliation with the worst. My greatest fears were coming to pass. The worst I could have ever imagined was being realized in front of my eyes. Slowly but surely, I was reaching rock bottom.

The little hope I had held on to was finally departing, making way for a new reality to sink in. There was nothing worse that could happen, nothing more that could be destroyed, nothing else that could be taken away.

I had nothing more left to lose.

From here, it was only an uphill path towards discovering a life that might not promise luxuries but held out a possibility of peace and dignity. Strangely, I felt all right.

I slowly walked down the narrow dark steps and opened the door to daylight.

The silent baheda tree stood wrapped in a cloud of mist. It held its ground and stood tall even when the sun ceased to shine. Its faith was probably bigger than its fears. Its resilience, stronger than its doubt. We stood facing each other for a while. I saw the path clearly.

My phone beeped again.

It was a text from Dev, 'In the area for a meeting today. Ashok uncle wanted me to stop by and check if you needed anything.'

'Please don't inconvenience yourself. I'm totally fine. Uncle worries for no reason,' I texted back.

'Regardless, a cup of tea doesn't sound too bad, I'm just a half-hour away. Of course, if it's not a bother for you.'

'Not at all. In fact, some company would be quite welcome today.'

'Sounds good. I'll stop by once I'm done with my meetings, say early evening?'

'Sure. See you then.'

The day was mellowing and a cozy afternoon sun drenched the surroundings in a warm, honey-gold hue. I sat in the verandah leafing through the pages of *The Forty Rules of Love*.

'Your guest is here, bhenji,' Premo announced.

Dev followed her, looking sharp in his navy blazer and a white dress shirt, while I sat in my oversized hoodie, worn-out jeans and comfy slippers.

'Hello, Tara. It's a pleasure to see you again,' he greeted politely, his well-defined jawline enhancing his characteristically warm smile.

'Same here, Dev! Thanks for coming all the way,' I added, growing a little conscious of my overly relaxed, borderline sloppy appearance.

'Premo, could you open the baithak for us please?' I requested.

'It's actually quite nice outside. If you don't mind, I could join you right here,' Dev suggested.

'Of course! I love being outdoors myself. Please, make yourself at home. It's rather basic around here.'

'But truly restful,' answered Dev, looking around at the quiet haveli.

'What would you like, tea or coffee?' I offered.

'Whatever you prefer. I'm good with either. So, you do seem to be doing all right I see,' Dev remarked.

'I told you so! You may go back and submit an all-clear report to Ashok uncle,' I smiled.

Dev laughed, 'Yes, I'd be in big trouble otherwise.'

'So, what brings you here?' I asked.

'Long story, but essentially some properties and projects that I'm managing in the area.'

'Business does demand travel,' I responded.

'That's right, but this is more personal than business.'

'I see. How long is your trip?'

'Well, I leave for Kasauli the day after. And that reminds me, if you'd like to send anything back for your children, I'd be quite happy to deliver it.'

'Thanks, Dev. I might take you up on that offer. I've been missing them terribly.'

'Of course. I know exactly how it is.'

I looked towards him but stopped myself from asking any questions.

There was a long silence, as though we were trying to piece together each other's lives, while still conscious and respectful of the boundaries that separated us.

'Well,' said Dev as he placed his cup on the table. 'I look forward to hearing from you. Thanks for the tea and the company.'

'You're welcome. And Dev, I truly appreciate your thoughtfulness.'

'Anytime. I am happy to stop by and pick it up, or if you feel like getting out for a bit, we could meet in the city over lunch or coffee. As per your convenience.

And you have my number. Remember what Ashok uncle told you! Don't hesitate to reach out.'

'Will do. Thanks again.'

'Who was that bhenji?' Premo came running to inquire as soon as the car turned the corner.

'Dev. He's an acquaintance of Ashok uncle. Anyway, I plan to have an early dinner and get some sleep tonight,' I replied.

The faint bustling of morning chores grew steadily louder, and pious chants of Gurbani infused the air. I looked at the clock. It was a few minutes past 5 a.m. The light in biji's veranda shone brightly. I leaned closer towards the window, trying to narrow my focus. There appeared to be a small figure sitting on the steps leading up to biji's room.

I strained my eyes harder, but it was still too dark to make anything out. Wrapping a shawl around my shoulders, I put on my slippers and headed down the stairs, curious to meet this unfamiliar, early morning visitor.

'Sat Sri Akal, bhenji,' Premo greeted me.

'Sat Sri Akal, Premo, who's that little girl sitting by biji's veranda with a book in her hand?'

'Oh her, that's Darshi's daughter. Darshi is not feeling too well, so she brought her along.'

'Seerat puttar, come here and meet Tara aunty. And talk to her in English,' Premo called out to the child.

'Bhenji, Seerat attends the local secondary school for girls. She's very intelligent.'

'Hello, Aunty. How do you do?' Seerat asked, her eyes bright and curious.

'I'm fine, beta. It's good to meet you,' I answered, fondly remembering my Mehar in her.

'What are you studying?' I asked.

'English. I know a little, but I want to learn everything. And I want to speak in English too, like an officer.'

'That's wonderful, Seerat.'

'But we don't have any English teachers in our school. We had one, but she transferred to Taran Taaran.'

'Oh, I could teach you English. It's easy. You will pick it up in no time.'

I had barely finished the sentence that two tiny arms gripped me in a tight embrace.

'Will you? Really? Thank you, aunty!' she exclaimed, before scampering away happily to inform her mother.

I followed after her.

Darshi heard the sound of my approaching steps and nodded her head in greeting.

'Darshi, I'd like to help Seerat with English lessons. Could you bring her to me in the morning, before her school starts?'

She nodded her head again as she continued to sweep in silence.

'Premo tells me you're not well. Hope you're doing better,' I asked, getting a little concerned with her unusual reaction.

'She's not better, aunty. This will take a long time to heal. He beat her up very badly. If the villagers hadn't intervened, he would've killed her,' Seerat blurted.

'Who would've killed her?'

'Seerat!' yelled Premo as she walked over. 'You talk too much. Go play now.'

'Nothing new, bhenji,' Premo added, walking up to me. 'It's the usual. Every now and then, her husband gets drunk and demands her hard-earned money to buy more liquor. If she refuses, he beats her up. This was the money that Darshi had saved for Seerat's school fees. She refused to give it, and this is what she got in return.'

I grasped Darshi by her shoulders and turned her around.

A bruised swollen cheek pushed up against a barely visible eye. Her deformed lip was scabbed over from bleeding and a fresh, protruding scar marred her chin.

Darshi swallowed hard, first choking on tiny sobs and then dropping to my feet as she began wailing. 'Save her bhenji. Save my daughter. I don't want her to end up like me. Please save my Seerat,' she cried, clinging desperately to my legs.

I stood still. I had no solace to offer, no words of comfort or assurance.

Five

'GOOD morning, Dev. I'll be in town later today to pick up a few things,' I texted. 'Perhaps, it would save you the trip if we met there.'

'Certainly! Would you care for some chole bhature? There is a great place I know of. It's not your typical fine dining, but you can't beat their authentic flavours. A truly local experience, in case you'd be interested,' Dev responded.

'Sounds really good,' I replied. 'In fact, I've been craving local Amritsari food for a while now.'

'Perfect then. Sounds like a plan. Kanha Sweets on Lawrence road. 1 p.m.?'

'See you there,' I confirmed.

After what seemed like ages, I was looking forward once again to the small joys of a simple life—warm sunshine, good food and pleasant conversations. Besides, there was something unusual about Dev's company—a rare calmness and maturity, like he understood life with great intimacy.

The day was beginning to warm up as I strolled down the busy marketplace. Buckets, mops, t-shirts and even bedsheets hung in a colourful array along crowded sidewalks. Large, overbearing hoardings of upcoming apartment complexes clamored for attention, while rickshaws, scooters and horse carts shared the road with gleaming chauffeured cars honking impatiently at pedestrians.

I walked quietly along. Suddenly, a polaroid camera showcased in one of the display windows caught my eye. How Mehar would delight in using this, I thought. I slowed down to a bare crawl, debating if I should go in and inquire about the price. Realizing it wasn't the most pragmatic idea, I forcibly dragged my eyes off it and prodded myself to keep going. I had barely walked another block when a wooden easel caught my fancy. A sturdy, tall and seemingly well-constructed easel. And that would make just the perfect present for Sid, the suggestion nudged me again, and painfully so.

Here I was, with little money which I planned to use judiciously. Mom had insisted I carry extra for contingency, but to me, it seemed like an unnecessary burden. My needs were basic and few. I had grudgingly agreed to take Rs.30,000 from her, and that was a burden enough.

I was saddened at the thought of having to curtail my desire to indulge my children. But I quickly reminded myself of how, for us as children, the most memorable presents were often the most straightforward ones—pencil boxes, cool sharpeners, rare candy and the experience of diving into a loaded goody bag filled with little trinkets and small surprises.

Some of the fancier gifts never quite delivered the same thrill, I argued.

Consoled by my own reasoning, I felt reassured that my children would sense love regardless of the price tag.

Assorted churan jars, rainbow-colored saunf, desi ghee matthis, aam papad, a pair of colourfully embellished Punjabi juttis for Mehar and a musical car that danced to Bollywood songs for Sidak completed my list.

Two bars of chocolate also made their way into the bag along with long letters I had written to each of them the night before. I kissed the letters before slipping them in, knowing the thrill this unexpected delivery would bring.

'How much longer?' I asked the taxi driver as I stared anxiously at my watch. It was already 1 p.m., and the traffic was barely inching forward.

'Madam ji, it's only a five-minute drive from here, but with the backup, it might take us 10–15 minutes.'

There was something about keeping others waiting that stressed me beyond any reasonable measure. I constantly timed myself with room to spare, even if it meant getting to places early and having to wait.

'Sorry, running late. Just caught up in some traffic,' I typed.

'Relax, this is Amritsar. Time and people both move at their own pace here. I'll see you when you get here,' read Dev's reply.

As I made my way towards the entrance, I couldn't help noticing the conspicuous image of Krishna on the signboard as though validating the seal of 100% pure desi ghee preparations next to it.

'Oh... Hi, Dev,' I fumbled as I walked in, looking and feeling a little out of sorts. I nervously adjusted the strap of my crossbody bag and switched the order of the bags I held in my hands.

'May I?' he offered, reaching for the bags.

'Thanks, but I'm quite all right,' I hesitated, swiftly moving both bags to one hand as I took a seat.

I sat across from Dev in this bustling restaurant. The clanking sounds of steel utensils, loud animated conversations followed by boisterous laughter and a hurried stream of servers hurling verbal orders across the kitchen appeared both chaotic and entertaining.

'Are you all right, Tara?' Dev asked, observing my curious absorption with the surroundings.

'Yes,' I answered, turning my attention back to him, still tense and uneasy. Not sure if it was the built-up stress from being late or the strange experience of being seated across a man who was unrelated to me in any typical sense.

'I hope you're okay with eating here. Otherwise, we could go to a different place.'

'Not at all,' I quickly interjected. 'This is perfect. In fact, dhabas were quite our thing during our childhood. Since we travelled a fair amount by car, the highlight of these road trips was always the next stop by some roadside dhaba. Dad was a firm believer in "volume breeds quality". The food was always fresh and consistently delicious,' I said, almost feeling my stress dissolve away into the conversation.

'I would agree with him. They know how it's done right. Besides, my association with this place goes way back. As a little kid, I loved coming here with my grandfather. And he himself had been a regular here since his college years. We're talking some 60 years ago, when this was a small shop inside the walled city. They've grown so much since then, but the flavours, he told me, were exactly as they were back in the day.'

'Really? That's fascinating.'

'Yes, some tastes develop into traditions,' Dev remarked.

'That's right!' I responded, finally beginning to relax.

Multi-sectioned steel thalis overloaded with steaming chole and aloo were hurriedly tossed onto our table. Its scrumptiousness dripped over the edges and soaked well into the crunch of oversized golden puris.

'Glad I gave my breakfast a miss this morning,' I smiled.

'Smart move! Please—enjoy now,' Dev offered.

I savoured the food, indulging in the rich flavours that burst forth with every bite. I felt deeply grateful for this moment of normality.

'Thank you, Dev. This was special. Haven't done anything like this in a long time.'

'Glad you enjoyed it and I could see you really did.'

'Yes, three puris for a woman my size, I'll have to skip dinner as well,' I laughed.

The server went along briskly after slamming a steel plate containing the bill buried beneath a loosely scattered sugar-fennel mixture, often eaten as a mouth freshener.

'Dev, I know it probably doesn't amount to much, but could we please split the bill?' I offered awkwardly, 'Nothing to do with letting you pay for a meal, it's personal. Just something that…'

'I respect your sentiment, Tara. And I promise you can pay for our next meal here unless you've already decided you don't want to see me again.'

'Of course, I do. And I guess…that would be fine,' I replied hesitantly to his well-reasoned response.

'Well, I should head back now. Here are the bags for Mehar and Sidak,' I finally offered.

'I promise, I'll handle these with exceptional care,' Dev smiled graciously.

'Oh, don't worry. Everything in there is rather inexpensive,' I clarified.

'Presents that come from mothers are always valuable. You can't put a price on these.

By the way, how're you going home?'

'Balwinder left for Chandigarh after dropping me. I didn't think I would need a car here. But the taxi driver who brought me here offered to drive me back. I have his number.'

'Not at all. I'll drop you home. And before you ask me—don't worry, my next meeting isn't until five.'

'You really don't have to do this, Dev,' I urged.

'I understand I don't have to, but I'd like to!' Dev replied.

We drove through the congested city streets on to open

country roads flanked by expansive green fields.

I stared out of the window, preoccupied with nagging, aimless thoughts that sped by faster than the fleeting landscape, leaving me with nothing but a blur at best.

'Tara, I hope you don't mind me saying something,' Dev broke the long, introspective silence.

'Of course not, go ahead. Are you going to ask me why I'm here?' I suggested preemptively.

'No. I won't ask you what brought you here, but whatever direction you take from here Tara, let it be a positive one. Your life matters,' he added.

I looked towards him in a questioning silence.

'Ashok uncle mentioned it in passing,' Dev clarified, his voice unwavering, and his eyes steady on the road ahead.

'Well, thank you for your concern, Dev, but honestly, it's too late to make my life matter anymore. I just want to do what is best for my children,' I said, fiddling with the bag that rested on my lap.

'What makes you think you know what is best for your children?' he demanded.

I looked up uncomfortably, my eyes as empty as my thoughts.

'You know, Tara, my parents always wanted to do what they thought was the best for me. If someone had asked me, I would tell them what I knew was clearly best for all of us. They could have saved a lot of pain and salvaged a lot of what they lost of their life.'

'I'm sorry to hear that,' I murmured.

'That's just life. The sooner we come to accept it and move on, the better off we are.'

'And this world is really vast, Tara. It extends far beyond what you've known and far beyond what you might think possible.'

I paused for a brief moment, 'It's not that easy, Dev.'

'It's not that complicated either. Look, you'll have your choices to make, but the fact is that you are more than this marriage. You matter as an individual. Your happiness matters. Give it a fair chance.

Sorry if I went overboard. Don't get me wrong. I'm certainly not trying to push you in any direction, Tara. I'm only giving you the advice I wish I'd been old enough to give my mother. Maybe she would still be alive.'

A stunned silence fell upon me. I looked at Dev. My burdened lips failed to part and my tongue fell completely numb. I wanted to say something. I fumbled for my voice, but the reservoir of words had dried.

'I... I had no idea. Take care, Dev,' I barely managed to stutter as I closed the door.

'Be well, Tara,' he responded. His expression was still untroubled and serene. But his eyes—they had suddenly become impenetrable.

As I walked towards the house, my mind spewed out a thousand questions and my heart sank faster than the setting sun.

Premo was sitting in the veranda shelling peas when I arrived.

'Bhenji, how was your day?' she greeted me exuberantly. 'I'm cooking your favourite pulao for dinner.'

'Did you see Darshi today?' I inquired as I approached closer.

'I haven't seen her all day,' Premo admitted.

'And, now that you mention, I haven't seen Seerat either,' she added.

'I wonder how she's doing. I must go check on her,' I mumbled.

'Bhenji, why do you want to go to the village? I'll have someone else check on her.'

'Why? What's wrong with me going there?'

'Nothing wrong, but...'

'Just come with me, Premo. I won't be able to sleep unless I see her. I have a bad feeling about this.'

'If you insist, bhenji,' Premo rose from her shelling, 'but I will inform bade bhenji that I tried to dissuade you.'

'Fine, Premo, you can defend yourself all you want. Let's go now. Please.'

We walked through the darkening fields towards a dilapidated cluster of tightly spaced homes.

Dogs barked. An unbearably potent stench emanated from the open drains. Women sat on steps directly above it, chopping vegetables and drinking tea, while kids played busily about the littered streets. It was a whole different world out there.

We entered the house through a barren courtyard. A tiny shack stood at the far end of the lot. To my left, was a modestly bolstered, thatched shed where Seerat stood collecting cow dung in a large metal bucket.

And to my right, lay a motionless man with his legs dangling partially off the manja. His parna, having fallen off his head, now lay covered in dust while flies hummed about his corpse-like body, which reeked of alcohol and urine.

My heart sank.

'Seerat,' I called out.

Seerat turned around. Her eyes lit up instantly as she dropped the bucket and bolted to the handpump to wash off.

'Hello, aunty,' she greeted me, with what I comprehended as a feeling of slight embarrassment mixed with a tinge of shame. 'I was making paathis since mother is unwell,' she began to explain.

'Well, I got you some books and a small surprise.'

'Really, aunty? You got me new books? Let me see!' she exclaimed, racing buoyantly towards me as I held out the bag.

Pulling out a book, Seerat dropped to the floor and began flipping through its pages, trying to speak full sentences as she went along.

'The boy plays with a ball,' she read, pausing to look up towards me.

'Well done, Seerat. You could be teaching English to others before you know it.'

She fixed her hair and stood tall, with new-found confidence brimming in her trusting eyes.

'And there's something else in the bag that you missed.'

'What is it, aunty?' she asked.

'See for yourself!'

'A chocolate! A big one too. Thank you, aunty. I knew Babaji has the power to make dreams come true. I'd been seeing this chocolate at the hatti for years now. I can't believe you just bought it for me,' she beamed.

'Where is your mother?' I asked Seerat.

'Sleeping inside,' Seerat answered, pointing towards the shack. 'The fever hasn't broken since last night.'

'Did she see a doctor?'

'She has no money; father took it all yesterday to buy his drinks.'

I looked at the listless man who lay oblivious on the bed next to an empty bottle, as an 11-year-old toiled with household tasks and a woman lay scorching in high fever without medicines or care.

I reached for my phone, 'Bittu, are you around?'

'Yes, bhenji, I'm home, do you need anything?'

'I'm at the pind, at Darshi's house.'

'What are you doing there, bhenji?' Bittu inquired.

'She is running a high fever. Could you request doctor saab to come here? I'll pay for the visit.'

'What are you saying, bhenji? Don't worry about it. I'll be right over with daddy.'

Doctor saab walked in behind Bittu, who carried his briefcase.

After attending to Darshi, doctor saab turned to me in a somber tone. 'Tara beta, I'm glad you called me. Her fever is touching 105 degrees. The infection has been spreading rapidly. Here's a course of antibiotics and a few other medicines I'm prescribing. The fever should break by morning. But tonight is critical.'

'Seerat beta,' doctor saab turned to her, 'who else is in the house?'

'No one,' Seerat shrugged her shoulders. 'Father will not wake up until tomorrow afternoon.'

'Doctor saab, I will stay back tonight and look after Darshi,' Premo offered.

'And I will get the medicine,' added Bittu.

'Bhenji. Come, I'll drop you on my way to the chemist,' he offered. 'Daddy will wait here to give the first dose and go over the rest of the medication before going home,' he explained.

I sat side-saddled behind Bittu, as he kick-started his Bullet. 'Thanks for doing this, Bittu.'

'Bhenji, thank you for giving me this chance. I think you can make a difference in their lives. I'm happy you're here for them.'

I refrained from letting my tears show. Who was I to be pretending to be this saviour when I couldn't save my own life? I was no different from Darshi. At some level, she was an extension of my own life. While appearances differed, the deeper issues remained just the same.

I opened the door to my room, turned on the light and placed my phone on the table. I noticed a missed call from Ashok uncle.

'Hi, uncle! I'm sorry, I should've called you once I reached.'

'Don't worry, beta. I have my sources for that information. But I was calling you about something different today.'

'What is it, uncle?

'Beta, I spoke with your mom a little while back. And

considering that for me you are no different from my own children, Ashu and Sonu, it might be a good idea for you to give some thought to this suggestion,' he continued.

'You know how quickly Sonu's hospital has been expanding in the last few years. He could definitely use some help in case you want to consider spending a few months in Delhi.

You have a house there. And you will also have aunty and Ashu to give you company. Besides, Ashu runs her own clothing line. She travels, designs and organizes events. You could possibly find something that interests you there. I mean, you two have always been close. It might work very well. Just some options for you to consider.'

I remained quiet.

'Thanks for the suggestion, uncle. I will give it a good thought, and yes, Delhi would be nice, and so would be the idea of being productive.'

'No beta, it's not about being productive, I just want you to open up new horizons. Try something you haven't done before. It's never about making money or being busy. Those are insignificant. The real point is personal growth. A lot of our own happiness and self-assurance comes from how we are evolving. Learning something new, trying something different. Stagnation of any kind can be dangerous. Life must feel like it's moving on.

However, as always, beta, the choice remains with you. I just wanted you to know this option exists. How was your meeting with Dev, by the way?'

'Very nice. He's quite a gentleman.'

'I wouldn't trust you to his care if I didn't know him so well. He's a rare gem.

Okay, Tara beta, my drinks are waiting for me. I better return to their company now,' he laughed. 'You take care of yourself.'

'I will, uncle. Good night.'

I called mom right away, 'Mom, why did you call Ashok uncle? Let me be absolutely clear, I have no desire to impose myself on his family. What he's doing for us is enough. I'm not at all comfortable living with them in Delhi or having them include me in their business. That's called overstepping and you know how I feel about being a liability.'

'Beta, it was just a well-meaning suggestion and he came up with it. You don't have to accept any of it but do keep an open mind.'

I remained quiet, my silence conveying how unconvincing her response felt.

'Look,' she began to explain, 'I talked to Premo earlier today and she told me about Darshi. The truth is that I don't want you to remain surrounded by the same negativity that you've been trying to escape. Their lives have been like this forever. You can't change anything.'

'Mom, I like it here. And I'm coping just fine. The fact that all of you are sitting out there constantly worrying about my life is what stresses me the most. Let me deal with whatever I'm going through. If there is anything I can't handle, I will absolutely let you know. I assure you.'

'Okay, beta. You know best.'

'And now you're upset!'

'No, why would I be upset? As a mother, I just can't help myself sometimes. Don't worry about me. Do what makes you happy.'

'Mom, just so you know, I met Dev for lunch today and thoroughly enjoyed it. I'm giving English lessons to Seerat, feasting on home-made besan ladoos that Bittu brought me and I'm more than halfway through reading my first book. Trust me. This place is doing me good.'

'Stay happy, Tara,' mom finally let out a little sigh of relief. 'God knows how I've been praying for a miracle.'

'Thanks, mom, it's all good. Just been a long day. Let me get some rest now. And you please stop worrying about me.'

'Okay beta, good night.'

I turned on the lamp and picked up the book from the nightstand, making myself comfortable in bed.

My thoughts immediately drifted to Dev. I wanted to say something. Something more, but without sounding too apologetic for his loss.

'Thanks for the wonderful afternoon and the valuable advice. I'll keep working on it,' I texted.

'And I will keep working on reminding you. The pleasure was entirely mine. Take care,' came his prompt reply.

'Safe travels,' I typed back.

Before long, I found myself struggling with pages that I seemed to be reading but not quite registering. I was clearly distracted and surprisingly awake. I closed the book and set it aside.

There was something on my mind, something bothering me with a nudge for an answer. Suddenly a slew of questions began swirling in my head. *'Why isn't Darshi leaving him? What is the extent of her abuse? Could Dev really mean that an unhappy marriage cost his mother her life? How far will Darshi go before she walks away? How far will you go, Tara?'* my mind rattled off, one question after another.

Intimidation, disrespect, humiliation, exploitation, bullying, undermining and cheating—I had endured every form of abuse. I had survived it all, but at the cost of allowing something to die within me—my happiness, my trust, my self-worth, my confidence, my conscience, and to some extent, my very desire to live.

Why had I stayed on? It clearly wasn't for money or lifestyle, given both hinged on his occasional generosities. I neither had love, nor respect, nor the remotest sense of stability or security.

Perhaps, I was just afraid to leave. Maybe clinging to a familiar pain felt safer than venturing out to find an unknown joy.

Quite early on in this marriage, I had developed a sense that his behaviour wasn't entirely 'normal'. I had seen nothing remotely close to this in my growing years. Yes, I had heard about domestic abuse and violence, but from what I knew, abuse came with physical evidence to show for it. Mental abuse, however, is this invisible tormenter that sneaks up and overpowers you while you're still trying to recognize its face.

Quite honestly, whatever little I knew about him didn't quite permit me to harbour too many illusions of a happy marriage.

Initially, however, I did try my best to project it, at least to my family that looked forward to my fond accounts of travel, pampering and family bonding. Once in a while, they would bring up a slight instance of something they found 'odd', but I was quick to write it off to his being moody or having a bad day. Gradually, my friends started making similar inferences: 'Did he just call you that?' or 'Why did he get angry and leave?' I figured it was far easier to stop socializing than it was to justify these embarrassing situations.

The few times that I did bring it to his family's attention, they conveniently camouflaged the issue. 'He has a bad temper. He can't help it,' explained his mother. 'Try not to make him angry and everything will be fine. And if he does get angry, never answer back,' she instructed. I believed this lie for many years and did only and exactly what pleased him. But his actions kept getting worse.

I was caught in this extreme cycle of violent outbursts, physical threats, rages and rants, power and control, and just as I reached the verge of my limit, he would flip a full 180 degrees, as though he wasn't even the same man. He would cry, beg for redemption, bring me flowers and even elevate me, in such moments, to the status of a deity. He would go any lengths to keep me from leaving. All with the sweet promise, 'It will never happen again,' and so I believed until I was proven wrong.

For all the weaknesses this man had, he had two disproportionate strengths that he used to his advantage. Logic and the art of manipulation. He could suddenly flip every situation such that he ended up the victim and I, the perpetrator. Each time, I was left absolutely convinced that everything that had ensued, I had inflicted upon myself with the choices I had made. 'If you had answered me the first time I called your name, I wouldn't have been angry. And when I got angry, if you hadn't tried walking away, I wouldn't have smashed the vase.' No matter what he did, he could always explain it as my fault.

'And what I got,' he would tell me, 'is what I deserved.'

He had managed to ingrain deep in my psyche, an unyielding belief that I didn't amount to much and didn't deserve much either. That I was lucky he was still by my side, despite all my shortcomings and my utter lack of accomplishment. I had grown to believe this and a part of me still questions if I really am capable of an independent existence.

While I can safely say the deeply rooted 'ride or die' family values I had harboured since adolescence had started to loosen their grip over time, what never did leave me was a deceitful hope—that only if I stayed, someday perhaps, he might change.

And now, for the first time, this hope had also departed. I don't know if it finally left me, or I eventually let it go. Whatever the case might be, it wasn't such a terrible thing.

My heart weighed heavy again as I caught myself spiraling down the darkness of my past once again.

In a flash of panic, I called Meeta.

'What's the matter, Tara?' she enquired as she answered the phone.

'Meeta, do you think I'm limiting myself by staying here? Should I consider Delhi, a better place with happier people, even if it means compromising my own pride? Maybe uncle is right. One can't remain stuck in a comfort zone, correct?'

'Tara, hold on, take a breather. What changed so suddenly? You were doing just fine this morning.'

'I don't know, Meeta. I don't know if I know anymore what's best for me. Mom and Ashok uncle seem to think I'd be better off in Delhi doing something productive with my life.'

'You sound overwhelmed, Tara. Whatever this storm is, let it blow over. Sleep on it. You don't need to decide anything today. You knew what you wanted before you came here and you will know what you want now.'

I took a deep breath. 'And what about Darshi? What if she's a constant reminder of my own pain?'

'Look, while I am concerned about that, I also believe life brings you everything for a reason. I can't advise you on what to do. But think of it this way, what if you can see in her life that which you've been unable to recognize in your own.

You were possibly too young to remember the poem dad wrote. For some compelling reason, I could never forget it. It was about a woman who went to fetch water from a well each day. One day, she suddenly saw the truths of her life in her own reflection, contained within its dark depths and confining walls. Once she recognized her prison, she was finally able to break free. He called it "aaina", the mirror.

Honestly, I see whatever you're going through as a positive thing. You are finally beginning to question. Which means you're finally beginning to care for yourself.

Relax and try to get through the night. We will talk tomorrow.'

I walked to the kitchen, made myself a cup of chamomile tea and headed over to biji's room. There was a strange peace that filled this space. I opened the window to let in the cool breeze as I pulled a chair by it. Peaceful moonlight streamed into this darkness, illuminating the old wooden charkha that stood in a corner and the portrait of biji and darji that hung on the wall above it.

'You know my wonderful children, this charkha is a lot more than just a spinning wheel,' biji's words echoed in my mind.

'What else can it do, nani?'

'Well, this brought us our greatest gift, our independence.'

'How, nani? How can a charkha bring us independence? It's not a weapon. It can't fight.'

'Beta, independence is not always won by fighting. It is won by deciding.

Bapu used this in the Independence movement as a symbol of self-sufficiency. He said when you become self-sufficient, you become mentally independent. And once you're mentally independent, physical independence inevitably follows. Keep spinning the wheel of freedom, my children. Be self-reliant and self-sufficient, and you can conquer the world.'

I looked at their portrait. They stood tall together, smiling harmoniously with wise, knowing eyes. Their love for each other seemed so vast that it still reached me here, decades after they were gone.

I closed my eyes, comforted by their love as the stars shone on.

Six

'HELLO, Tara. How've you been?'

I read Dev's message as I took a sip of water.

Putting the glass aside, I responded, 'I'm doing well. How about you?'

'All well here. I'm in the area this week, why don't you join us for lunch at my tayaji's farm one of these days? The orchards are in full bloom. And, while you're here, perhaps, I could also introduce you to someone special. I'm sure you'd enjoy meeting her.'

Reading through his words, I was suddenly struck by how overbearing my self-absorption with my miseries had become. I hadn't even bothered asking Dev about his family.

'Of course, I would love to meet everyone. I'm sorry we never got a chance to talk about your family before,' I responded apologetically.

'Well, if you figure everything out in just a few meetings, there'd be nothing left to discover. No fun in that!

So, is Wednesday good for you?' he suggested.

'If it works for you. Not like I have any schedule or commitments here.'

'You should! But more about that when we meet. I'll pick you up at noon.'

'I'll see you then,' I replied.

I stared at my phone, gripped by a slight sense of unease as I returned to questioning my sensibilities once more. And once more, I needed validation. I called Mala.

'Mala?'

'Hi Tara. How's everything going?' she inquired.

'Not too bad. I'm holding up better than I imagined,' I answered wryly.

'But Dev just called. He's inviting me for lunch at his tayaji's place on Wednesday.'

'That's sweet of him,' Mala affirmed, in her characteristic perky tone.

'It is. And even though I accepted the invitation, I'm just a little reluctant.'

'Reluctant, about what?'

'I understand Ashok uncle treats him like a son, and somewhere in his heart, Dev relates my situation to his mother's, but I'm afraid I might be too much of an obligation for him to constantly cater to. It's not like I contribute much to his experience. Besides, isn't it a little odd for me to interject myself in his life so randomly?' I rattled on.

'I mean, he was nice enough to offer to introduce me to his wife or girlfriend, whatever their status might be, but what would she think of this as a woman? Is it respectable for me to be having lunches like that or be driving around with a man I am not connected to in any sense, especially now, when my own marriage is in shambles?' I croaked, my statements sounding as incoherent as my sentiments.

'Goodness gracious, Tara! What day and age are you living in?' Mala huffed. 'And it's not like you are piling on or imposing on him. He's volunteering to spend time with you. He's the one inviting you. Remember?'

'I agree. But what does he have to gain from all this? In the end, it's an obligation that uncle has forced around his neck. He feels a compelling sense of duty towards me. That's all,' I conjectured in a small, dismissive voice.

'People connect over different things, Tara. And that's a huge leap of assumption that you don't contribute positively to his experience. That's what you need to change about yourself. That man, I tell you,' Mala fumed, her voice rising in tandem with her temper.

'Tej has completely messed up your psyche. He's somehow got you convinced that you're totally worthless and completely undesirable. Get over it, Tara. There's another perspective beyond Tej's. And for heaven's sake, don't get caught up in this analysis paralysis. Learn to appreciate people who see you for what you're worth. People who genuinely and selflessly care. And contrary to your belief, yes, such an emotion can exist in humans,' she remarked, her words bordering between wisdom and sarcasm.

'So… if I understand this correctly, what you're saying is that I should go.'

'Clearly, you should! He seems like a decent, good-hearted person. And if there is any reason for you to believe otherwise, you will know it, Tara. Besides, I trust Ashok uncle's endorsement over anything in this world.

Relax now! Get out of the house and try to have a good time. Meet new people, gain new experiences. Laugh a little. That's what life should be about!'

'Huh,' I let out a deep breath. 'Thanks, Mala. I feel better. You always make it sound easy.'

'Anytime, my princess,' she remarked. 'You're welcome to chew my ear with your most distorted conclusions and I'll patiently keep calling out your foolish notions! Now take it easy. And please, snap out of this mourning business. Love you.'

'Bhenji, I ironed your clothes and left them on your bed. Do you need anything else?' Premo checked in.

'Thank you, Premo. Just let me know when Dev gets here.'

I hurried down the steps as I scanned my watch, pulled up my sandal strap and snapped in my earrings.

'Bhenji, wait!'

'What is it, Premo?'

'Just one-minute, bhenji,' she urged, scurrying about the kitchen looking for whole red chilies.

'Bhenji, this is the first time you've dressed up since you got here. This is to deflect any buri nazar before it reaches you. Rab mehar kare…you look beautiful,' she gasped, swiftly circling the chilies over my head while muttering strange incantations before throwing them on a hot griddle.

'And,' she confirmed, 'it's a very good thing that you're wearing a black suit. That's added protection,' she explained, her lips curving ever so slightly in a discreet, tactical smile.

If not for mom, I had found Premo to do this. What had anyone to envy about my life anyway, I mused.

'Bhenji, Dev ji is here. I will keep dinner ready for you.'

'Thank you. Also, remind Seerat about the class tomorrow morning. She must come,' I repeated as I headed out the door.

'I will, don't worry, bhenji.'

'It's good to see you again, Tara,' Dev stepped out of the car to greet me.

'Good to see you as well,' I replied, taking a seat in the car.

'Just so you know, the presents were safely delivered,' Dev confirmed, backing out of the driveway.

'Really! I'd been dying to ask but didn't want to bother you with it. How are my Mehar and Sid?'

'You should've seen them. They were beside themselves with

joy when I handed them the bags. Ashok uncle was there too. In fact, we all had lunch together and I got to learn a lot of fun facts and cool history trivia,' he laughed.

'Here, I knew you would want to see this,' Dev handed me his phone.

Mehar and Sid clung to Ashok uncle wearing ecstatic smiles and amused expressions as floating clouds framed them perfectly in a soft white cocoon.

'Ah! I don't know how to thank you for this, Dev.' My eyes gleamed. 'Really. You have no idea how heartening it is to actually see them this happy.'

'I do,' he added, turning to look briefly out the window. 'I understand that rare joy only a mother is capable of kindling.'

'I've been longing to speak to them but end up holding back for fear of having to explain everything. But now that I'm better and have enough good things to talk about, I'll call soon.

Although, how nice it would be if they could join me here for a weekend—just running around the fields, splashing in tube wells, but…it's complicated right now,' I sighed.

'Don't worry. That too will happen when it's time.'

'I hope so!' I added.

'And we're almost here,' Dev indicated pulling onto a long, narrow dirt road, as thick clouds of dust arose from the ground, obliterating the world behind us.

We stood in front of tall metal gates, guarding a property that remained fortified within its 15-foot towering walls. Dev beeped the horn and slowly, the gates opened, revealing an awe-inspiring structure that seemed both out of place and out of this world.

The commanding stone carport was connected to two flights of stone steps leading up to a circular patio. And another flight of steps led to the stone-walled main mansion.

'It's quite an unusual property for this area. Very interesting architecture,' I observed.

'Indeed. It's my tayaji's "grand" vision. Too grand, in my opinion, but to each his own,' Dev remarked casually.

'He's rather "British" in his temperament as you will soon discover. And the design of this house is inspired by or rather replicated from some villa in Italy he'd briefly stayed at. You will find a picture of that villa hanging in the foyer. As children, we were fascinated by the stark similarities and often referred to it as our twin home in Italy,' he laughed.

'I would be fascinated too. It makes for a great story,' I concurred, soaking in the opulence that surrounded us.

'It's interesting how we are often in love for reasons other than we realize,' Dev stated. 'Tayaji's passion was centered around building this house, which he did, but it wasn't necessarily about enjoying it. For the longest time, he would visit only once a year, although he's been here for almost two years now, the longest ever. But he can't wait to go back! I often wonder if this home was a means to an end or an end in itself.'

'Isn't that true for so much else in life? I would've thought that of my marriage, turned out it was merely an event that cost us the love itself. If there ever existed such a thing...' I paused.

Dev glanced at me abruptly and just as quickly pulled back.

'We do share a lot in common,' he observed.

'What makes you say that?' I questioned inquisitively as I unbuckled my seat belt.

'I've seen a lot in life, Tara. And with experience one develops an eye for recognizing that which resonates at a deeper level. And as vast as this world is, it's really a handful of things that define what the world means to each one of us. And we spend our life looking for exactly that. Isn't it?'

'Good afternoon, my lovely lady. How do you do?' greeted a cheerful man standing outside the entryway sporting a flat cap, wellington boots and an olive quilted jacket with a corduroy collar. He held a pipe in one hand and extended the other to receive me in a firm handshake.

'How do you do?' I responded with a gracious smile as I followed him inside the house.

'Pleasure to have you join us. Welcome. Make yourself comfortable,' he said, pointing towards the sofa draped in luxurious peach velvet. 'Would you care for a cup of earl grey tea, or would you prefer some masala chai instead?' he offered, his frameless glasses resting on the tip of his pointy nose.

'Whatever you'd like. I'm good with either.'

'All right then, let me go instruct them in the kitchen. It has taken me all these years, but they still would not learn how to brew a perfect English cup.

Dev, why don't you show her around in the meantime.'

'Certainly,' Dev responded.

'Tara, make yourself at home, darling,' his uncle offered, disappearing past the hallway doors.

I turned to Dev, a little amused, 'You were spot on in your description. He's very British, but a charming man indeed.'

'Runs in the family,' Dev winked.

'Come, let me introduce you to my one and only.'

'Oh, yes, I've been waiting,' I replied, picking up the flowers.

'Where is memsahib, Jindu?' Dev questioned the man polishing the brass doorknobs.

'She's been in her bedroom all morning,' he answered reverently.

'We'll meet her upstairs then. She has not been too well lately,' Dev clarified as he led me up the winding staircase that displayed a stunning monochrome photo gallery along its wall.

'Sure,' I added, following quietly behind. I wondered if somehow, I could be the reason behind her 'not feeling well'. My heart raced erratically.

Dev knocked on the door before pulling it open.

'Why are you late? I've been waiting for the last 20 minutes,' spoke a meek, trembling voice, as though pouring every ounce of strength into those words.

'See, now I'm here, beeja,' Dev walked up and pressed a gentle kiss on her forehead.

'I'm sorry it took this long, but look, someone's here to meet you.'

'That's my sweetheart beeja,' said Dev, introducing a fragile, radiantly beautiful woman.

'And beeja, this is Tara,' he added, completing the introduction.

Beeja sat on her bed, bolstered against two large pillows. Her ash hair complimented the deep folds of her pearl white skin, and her wise eyes intensified with the spark of the vibrant lipstick she wore. It was a joy to behold her charm and spirit. I stood in awe of her compelling beauty.

'Finally! Hai Waheguru, tera lakh shukrana, you made me see this day before I die. Quick, hand me my glasses, Dev,' she said ecstatically, as she leaned forward and strained her eyes to capture the first look.

'Beeja…she's…just a good friend,' Dev clarified, a little embarrassed, as he reluctantly handed her the glasses.

I, too, felt a surge of warm blood rushing to colour my cheeks.

'Oye chup kar! That is still a huge improvement. You have never introduced me to anyone before, be it a friend or a non-friend. And my hair hasn't turned gray sitting idle in the sun.'

'Beeja, you don't understand. She is related to Ashok uncle

and just happens to be here in Amritsar. That's all.'

'You stand aside. Let me meet her,' she insisted, putting on her glasses.

'Come beta, sit next to me, what's your name again?' she asked, brimming with elation.

'Sat sri akal, beeja, I'm Tara,' I stepped forward, offering her flowers that paled in comparison to the bright cheer she wore on her face.

'Oh, this house is blessed today to have a girl walk through its doors. May Waheguru shower you with his choicest blessings,' she said as she tucked my hair behind my ears, looking intently from behind her round metal-framed glasses.

'What a beautiful child, Tara! Shining like a star!' she muttered.

'Look,' beeja excitedly untied the knot in her dupatta, 'Dev gets patase each time he visits me. Exactly five of them. But today he gets only two, while you get three,' she emphasized, fondly holding them out in her hand.

I looked up at her, a little surprised.

'What, Tara? What happened?' she asked, trying to comprehend my silence. 'Oh, I forgot, girls don't eat sugar these days. I get it. I have something else for you,' she quickly added, fumbling around the drawer.

'No, beeja. It's not that. Actually, my biji too used to give us patase, whenever we visited her.'

'Well, it was somewhat of a common tradition back then. These popular bribes always worked with children. Kept them coming back,' beeja chirped, breaking into a contagious laughter.

'It did,' I nodded in agreement. 'I'd been missing her terribly since I got to the pind, but today, for a moment, I felt as though she had returned.'

'May you live a hundred happy years. Just think I'm your biji,' she offered warmly.

'Beeja,' Dev interrupted, 'Don't overexert now. Have you been out at all this morning?'

'Who would take me out? These wretched doctors tell your taya, Pritam, I shouldn't go out, and that I shouldn't even talk. You tell me, isn't that what dead people do? Take me out now. My manja must be waiting for me in the orchard. I want to sleep there for a little while.

But before that, leave me alone with Tara for a few minutes. I need to talk to her.'

'Beeja, why don't you do it another day? She will be back, I promise.'

'Oh, stop being a killjoy. Nothing will happen to me if I lighten my heart and enjoy a few moments of my life. Go now.'

'Don't be too long,' Dev insisted as he hesitantly closed the door behind him.

'Tara beta,' she spoke in a hushed whisper, 'could you bring out the wooden case from the chest drawer behind you?'

I stood in the meager stream of filtered sunlight that had managed to sneak its way past the thick velvet curtains and fell directly upon the chest, lending it a mysterious luminosity.

'This one, beeja?' I turned to check with her.

'Yes, bring it to me,' she indicated.

Beeja unravelled a carefully stored piece of paper and placed it tenderly in my hand.

'This is what keeps the strings of my heart bound to this world,' beeja shared.

'This boy, Dev, I gave him everything I could, both as a grandmother and as a mother, yet there was something very precious that I lost in him. I could never revive it despite my greatest efforts.

Now I entrust you with this task. Don't refuse. It will greatly relieve me of my burden and allow me to die in peace,' beeja implored, her expectant gaze locked in anticipation.

I smoothened out the creases. It read,
Why dream when you know it will be broken
Why love when it's just a lie
If love was true and so eternal
Why did you leave me, why did you die?

'I found it under his pillow one morning. My Dev was so full of love and dreams. But after the turmoil he experienced with his parents, especially his mother's loss, something broke inside him. He retreated to a place so deep within himself that no one could reach him. Not even me.

I often told him stories of love and possibilities. I bought him all kinds of poetry books but his heart was sealed. He just wouldn't allow himself to be vulnerable again.

By Waheguru's grace, he did not become bitter, instead he found his comfort in giving. Notice how he is always making everyone around him happy. But what happened to his own happiness in the process, I do not know.

You tell me, Tara, does one bad relationship mean all relationships will be the same? His dadu and I had the most wonderful life because we were friends first, we were friends last, and we were friends throughout the journey.'

Beeja paused, still holding my hand with hopeful eyes.

'But beeja,' I hesitated.

'Don't say another word. I have a feeling he sees in you what he's lost in himself. You can help him.'

I was rendered speechless 'But, I mean, how would I…'

'His dadu and I were all he ever had. He's gone, and soon it will be my turn. I know for the first time he's found a friend. I see it in his eyes. He's beginning to believe.'

'Beeja, I'll try to be a dependable friend,' I uttered vaguely, unsure if it even meant anything.

'God bless you, Tara. He's a precious soul, my beeba munda. While I wish he had a life-long journey as we did, even a short walk with a good friend will do.'

I smiled, my heart warming up to her selfless love that was watering this unfounded hope in barren wilderness.

'And I understand when you insist you are just friends, but remember, good people make good friends, and good things come out of good friendships,' she added.

'Don't worry, beeja. You're not going anywhere yet.'

'This is where I complete my task, and by His grace, I have finished my job well. Waheguru, tera shukrana,' she added as she folded her hands and looked up in gratitude.

'Beeja,' called Dev as he knocked on the door.

'Hide it,' she muttered, pointing to the paper I held in my hand.

'You better be done with your talking for the day. Time to get some fresh air now,' Dev insisted.

'Yes, I'm tired of your taya and his medical friends from England who give him the advice that somehow cutting me off from sunlight and locking me up in this mausoleum of a room will help me bloom back to health. Even our maali knows better than to plant failing flowers indoors.

We all need a little sunshine, don't we, Tara?' she beamed.

'Yes. We all need a little sunshine!' I smiled back.

Beeja sat on the manja perched in the middle of their fruit orchard, sipping on fresh kinnow juice. I sat by the edge of the bed, holding her hand. She was 87 but infused with a desire for life that was respect-worthy.

'Do you smell the citrus? Soon there will be mangoes,' she said, her eyes gleaming with sweet nostalgia.

'You know, his dadu and Dev planted this orchard when Dev was barely seven. The trees have grown up with him. What fun were our days here in this simple home! And those adventure-filled years,' she recalled wistfully.

'Beeja, Tara is right here,' Dev disrupted her sweet longings once again. 'I promise she will be back. You look tired, get some sleep now. Besides, tayaji is calling us for tea. And he tells me your attendant is on her way over.'

'That's all I will do when I'm dead, but all right, it's the Englishman's order, you better learn to respect time and tea, as he will tell you. I will rest now, but Tara, come back and see me again.'

'I will, beeja. I wouldn't miss it for anything.'

'Good girl. Come see me again,' she repeated as she lay down and restfully closed her eyes. The placid expression on her face was one of a weary traveller at the sight of a distant rest house after having walked for days on end.

We were greeted by an exquisitely displayed tea station complete with a tiered cake stand adorned with scones, butter cookies and macaroons.

'Try these, my love. Macaroons from Ladurée, Paris. My friend just returned from his travels,' Dev's uncle presented.

'They're delicious. Thank you again for hosting me,' I offered politely as I bit into a rose-flavoured macaroon.

'I always enjoy meeting and entertaining people. As a matter of fact, I've had some of the most interesting conversations over a good cup of tea,' he said, fixing his hat as he drew in a puff from his pipe. 'You seem rather intrigued by my pipe.'

'Not at all, just haven't seen one in a long time.'

'You're right, your generation does not get to see much of this anymore, but trust me, Tara, pipe smoking is a lost art that only people who have experienced it in its heydays will ever appreciate.

Come, darling, let's have lunch now,' he offered.

An 18-seater rustic wood table set in the centre of a high ceiling dining room awaited us, with pleasant aromas and fine china displayed in an impeccable table setting. The grand wood-burning fireplace kindled beneath the large gold-framed mirror, which reflected the dazzle of the ornate Venetian chandelier. The floors were a dark gray polished stone—stately and inviting.

'Well, as little children, their summer assignments often included lessons in table manners and practice sessions on how to eat properly with a fork and knife. Jen was quite particular about it and had a rather hard time watching people eat with their hands.

Jennifer, my wife. She's no longer with us.'

'I'm sorry,' I added.

'Don't be. There's little a man can do about fate.'

'Hope the food is not too spicy for you? I think they finally perfected the chicken tikka masala in this household,' he added diverging from the conversation.

'Oh, it's actually the best I've tasted in a while. Takes me back to our first winter holiday in England. Back then it was a whole different world. Even air travel was an experience. People dressed up like they were going to attend some important event,' I laughed.

'That's right, those were some fine times!' his uncle added, sipping on warm lemon water.

'So, what is it that you remember best about your first trip to England?' Dev asked curiously.

'The first snowfall, a trip to Hamley's, the London underground and the Big Ben... Actually, being the bookworm I was, I lived the entire trip imagining myself to be Alice lost in wonderland. I think that's what I truly remember the best,' I smiled.

'Travel awakens our imagination like nothing else can,' Dev affirmed. 'So, you're a dreamer then?'

'Well, I never thought of it that way, but I prefer to live in the world of stories. It's my happy place,' I replied.

A helping of warm cinnamon toasted apple pie served with vanilla ice cream concluded this lavish lunch.

'So, Dev, what's the plan for the rest of the evening?'

'I have a meeting with the contractor at six, other than that I'm pretty open. Do you need me for anything?'

'No, not really. I'll be off hunting with the Major this evening. Make sure you check on your grandmother tonight.'

'Will do.'

'I think we should head back now,' I suggested looking at my watch.

'Thank you for the wonderful afternoon,' I added, turning to his uncle.

'Anytime, love. My regards to Ashok when you speak to him next and remember me to your family.'

'Most certainly will,' I added with a slight bow as I made my way to the door.

'Sorry, Tara, if any of this made you uncomfortable,' said Dev as soon as we sat in the car. 'I had no idea beeja would put you on the spot like this. It's tough to predict people once they get past a certain age. They start behaving like children again. I guess she was simply overjoyed to meet you and ended up reading a little too deeply into a non-existent situation.'

'Not at all, Dev. In fact, I truly enjoyed spending this afternoon with her. Both sets of my grandparents have been long gone. You are blessed you have her. Never apologize for her love.'

'You must know I appreciate your understanding,' Dev added,

maneuvering his way past gaping potholes and jarring bumps.

'And I appreciate all that you continue to do for me,' I answered.

'Good then, we're even,' he smiled.

The journey back seemed rather short, between casual conversation and pleasant observations.

'And if you could drop me right here,' I requested, pointing towards the white gate by the side of the road.

He looked out the window at the towering dome past the modest boundary wall.

'Do you come here often?'

'Twice a day. I'm starting to find my comfort here. I can't say I grew up with it, but in a strange way, I have returned to it.'

I closed the door and leaned forward, 'Well, it was a great afternoon. Thanks, Dev, and take care.'

'You as well. Good night, Tara!' Dev reciprocated.

I walked into biji's room and placed two of the three leftover patase in the almirah.

'One for me and one for Seerat,' I smiled.

'Premo,' I called out. 'Did you get a chance to remind Seerat?'

'Yes, bhenji, she will be here at 6 a.m. tomorrow.'

I ate a light meal under the silent starlit sky.

I felt a deep sense of grounding that I had not felt in a long time. Perhaps, the reason why mom always encouraged us to know our roots.

Seven

'GOOD morning, Aunty,' Seerat chirped bright and early as she walked through the front door, dressed in her school uniform. She held a flower and a textbook in one hand and a roll of parantha in the other.

'Good morning, early bird. Look at you—all dressed for school while I'm still lounging around in my night suit.'

Seerat giggled, handing me a pink rose. 'I always wake up early. The speakers from the Gurudwara are so loud that I can't sleep, even when I want to. Besides, I have to help mother in the mornings, so she is not late for work. Otherwise, they cut her salary.'

'Oh, do they?'

'Yes, but aunty, when I grow up and become an IAS officer, it will all change. Mother will not need to work so hard or be beaten up by father. I will take her away from everything.'

'You want to become an IAS officer, Seerat?'

'Yes! And then people will salute me when I walk out holding my files, dressed in a saree like a madam,' she giggled, the dream written clearly across her optimistic eyes.

'Aunty, how long did it take you to learn to speak like this?' she questioned.

'Like what?' I asked.

'I heard you talking on the phone the other day. You speak English so fast and so good. I couldn't understand anything,' she chuckled with carefree innocence.

'I can't remember exactly, but let me tell you something, Seerat. We can keep staring at the mountain, wondering how high it is, or we can start climbing it. And there's a chance that you will stumble at times, but the important thing is that you don't stop. Study, even when you don't understand. Speak, even if it is incorrect. Nothing is too difficult once you commit to it.

And with that, it's time to start,' I reminded her.

We spent the next hour reading, writing and practicing our speech, interspersed with solving riddles that Seerat delighted in posing.

Soon, the cool sapphire morning gave way to the warmth of the golden sunlight sprinkling tenderly upon the trees and fields alike, slowly embracing the world in its welcoming glow.

Premo walked up with a glass of warm milk. 'Drink your milk and run off to school. It's 7 a.m. You'll be late otherwise. And you know your Master ji. He'll be waiting at the gate with his stick!'

'I must go,' said Seerat closing her book. 'I will come back with mother in the evening,' she confirmed, hastily strapping on her bag.

'And Master ji, he only walks around with a stick, he can't even beat an ant!' she chortled playfully, handing the empty glass back to Premo.

I watched her run off, her backpack bouncing on her shoulders and red ribbon braids swinging behind her.

'Seerat, wait!' I called out.

She turned around. 'Yes, aunty. Did I forget something?'

'No, I did. Come back quickly. I have something for you.'

I took out a patasa from the cupboard and placed it in her hand. 'A token of good luck for my future officer!' I affirmed with a salutation.

Those brilliant black eyes grew even brighter. 'This is the best day ever. Never leave,' she cried, arching her heels as she wrapped me in a tight squeeze.

I smiled, watching her trot off into warming daylight.

I took in a deep breath as my thoughts returned to me, a little idle, a little empty.

I closed the cupboard and walked out, chewing the patasa and ruminating on my thoughts.

Suddenly, in a flash of inspiration, I'd found my story for Mehar and Sid.

I could finally explain why I was here and be somewhat convincing about it.

I dialed the school. After a few anxious minutes of waiting, Mehar finally came on the line.

'Mama, why didn't you call last week? I missed you so much.'

'I did too, Mehar. But you would be thrilled to hear what I have to tell you.'

'What is it, mom?'

'You know how all these years I've wanted to do something. And you've also heard about how I grew up wanting to be a teacher.'

'Yes, wearing nanima's sarees and teaching flowers in the garden how to count. I remember,' she added, a little amused by the embarrassing account of her mother's childhood fancies.

'That too,' I laughed. 'Well, guess what? I'm teaching.'

'Really? Where? But how is it possible, mama?' questioned Mehar, her voice skeptical, but optimistic.

'In Amritsar, at biji's house. I've taken on an assignment to teach English to a group of village girls. But Mehar, papa can't know.'

'Oh mama, I'm so happy to hear this. Could I come during my next break and teach with you as your assistant? Please!'

'I hope so, Mehar! You know, an 11-year-old girl Seerat is my first student and she wants to grow up to become an IAS officer.'

'Mom, this is the best thing you've told me. I'm very happy.'

'I love you, my doll. Where's Sid? Let me speak to him now.'

'He's on a field trip. I will tell him everything when he returns and we'll call you together next week. You know we're only allowed two calls and I already called nanima earlier this week.'

'That's fine, my sweetheart. Don't worry. We will talk next week. And remember, mama loves you. Too much!'

'I know. And we love you too. Keep sounding this happy, mama. And, oh, I forgot, thank you for the goodies. My friends loved the churan. Send some more packets if that uncle is coming to Kasauli again.'

'I'm glad you liked it. I'll send a bunch, or hopefully, bring some myself.'

'Yes, Miss,' said Mehar, as if responding to someone else in the room.

'Okay, mom, I have to go. I love you.'

'Bye, love,' I said as I hung up and held the phone next to my heart. I closed my eyes and let out a little prayer, 'Keep showing me the path and I promise I'll keep walking.'

Just then, Bittu strode in greeting me with a buoyant 'Sat Sri Akal, bhenji.'

'Perfect timing Bittu, I was just about to sit down for my cup of tea. Come, have a seat.'

'I saw Seerat on my way here. Everything okay with Darshi?' asked Bittu, pulling up a chair.

'Yes, she seems to have recovered well, thanks to you and doctor saab. She might come by later this evening, but Seerat was here for her lessons with me.'

'Wow, bhenji, what are you teaching her?'

'English.'

'O balle! Very good idea, bhenji. This could change the future for our girls. I say if you're teaching one, why don't you teach all? You should visit the school and see for yourself. It's in a sorry state of affairs.

Anyhow, bhenji, I came to inform you about dinner tomorrow at our house. And you must come. Before you say anything else, let me tell you that I'm bringing Preeti, my girlfriend of four years, to finally meet mummy ji.

But there's a slight problem. More than wanting a wife for me, mummy ji wants a successor for herself—someone who will cook and manage the house so she can finally retire. But Preeti is going to be a doctor. She's much better at cutting people than she is at chopping vegetables. Not only that, but mummy ji's sole mission in life has been to find a daughter-in-law who is head and shoulders above the community. And Preeti,' he laughed, 'she's so far above the community, that she doesn't even belong to it. She's a Kashmiri Pandit,' he crackled. 'I'm afraid mummy ji might have a heart attack when she finds out. As a precaution, I've asked daddy to remain on standby,' he bantered on, uninterrupted.

'But Bittu…'

'Bas, thank you, bhenji,' he stood up and folded his hands. 'Please handle it tomorrow. 7 p.m., be ready. Preeti and I will come,' he repeated, heading out the door.

I shook my head as I exchanged an exasperated glance with Premo, who was busy hanging clothes on the line.

'7 p.m. tomorrow! He's coming with his fiancé and I need to go convince his mummy ji. What in the world would I say to her?'

'Bittu is a good boy and bright too,' said Premo wringing out a towel, 'but sadly, he hasn't done anything with his life. Wasted it in "sardari" riding around on a bullet and twirling his moustache all day long. If I were in his mother's place, I would be more worried about how he would feed his wife and children after marriage, than who he marries,' Premo mumbled skeptically.

'So, is it even a good idea for him to be married then?'

'What else will he do? This will put some responsibility on his shoulders. Maybe, he will grow up. Otherwise, with the company he keeps, God alone knows where he might end up.'

'Look, Darshi is here,' Premo pointed towards the door.

I looked over my shoulder, placing my empty tea glass on the floor. 'What a surprise! I thought you were going to come later this evening.'

'I had made some kadah for the gurudwara and thought of bringing you some.'

'Oh, thank you. Well, you look better,' I observed as I stood up and walked over to her.

'Bhenji, God knows what would've happened if you hadn't come that day. More than myself, it's Seerat I worry for.'

'Don't think too much,' said Premo collecting the empty glasses, 'Just thank Waheguru it's behind you.'

'Premo is right. And Seerat is doing so well, I'm sure she'll make you proud one day,' I offered reassuringly.

'Bhenji, Seerat is very happy to be learning English from you. But as a mother, I can't help but be afraid,' Darshi hesitated.

'Afraid? Of what?'

'Afraid that she's too little and her dreams, too big. When they break, they will shatter her too.'

'Darshi, it's a good thing to dream,' I insisted.

'Only when dreams are within your reach,' she sighed. 'Unfortunately, she's harbouring a dream that will never see the light of day.'

'Who are we to determine that? You and I are here to give her wings. Let the wings decide where they take her.'

'Bhenji, you have no idea how we live. If her father even has an inkling about her plans, he will bury her alive. How many times he's beaten me for wasting money and time at school! He's slapped her too. But this girl does not flinch. She just keeps repeating, "I will be an officer one day and then father can't slap me."

But maybe she won't be an officer. Then what?'

'Look, Darshi, if she truly wants it and works hard for it, nothing can stop her.'

'Bhenji, it's different for you, but for us village women, truly wanting something is never enough. Means and freedom are both needed. Unfortunately, she has neither.'

I remained quiet. Maybe it was not so different, after all. Perhaps, it was a man who decided how much of her own life a woman would be entitled to.

Premo rushed through the door, looking completely distraught.

'What's the matter, Premo?' I questioned.

'Darshi,' she muttered breathlessly, pointing repeatedly towards the door. 'Your…' she stammered, 'your husband is at the door. He's drunk and keeps asking who you're sleeping with in here. I told him you're with Tara bhenji, but he refuses to believe. He says you left the house wearing a new suit and carrying a bowl of sweets; must be for some lover of yours.'

'Where is she?' he bellowed, standing at the door. 'I will grab her by her hair and drag her through the village streets for everyone to see. Come out both of you.'

Darshi trembled in fear. I felt sick to my gut. Mustering some courage, I walked towards him with hesitant steps. 'Darshi is with me and I will bring her home. There is no one else here. Leave now, or I will call the police.'

'Who are you to tell me that? Never seen anyone here before.'

he stuttered, grabbing the wall for balance.

'I am,' I paused for a moment, contemplating my response, 'I am Sardar Sahib's granddaughter and this is my home.'

The colour vanished from his face. He stared at me, pale and stunned, as though he was looking at a ghost.

'Forgive me bibi ji,' he said, folding his hands as he dropped to his knees. 'Forgiveness, please. Sardar Sahib was our karta dharta. Long live his legacy. I did not expect you here.'

I stood there, bewildered by his response. I looked towards Premo, who folded her hands and indicated with a swift wave to let him go.

'I will bring her home soon. You may go now,' I said, shutting the door close as he retreated obligingly.

Darshi dropped to the floor, wiping the droplets of sweat from her neck with the edge of her dupatta. 'Bala tali.'

I turned to Premo, 'Why did he give in like that? It's not like I could've done anything.'

'Bhenji, the village can never repay Sardar Sahib's debt. His word remains sacrosanct to this day. But my fear, when I saw him at the door, was that he would beat her black and blue again. This wretched fellow is always on the prowl, hunting for reasons.'

'But Darshi,' I said, turning to her in dismay, 'why do you live in such terror and torture? Why don't you leave him?' I implored, offering her a glass of water.

'Bhenji, I have a daughter. Even though he's a worthless man, at least there is a man in the house. If I were to leave him, the world would only point fingers at my character. Then who would marry my Seerat?'

'Isn't he the one doing exactly that?'

'Yes,' she sighed, 'but that's between him and me. Even my brothers will not take me back if I leave him. With all the responsibilities and no place to go, what can I do? Bhenji, if you were in my shoes, what would you do? Would you really leave?'

I sat there, speechless. I couldn't get myself to utter, 'Yes, I would.'

'So much for an early morning drama,' sulked Premo as she turned off the stove. 'Don't let it bother you, bhenji, just rest now. I will walk Darshi home,' she offered.

I sat motionless on the veranda as birds fluttered in and out of the tree. Premo tendered a dose of consolation to Darshi on her way out and I watched the two of them depart.

Soon, a notification popped on my phone. It was an unknown number.

'Hello, Tara beta. This is your beeja. I got your number from Dev. I wanted to invite you for tea tomorrow afternoon. They are also harvesting the kinnows. We can sit in the orchard and talk. I'm sure you will enjoy it. Would you come, Tara?'

'Yes, beeja. I would love to join you,' I responded.

'Very well then, I will send the driver around three,' she replied.

'I'll be waiting, beeja.'

I set the phone aside and picked up a wooden stick, scribbling aimlessly in the dust.

Why had I chosen to stay in this marriage all these years? I had left home on numerous occasions only to return—sometimes at his pleading, sometimes for the children who missed their 'home' and sometimes thanks to my own insecurities. I had many reasons to walk away, but always an excuse to return.

Why was it so difficult to leave? And why wasn't I still sure if I had only managed to escape until found, or had I finally walked free this time around?

On an impulse, I dialed Tej's number.

'Hello, Tej.'

'Oh well! Hello! That's quite bold of you to call me from your new number.'

'How did you remember me today? Did you run out of money, or did you finally realize your stupidity?' he jeered in a caustic tone.

'Neither, really.'

'Well, in case you harbour any doubts about your smarts, Tara, let me inform you that I have known your whereabouts all along. From Chandigarh and Mercedes, to pind and taxis. Progressive indeed!

Anyway, I knew this call would eventually come. Missing the comforts, I imagine. Everyone told me—give it six weeks and she'll come begging to be taken in. Well, I guess I overestimated your resilience.'

'Actually,' I interrupted him, 'I was calling to let you know I will not be returning home.'

He laughed even more contemptuously.

'What a brave girl! All right. Try it out. Let me see how long you last. Oh, forgive me, I forgot you're totally well equipped to fend for yourself. Bachelors in English Literature, right?' he remarked disparagingly.

'Good luck with that,' he snapped as he hung up on me.

I stared at the phone, his arrogance and condescension still ringing in my ears.

I was jolted out of my stupor by the shrill sound of shattering glass in biji's room. I rushed inside and noticed a rat jump off the trunk and scurry underneath it. A photo frame lay on the floor, with shards of glass scattered all around it. I flipped the frame over and knocked it a few times to get rid of leftover glass.

The photo was still intact. It was one of mom standing on a pedestal, sporting a medal around her neck. Her hair braided and eyes beaming with pride—'Punjab Women's Hockey

Championship. 1965, Roshan Studio' it noted.

And that's what love and freedom must look like, I thought. I ran my fingers across the precious picture and decided to put it safely inside the trunk until I bought a new frame for it. I pushed aside the blanket and lifted the lid. The trunk was one of the massive steel petis, used mostly for seasonal storage.

One end of the peti contained bulky velvet rajais, in green and sapphire emanating a familiar musty smell. While on the other side, a worn-out leather briefcase rested on top of neatly stacked red and white checkered khes.

I remembered seeing this briefcase in darji's hands on more than a few occasions. Reluctantly but curiously, I opened the bag which mostly contained certificates, legal papers, some pictures and a few letters. My first instinct was to put it back exactly where I'd found it, but a strange inquisitiveness came over me.

Well, it could not exactly be termed as violating privacy, I reasoned. Perhaps, a softer verdict would be 'discovering personal history through relics and memorabilia'.

Satisfied by my reason, I closed the peti and brought the briefcase up to my room. Making myself comfortable on the bed, I began sifting through the photos, mostly black and white and a few colored ones now faded to a much lighter version.

Photos of the three of us—Mala, Meeta and me—climbing the banyan tree, splashing in a tube well, milking the cows and eating mangoes in the courtyard out of metal buckets filled with iced water. Everyone appeared youthful—mamas, maasis and even darji and biji.

However, something was apparent in all these pictures, towering way above the pleasant memories. A deep contentment, a bond of togetherness and the endearing simplicity of a life we had grown up with.

As I collected the pictures and returned them to the briefcase, a blue letter carefully preserved in a clear plastic bag caught my eye. It was addressed to darji.

Sat Sri Akal Sardar Sahib ji.

As you visit your land after all these years, I imagine you would find the smell of this soil still fresh in your breath and blood. I trust you will bring back this mitti that runs in our veins but which we no longer hold in our hands. How's my Lahore? Pay my greetings to it. Sadke isde. Are the bazaars still the same? Is there anything left of our home?

I've been on this bed for weeks now. This wretched fever has rendered me unable to serve my family as I normally did. I pray even if my days are numbered, I go away fulfilling my duties every minute of those days. After all, my family is the reason I live, and you, Sardar Sahib, have given this gift to me.

I was all of nine when they dressed me up as a bride. I knew I had a husband many villages away, and one day, I would grow up and join him at his home. That afternoon, I was playing outside when the sound of my mother's wailing reached my ears. She ran to me and held me against her bosom, weeping frantically. Finally, when she looked at me, it was as though she was looking at a stranger.

Slowly, the village women began converging around me, beating their chests.

'What a curse! You will never have a family. You will never have children of your own,' my mother howled like a screaming wind on a cold, stormy night. 'Your life is over even before it had started.' I cried too, not understanding what had happened, but knowing some great misfortune had befallen me.

Months passed. I talked and ate little. Then spring came and so did my friend's wedding. But that day, I was asked to sit outside, among the widows, so I would not cast my unfortunate shadow on her future. That night I cried for myself.

Days and seasons slowly began to pass me by. Until finally, one day Maa ji came like an unexpected blessing. Mother was worried that I would be sent off to live alone with your family, but Maa ji had greater plans in mind. She had dared to stand up against my fate, forcing it to surrender to a happiness that she dictated, and you conferred.

My daughter-in-law will not live the life of an unfortunate widow, she said. We will still take the muklawa when she turns 18, but with my younger son, who will honour and love her as his wife.

You probably sacrificed many of your own dreams in the path of your responsibility towards the household. You were the unfortunate bridegroom who never wore a sehra.

I still remember our first day together. The scent of mango blossoms filled the air. A mynah sang a song of timeless longing while you pensively paced the corridor. Day turned into night, and you remained in deep deliberation. I grew worried. The next morning when I brought you tea, you spoke your first words to me.

Words that forever transformed my life—'This day, I wholeheartedly accept you as my wife. I will live and die for your honour and I will do my best to be the husband you idolized growing up.'

We built this family on the unshakeable foundation of respect and duty towards each other. And love emerged out of it, like the inevitable fragrance that comes from a well-

nurtured flower in full bloom.

You have never raised your voice, nor have you ever raised a question. Your acceptance of me—my strengths, my weaknesses and my mistakes, was unconditional.

I hope I have been able to serve you as well as you have served all of us.

Of that house in Lahore, where I first set my foot and we started our family, offer my ashes to its grounds. It gave us countless joys and innumerable blessings.

I leave the children to your care, and you to theirs.

My heart will continue to beat within the walls of this house and inside each of your hearts. I will never be gone.

Yours,
Amrit.

I folded the letter and placed it under my pillow as I lay staring at the ceiling.

Respect, duty, care and sacrifice. If this is what marriage was all about, no wonder what we had never lasted.

Marriage—a word so simple yet so deeply complex. So overly used, yet so little understood.

Eight

'Easy, Darshi,' I cried, sweeping the hair off my eyes as she continued to massage my head with relentless vigour.

'Bhenji, this must be done with a firm hand. Otherwise, the oil does not seep in. Your head will feel much lighter afterward,' she giggled, tying my hair up in a knot.

And good it felt indeed, as I basked in the lazy afternoon sun, relaxed from a warm oil massage.

'Oh, bhenji, I must tell you, whatever you said to my husband the other day worked like a charm. He became straight as an arrow. Well, he still drinks plenty but leaves me out of the muck. That's the thing with these men, the minute they know you have someone powerful backing you, they retreat like cowards.'

'I don't know about the rest, Darshi, but we got lucky for sure.'

'Bhenji,' Darshi spoke with a newfound spark in her voice. 'I was thinking, now that he's off our backs and you're feeling better, we should resume our afternoon sessions under the pippal tree. It's finally beginning to warm up and I could tell the other women to join us too. I even have a new song for us.'

'You just love to sing, don't you, Darshi?'

'Yes. It's like…,' Darshi searched for the right words, 'it's like jumping into that nahar and being swept away by its current, leaving everything else standing along the banks.'

'That nahar, where I almost drowned?'

'Mala bhenji was the one who pushed you in,' she chuckled.

'Yes, her adventures often came at my expense. It's a miracle I'm alive,' I shook my head.

'You know, Darshi, I grew up hearing that life's whole journey is about finding that one thing which can make us forget everything else. Maybe singing is that for you.'

'Then what is your one thing, bhenji?'

'I'm not as lucky as you are. I haven't found it yet, although my children come close.'

'Bhenji, we all have children, but there must be something that is just about you.'

'Right now, there's nothing that is just about me. When I find it, I'll let you know. How's Seerat doing?'

'She's happy. Thanks to you, she sits there all day long, embellishing her dreams with newfound hopes,' Darshi giggled. 'She chants your name more than she's chanted Waheguru in her entire life. The whole school knows about you and now all the girls want to meet you. Bhenji, would you go to meet them? It would mean a lot to those girls.'

'Of course, I'd love to. How many girls are there in the school?'

'Around 600.'

'Six hundred! That's a huge number!' I exclaimed, a little surprised.

'Yes, this is the only school in the area. Girls from five villages come here. Some walk as much as an hour each way.'

'What a hardship to bear at this tender age. I'll make it a point to visit the school this week,' I assured her.

I looked at my phone.

'Darshi, I should start getting ready now. Beeja's driver would be here soon,' I remarked distractedly, as I read the message from Bittu. 'Mummy ji has put her foot down. She refuses to meet Preeti. Daddy thinks she will eventually come around. But I don't know how long this might take.'

'Don't be disheartened, Bittu. Mothers are special. Trust me, she only has your best interest at heart. It just might take her some time to realize that this is where your joy lies. Keep your faith. Everything will work out,' I wrote back.

'I have already pledged that if she accepts Preeti, sukh naal, I will walk barefooted to Darbar Sahib for 40 days straight,' Bittu replied.

'God willing, it will all end well.'

'Please pray for us, bhenji,' he texted back.

Soon after, I was on my way to meet beeja.

'Madam, Mata ji is in the orchard. She asked me to show you there,' the gardener offered as I stepped out of the car.

Beeja sat in her wheelchair with a shawl spread over her knees and another wrapped around her shoulders. A dainty pink flower hung playfully above her right ear and a string of pearls adorned her long, deeply creased neck, with crimson lipstick adding a timeless charm.

'Beeja, you look gorgeous. You inspire me to fall in love with life all over again.'

'You should! No one deserves your love more than this life—this thrill, this exhilaration of falling in love with the same thing over and over again and discovering something new each time is delightful. By now, one would think I should understand life. Well, it never fails to surprise me.'

'I love how you look upon life with so much adulation, beeja.'

'Well, why not! People come and go, but this life—it was there when I opened my eyes and it will not leave me until I finally let it go. How can I offer it any less? Come, sit here, close to me,' she said as she gently beheld my face in an affectionate gaze.

'Just as beautiful as I remembered,' she murmured, straining to fix her unsteady glance on my face. A pleasant smile emerged in her eyes.

'That noor, that light!'

'Did you say something to me, beeja?'

She shook her head, dismissing it. 'Nothing. Old people often amuse themselves through the art of self-conversation and I happen to have mastered it. But tell me, what would you like, tea, coffee or juice? All three is also an option,' she proposed.

'Anything you like, beeja.'

'If you'd take my recommendation, try the farm-fresh blend of Kinnow and Malta juice. It is sweet. Like nectar.'

'Certainly! That's what I came here for.'

'For the juice, not for your beeja?'

I laughed, 'No, I meant, I came to have juice with beeja.'

'Hmm, smart girl. I like it,' she affirmed.

'Talking about my relationship with life, Tara, it has been interesting as far back as I can remember. There's one thing you should understand about life. It gives you only what you expect from it. I wouldn't say life is unfair, but it is certainly biased towards those who demand of it. Never settle for what it brings you. Have the courage to ask life to deliver what you want.'

'But beeja, not everyone has it in them—this courage.'

'We all have courage in us, Tara. What we don't have enough of, is trust. The first sign of trouble, and we run back to safety. This courage is not about some abstract bravery or fearlessness, it's about trust. The trust that tells you that no matter which way life takes you, or however much it tests you, it will not let you down.

Now, Dev tells me you have two children.'

'Yes, beeja. Sidak, my son is 11, and Mehar, my daughter is 13.'

'God bless, you do not look like a mother of two!

And he tells me things are not going so well in your marriage.

Sorry, if it's a personal question, but when you call someone beeja, you sign away the right to question.'

I smiled, 'Yes. It's been a struggle, but I'm doing my best to cope with it. Let's see what life has in store for me. It's hard to tell if what I'm doing is right or wrong.'

'Don't live your life between right or wrong. Wrong isn't what you do, wrong is when you fail to be you. Start being you. Start surrounding yourself with what is yours. It will always feel right. And if marriage fits into this scheme of things, good. If not, so be it.

Look at how much I've been talking. That's what happens when Dev is not here to restrain me. I didn't even let you drink your juice. Go on, take a sip, you still have the whole pitcher to finish,' beeja laughed.

'When Dev was a little boy, he could finish three of these in one go. What a handful he was! He loved running around this orchard and climbing on top of trees while his dadu chased after him, huffing and puffing.'

'He doesn't appear anything like it now,' I remarked.

'Yes, he changed after his mother passed away.'

'What happened, beeja?'

'Her failed marriage. It became a noose around her neck that kept tightening with each passing year. She gave in to drinking, depression and medication. Honestly, she had died long before she killed herself. It was traumatic. Dev was the one who opened the door to find her surrounded by a puddle of blood.

We brought him home with us. His dadu and I tried to fill his life with every adventure—fishing, flying, horse riding, travel, but a mother is a mother. Irreplaceable. You cannot compensate for the warmth of that lap. And how she loved him!'

A deep silence swept over us momentarily. For the first time, I had a fleeting glimpse of a deep despondency that resided inside beeja's heart. Her empty eyes and her quivering lips, conveyed a silent saga of an unfathomable loss.

'But forget that,' said beeja snapping out of her thoughts.

'Here, I have something to show you,' she said, handing me the box kept by her bedside. 'Our family album,' she presented, with discernible pride.

I leafed through the pages, leisurely sipping on the freshly-squeezed citrus juice, that contained subtle notes of honeysuckle and a hint of acid.

'Wow, beeja, look at you, on these horseback adventures!'

'And this is precisely how I like my women to be. People liked to call me a feminist even back in the day, but I don't think it's about equality as much as it's about the freedom to be who we are.

And for all the feminist perception, I admit, I couldn't have achieved half as much if his dada hadn't been my champion and my best friend. We were so young when we got married,' she blushed. 'I was only 18, and he was 22. We met at a flight school.'

'You flew as well, beeja?'

She gushed, 'Don't ask me what I did, ask me what I didn't do.'

'Flying, riding, law school, classical music, you name it. I tell you, when I go from here, my life would be waiting to rest. I squeezed every ounce of it. I spent it well!' she concluded with a happy heart.

'How about your family, Tara? Brothers, sisters, parents?'

'Mom lives in Chandigarh, and I have two sisters who live in the US and Canada.'

'Teen Deviyaan, very nice. You know, that movie was a hit in our time. Cinema was also my passion. I did want to marry Balraj Sahni and act in movies someday, but Dev's dada came before Balraj could. We were neighbours, almost. I mean Balraj was from Rawalpindi, and I was born in Islamabad.'

I laughed, 'You're funny, beeja.'

'And this is Dev's father and standing next to him in the saree is his mother,' she said, pointing to a handsome couple that greatly complemented one another.

'Beta, I looked at this family album yesterday, and I had a thought if you don't mind me sharing it. I don't believe in keeping things restricted to my heart. I like to put them out into the world and let them go where they must.'

'Always a good idea. Please, beeja, go right ahead.'

'You know, I was thinking that your photo will look quite nice in here. In my family album.'

I laughed heartily. 'Thank you, beeja. I'm honestly flattered, but you forget I'm married, and I have two children.'

'I don't call that kind of a relationship marriage. It finishes with one signature. And for your children, I would love to see them play in this orchard. This Englishman's wife Jennifer also had a daughter. You can ask him. I loved her like my own.'

I remained quiet, trying not to argue with her fantasy but felt deeply touched, nonetheless.

'Maata ji, doctor saab is here,' announced the attendant.

'Tell him to come tomorrow. I have guests today.'

'No, beeja, please go for your checkup. I'm not too far. We will spend time again. I'm sure if Dev was here, he would have wanted that too.'

'Your request is enough. You're just as important to me. I will not refuse, but come soon,' said beeja, affectionately stroking my hair.

'Now remember what I told you,' she repeated 'and start demanding of life like you own it. It will bow and surrender. And sometimes, surprise you a little. But surprises are good. Welcome life and opportunities with abandon, my dear. Until next time!'

The attendant wheeled beeja off. She waved her way out of sight as her instructions to the gardener trailed behind her.

I waved back with a grateful heart.

※

Chewing on the last bite of parantha, I looked at my watch. It was 10 a.m.

'I must get going, Premo. Seerat will be waiting at school.'

'Bhenji, your tea?'

'Later. This should not take too long.'

I sauntered across the tree-lined driveway, as a fog-laden morning sun played peek-a-boo, occasionally glancing through the clouds and piercing briefly past the patchy tree shade, as though writing its own story in a language unknown to the world.

A gateless yard bearing overgrown grass led me to a desolate, weather-beaten building shaped like a shoebox.

Seerat sat on the steps of the verandah, reading aloud to a captive audience that hovered around her.

'Is that your aunty?' a girl tapped Seerat on her shoulder as she pointed towards me.

'Yes!' Seerat darted forward.

Following her, a bunch of young girls in blue uniform with curious faces and quiet eyes began swarming around me.

'Why aren't you attending classes? It's rather early for recess,' I inquired, looking at my watch.

'We don't have any classes to attend. Three of our teachers are on leave today, so only two classes are in session. And the headmaster does not allow us to sit in classrooms unless teachers are present.'

'You only have five teachers for the entire school? But I see a lot more students than five teachers could teach.'

'653 girls in all,' Seerat confirmed with obvious pride.

'Aunty,' whispered a tiny voice to my right, tugging on my shirt.

'Can you make me a doctor too?" she questioned, with a penetrating gaze that sent a shiver down my spine.

'I want to talk in English,' added another.

'I want to become a teacher,' chimed another, as muffled voices of intense yearning steadily grew louder.

'Quiet down,' said Seerat stepping on the verandah. 'Whatever aunty teaches me, I will teach you all. Happy? Now, let her meet the headmaster.'

I stood among a sea of hopeful eyes as a feeling of betrayal cut through my heart. Caught in a dark storm of desperation, these eyes seemed to be longing for that first ray of sunlight.

What could I do to change their lives? What had I to offer? Neither guidance nor the means to help them realize their dreams.

After all, how could a person, who had long forgotten how to dream, talk about following them?

I suddenly remembered beeja's words, 'Courage. We all have it in us. We just don't trust it enough to depend on it.'

I made my way through the busy corridor, lined with chipping paint and empty classrooms, to be greeted by an older bespectacled man wearing a gray turban.

'What an honour to have Sardar Sahib's granddaughter visit us,' he offered respectfully stepping forward with a bouquet. 'Welcome, beeba ji,' he greeted me, pulling out a chair.

'Beeba ji, this school and this land was your grandfather's gift to the village on the occasion of your mother's birth.

'He saw women as the cornerstone of a harmonious society. "We neglect them, we neglect our future," he would say. What a great man. Back then, he personally went from house to house, securing pledges and commitments from families to educate their daughters. Those were the days of free books and free kitchen. What a reputation this institution commanded across Punjab! The famous heart specialist, Dr Ranjit Kaur, is a product of this school,' he said proudly, pointing to the off-centered picture that hung on the blue wall behind him.

'What is the situation now? I hear the school only has five teachers for over 650 students. How do they learn?'

'Beeba ji, the truth is they don't. If you've ever played ghar-ghar, you'll understand how it works. We keep pretending to teach and they keep pretending to learn.

I have spent over 40 years as the headmaster of this school, beeba ji, I have known the good days when education was a reality. Those were the days of progress and growth, then came stagnation and now there is decay. Despite my best efforts, the situation keeps going from bad to worse. I've seen generation after generation born with a promise that fails to blossom. My father often said that we may starve for food, but the day we begin to starve for opportunity, we should know we are indeed poor.'

'Is it not possible to get more teachers then?'

'Occasionally, we get a few teachers through quotas, but within weeks they transfer to bigger cities and better schools. Well, what can one do? Teaching these days has reduced to a mere profession. And for these girls, unfortunately, they will grow up one day like thousands of others, who become so weary of carrying the burden of unfulfilled dreams that they eventually abandon them. Some will trade them to bear children in adolescence and others to conform to this unforgiving society.'

I looked past the door, at hundreds of questioning eyes and expectant faces that remained tuned to our dismal conversation.

'Thank you. I will come back,' I said, pushing the chair back as I stood up.

The girls followed me to the road in gloomy silence.

'Aunty,' finally, a trembling voice muttered, 'will you ever come back?'

'Yes. Yes, I will come back,' I affirmed, if that was to be any comfort for them or me.

※

'Mom, I visited the school today.'

'Which school?'

'The one that darji started.'

'Is that school still operating? The last I heard, they didn't have the money to even keep the lights running. I thought they were planning to shut it down.'

'Not too long before that happens, unless we do something about it.'

'What can we do, beta? We got it off the ground and handed them the keys. It was for the village to keep it up. We are neither physically present, nor do we have the resources to sustain it endlessly.'

I remained quiet.

'Tara look, I can imagine how you're feeling,' she said after a determined pause, 'It's easy to get sucked into nostalgia, but the past can never be recreated. You must look towards the future.'

'I am looking towards the future, mom. These girls want an opportunity.'

'Beta, there are millions of people who are disadvantaged and suffering. And we have more than our fair share of problems to deal with. How many lives can we change? It will be a miracle if our own lives get back on track.'

'Mom, Seerat believes in me. And she believes in her dreams. I cannot let her down.'

'If you're taking it so personally, Tara, I don't mind sponsoring her for an education at a better school. Maybe you will find your joy in watching her succeed.'

'That's the easy way out, mom. But it does not change anything. Neither for her, nor for me, nor for the hundreds of girls who are slowly walking towards their own pyre.'

'You won't understand, mom. I see the same helplessness everywhere that I feel within myself—women crushed, defeated, disadvantaged. This termite of oppression has infested our social fabric. It is busy weaving a hollow future while we stand there and watch it unfold.

This happened to me, it is happening to Darshi, tomorrow it will happen to Seerat and maybe even to our Mehar.'

An uncomfortable silence followed.

'Look, mom, you raised us in a loving, protected home. We never had to fight for survival. While you did so much for us, I am ashamed of how little I've done to help myself. If I were standing on my own two feet, maybe I wouldn't still be standing here. Maybe I would've had the courage to walk away.

That courage which I couldn't find within me, I find in these expecting eyes. Their faith in me is unshakeable. Perhaps, they will never find another person who comes along with the same promise of hope. And perhaps what they see in me today, somewhere along the way, I will also begin to find in myself.

I want to try. Even if I fail. At least, I would know I dared. For once, I dared to change something. For once, I dared to question.'

'Tara, I hear something in your voice that runs deeper than your words. I'm with you in whatever you wish to do. And you should know, I'm already proud of you.'

I looked out of the window. A sea of yellow mustard fields stood silent beneath the hazy, late afternoon sun. Women carried enormous stacks of hay bundled in colourful muslin sheets. Birds resting in a distant tree took to the blue skies and the gushing water from the tube well rushed to kiss the thirsty ground. All seemed as it should be. I felt better. And perhaps, unreasonably hopeful.

'Hello, Dev. Are you back in Amritsar?' I texted.

'Hi, Tara. What's up? Everything all right?'

'Yes, everything is good. Just been dwelling on an idea. Wanted your perspective on it.'

'Of course. I will be back in Amritsar the day after, but I'm certainly available to speak on the phone today, say in half-an-hour, if you'd like.'

'Don't worry, nothing pressing. We'll talk once you're back.'

'All right, then. I'll text you Sunday morning.'

'Sure thing!'

I stared at the message trail. Why was I reaching out to Dev of all people? I never reached out to people, let alone those I barely know. But it didn't feel that way with him.

Why are some strangers not strangers enough?

Could it be the notion, I tried hard to rationalize, that perhaps he'd be more objective than my family in his feedback? Or was I just looking for an excuse to speak with him?

There was no denying that I had been starved of social relations for years. My life had mostly remained confined to my family and one friend I'd known since my first day of kindergarten.

I longed for the possibility of interacting with someone who saw me with a fresh perspective. Someone who didn't weigh me or judge me. Someone who neither loved me nor despised me. Someone who didn't expect Tara to show up perfectly put together, rather tried to view Tara in her entirety—good, bad, ugly. Someone who expected nothing and to whom I owed nothing.

Someone I could respect and deeply trust.

Maybe, I already trusted him. A lot more than I thought I was capable of trusting anymore.

I visited the Gurudwara to offer my daily prayer and returned with my daily dose of strength and guidance. Over the days, it had started to weigh up. The scales seemed to be tipping favourably. Finally.

Finally, I was smiling more than I was crying, and the warm days were surpassing the cold ones. 'Spring is around the corner', whispered the sweet whiff of flowers that came drifting my way at this thought.

Nine

THE alarm went off. I peeked through a partially open eye and hit the snooze button. It was 5 a.m. The book rested heavy on my chest and the lamp was still on.

'I must've been really tired not to realize when I dozed off,' I mumbled, reaching for the phone.

There was an unread message from Dev.

'Hello, Tara. I'm back in Amritsar. Regarding the idea you wanted to discuss, how about we meet and talk over lunch tomorrow? It's Sunday, and as usual, beeja is busy curating her "Sunday special" menu. If you don't have other plans, I could pick you up around 11:30.'

The thought of beeja delivered my first dose of early morning cheer. And the sound of water boiling in the kettle downstairs came a close second. I decided to wait until later in the morning to respond.

I pulled myself up against the headboard, anchored in the newfound serenity of a quaint morning routine that awaited me. These predictable practices had now taken on the proportion of important daily rituals. Tea beneath the deep blue canopy of the early morning sky, slurped out of steel glasses to the sounds of chirping birds and crowing roosters. Watching steam from the glasses rising to mingle with the mist. That faint melody of distant traffic slowly beginning to hum. And the walk down the crooked trail to a peace-inducing half hour at the Gurudwara, followed by a 6 a.m. English session with Seerat.

Seerat was never late and she loved to talk. She often shared stories of her animated dreams, mostly happy ones, that would make me laugh. And then, once in a while, she would talk about her friends and their struggles. Another one of her friends had recently been married. And every so often she would ask for my help in composing short letters in English, so her friend would have a way of staying connected with the language.

Biji's almirah had been restocked with jars of patase, which Seerat gladly helped herself to, before leaving for school.

Having Seerat by my side was like having my Mehar share my mornings.

I missed them, my Mehar and Sid.

I looked at my watch. It was just past 8 a.m. Without further deliberation, I dialed the school.

'You spoke to her last time, I go first today,' I heard Sid's voice approaching the phone.

'Mama, I'm not talking to you. I had been missing you so much, but you never called.'

'I know you have your reasons to be upset, Sid, but what if I give you a reason to be thrilled instead?'

'It better be something good,' he responded, still choosing to sound grumpy to conceal his curiosity.

'Something good? Hmm... What do you think of me giving you—a real, big, tight hug this Friday?

I am coming up to visit you, my munchkin. How's that for an early morning surprise?'

I could hear the celebratory pounding of Sid's feet interspersed with 'Yes! Yes!' as Mehar snatched the phone from him.

'What? You're coming to Kasauli?'

'Yes! And you get to stay with me at Ashok uncle's house.

We'll spend the entire weekend together.'

'Yay, this is the best news ever! Monday to Friday. Five more days to go. Oh, don't forget to bring me churan. And Sid is asking for aam-papad,' Mehar rattled hurriedly.

'I'll bring it all. Don't worry.'

'Come soon, mama.'

The ecstatic sound of a high-five and giggles was interrupted by a stern reminder, 'Children, time to say goodbye and head to Sunday morning assembly.'

I blew a kiss into the phone, 'To last you until Friday,' I whispered. 'Now run off before your matron brings out the stick,' I laughed as they suppressed a chuckle.

An intense rush of joy coursed through my body. It was turning out to be a happy morning, indeed. Next, I dialed mom.

'Mom, I'm going to see Mehar and Sid this Friday. You should come too. It'll be wonderful.'

'How come this sudden plan, Tara? That's quite unlike you.'

'I don't know how or why I decided, mom, but I'm happy about it,' I answered with careless abandon.

'And I'm happy for you, my child. I'll arrange for Balwinder to pick you up and we can drive together from here.'

'Sounds good,' I confirmed.

'I will not be home for lunch today,' I informed Premo, heading out the door.

'Going to see beeja again?' she inquired playfully.

'Yes. And Dev is here as well. I would like to discuss the school situation with them.'

'Hai, bhenji, I pray something good comes out of it.'

'I hope so too. I'll see you later,' I added, closing the door behind me.

'How've you been, Tara?' Dev greeted me as I made my way

over to the car. He narrowed his focus, as a mischievous gleam emerged in his eyes.

'Actually, I don't even feel the need to ask you that question anymore. It's written all over your face,' he observed. 'I must say this place is working its magic. You keep looking better each time we meet,' he laughed.

I nodded. 'It's nothing like that!'

'Of course, it is! You're beaming with joy. Come on, out with the secret,' he demanded.

'Not much. I just spoke to the kids this morning, and I'm going to see them on Friday.'

'Now, how's that not a big deal? That's great. I'm glad you're doing this.

In fact, I will be in Kasauli Thursday through Saturday. We could drive back together if it suits you,' Dev offered.

'I'll tie up the details and let you know,' I responded, taking a seat in the car.

'So?' he asked, turning on the engine.

'So?' I beamed, turning towards him.

'So, it seems like the advice was well taken. I'm happy to see this smile return. Do me a favour, just be kind to this smile of yours. It seems to be looking for a permanent home.'

I gushed, 'The smile says thanks for showing it the way back. It had been lost and wandering too long.'

'Don't worry, let your smile know that this time around, I won't let it out of sight,' he added with a wink.

I smiled again. And smiling, I realized how unnatural it felt—a little burdened, a little undeserved, a little out of place. Why was a measure of guilt and fear attached to it? Like it had landed on the wrong door. As if it was just a matter of time before it realized its mistake and departed.

We drove past the tall metal gates, as sprawling lawns bursting forth with delightful yellow and white blooms welcomed us in. Tayaji, who stood in a far corner of the garden, waved enthusiastically, holding his pipe in one hand and a putting stick in the other.

'Practicing his shots as usual,' Dev remarked.

We pulled up to a stop under the carport. Beeja was waiting by the entrance, her impatient eyes harboring a secret that she clearly couldn't wait much longer to give away.

She propelled her wheelchair forward as I rushed up the steps to greet her.

'Tara, see what I have for you today!' she exclaimed, holding out a gajra.

'It's mogra. I had two of these made for us this morning,' she beamed ecstatically, turning sideways to flaunt her flower-adorned hair.

'But first,' she instructed, 'close your eyes and soak in the fragrance. His dada often brought me these mogra gajras. He knew it could make me smile any day, no matter what. And how he loved to make me smile,' she recalled nostalgically.

I held the gajra in my hands and inhaled the delicate fragrance arising from the moist flowers.

'Absolutely divine, beeja. Thank you,' I said, extending a hug.

'Come, let me clip it in your hair,' she offered, reaching behind my ear as she tucked the flowers in.

'The lunch table is laid out in the backyard. You all start. I'll join you in just a few minutes,' beeja proposed, tapping me lightly on my shoulder.

'No way, beeja. We all start together,' Dev insisted, grabbing her wheelchair as he steered her away.

'Oye wait, I still have to instruct the cooks on...'

'Not needed. By now, they know exactly what to do. You gave them the same instructions last Sunday, and the Sunday before, and the one before that,' Dev insisted.

Seated at the head of the rustic wooden table, beeja announced, 'Attention. I have a special addition to today's menu.'

'A special addition?' Dev turned to beeja with a puzzled curiosity. 'That's new!'

'Yes!' She affirmed. 'After a long time, I felt like drinking champagne. I figured I finally have the "right" company for it. With this Englishman and you, and your constant worrying, drinks do nothing for me. Company is very important for the right effect of wine. So, for today, I decided to chill my favorite bottle. Go, bring it from the refrigerator. Good boy!' beeja entreated Dev.

I laughed, 'Beeja, thank you. I haven't had wine since I got to the pind. I was almost beginning to miss it.'

'Then fine, from now on, we will only have kinnow juice mixed with champagne—our homemade mimosa for two.'

We laughed, ate and drank champagne under the patchy canopy of lush trees and clear skies. Conversations got louder and happier with the warming daylight.

Slowly, lunch transitioned into tea-time.

'So, you wanted to discuss something, right?'

'Yes. Thank you,' I answered, taking the cup of tea Dev had just poured.

'So, there's a young girl named Seerat I recently started teaching. And I have been rather troubled to discover how desperately Seerat and hundreds of others like her are struggling to carve out a better future for themselves. They are striving for a change, so their lives don't repeat the stories their mothers have lived. Stories of oppression, fear and abuse. Now, mind you, these are bright, capable girls with ambitions of becoming doctors, teachers and scientists. The only thing holding them back is the lack of access to proper education.

Sadly, they do attend a school, but only in name. There's no real learning that takes place.

And fortunately, or unfortunately, these girls seem to have pinned all their hopes on me. As though I will somehow wave a magic wand that will make all their problems disappear. But Dev, I don't possess such a magic wand that will help manifest their dreams.

I mean, other than taking these insignificant English lessons, I don't know what else I can do to make a lasting difference. I met the principal a few days ago, and he too painted a rather grim picture. They don't have enough teachers, books or resources. And even basic infrastructure, like dependable electricity and toilets, is simply not there. With ever dwindling support for this institution, they might shut down entirely in months to come.

At one level, this feels very disheartening, yet, at another, it's equally compelling. I haven't been able to sleep. I'm consumed by this single question—what can be done to change this? And I know something must be done. I just don't know what.'

'Tara, beta,' said beeja, her voice brimming with compassion. 'I am pleased to hear that you're thinking about this. In fact, Dev's dada and I had started a charitable grant for underprivileged girls. I am happy to write you a check. Go, do what you must to improve their lot. They deserve better.'

'Beeja, I'm truly touched and honored by your generosity and support. But the issue runs far deeper. They will exhaust this money in a few months or years at the most. And then it's back to where it is today. What is needed more than money is a way to change the system. To start a cycle that will sustain and grow itself.'

'Tara,' Dev added after a contemplative pause. 'Why don't you get to Chandigarh a day early? The Secretary of Education knows me well. He would possibly be the best person to answer our questions and recommend the way forward.'

'Really, Dev? Would it be possible to meet him?'

'Of course. Put together a small presentation and highlight some key issues. We'll take it from there.'

'I'll be on it!'

'And let me know if you need help,' he offered.

'Certainly!' I replied, feeling infused with a new hope.

'I'm glad you two are working together on this. Dev is a smart boy, Tara. He has a solution for everything in life. My advice—keep him handy for such situations,' beeja laughed as a trace of tiredness crept into her eyes.

'I must rest now. This has been one of the better days this year. I will sleep well tonight.

And Tara, and if I don't see you before you leave, I will see you again, very soon.'

'Rest well, beeja,' I gave her a goodbye hug.

'Dev, we should get going too,' I suggested, looking at my watch.

'Wait a moment, I have something for you.'

'For me?'

'Yes, something small. I thought you could use it.'

Dev returned after a few minutes and handed me a journal.

'A dairy? For me?' I asked, a little surprised.

'I relied a lot on writing while I was growing up,' Dev admitted. 'Words have a way of penetrating our minds in a way that thoughts can't. You'd be surprised at how well they grasp emotions, often compelling the drifting fog of feelings to commit to a comprehensible form of reason. Like distilling murky thoughts for pure essence.

Try it. It will do you a world of good. And a small piece of advice. While you're at it, try not to impose any limits or conditions on your writing. Allow it to be bold. Allow it to be free. Allow it to question. If it wants to be irrational, unreasonable, rebellious, so be it.' He paused to look at me, 'But allow it to be true. Authentic. You. Let your writing be truly you, Tara,' he repeated. 'You might uncover many secrets you've kept from yourself.'

I smiled. 'Only if I had secrets to uncover! But that's very thoughtful, Dev. Thank you,' I responded. 'I used to write a lot as well when I was younger. Not sure when or why I stopped, but thanks for bringing it back.'

'What did you write about?'

'Nothing in particular, just a bunch of random stuff. Anything that left me curious enough to go looking for more.'

'Then do it again. Be curious. Don't settle for answers others hand you, form your own conclusions,' Dev urged in an impassioned manner.

I looked at him and that selfless concern. That desire to give and keep on giving. Did such people even exist?

'I should get going now,' I suggested.

'Very well,' he stood up. 'I'm sending you home with your new friend. Time for you two to get creative or get disruptive. Whatever you do, let's stir something up.'

I laughed. 'I have a feeling we'd get along.'

Dev held the car door open for me.

'Dev, I can get my own door. I'm not used to any of this. Really, I'm no queen.'

'One, it's never too late to get used to it. Two, I'm not treating you like a queen, only the way a lady ought to be treated. With respect. Always. Sometimes, courtesies are just another way of adding texture to the mundane and ordinary. And a little indulgence is always fun. Enjoy it.

By the way, I have a few bottles of wine in the car for you to take home. You won't find it at any of the local thekas.'

I laughed. 'This is totally not needed. I don't need to drink like that, I mean...'

'Again? Never apologize and never explain. Whether or not you want to drink is up to you, but when you want it, it should be available. Didn't beeja tell you I also have the best foresight?' he grinned, closing my door.

'So, did you decide on purpose not to marry, or did things not work out for you? We never quite had a chance to talk about it,' I asked.

'Finally. You feel comfortable enough to ask. Good,' he replied warmly.

'I have been in a few relationships, one of them actually held promise. We lived together for over four years. But then, marriage requires a lot more than just an ability to get along. I knew clearly from the beginning that I would only marry when I meet that person, the one I've known all along was "right" for me. I mean, I went through life holding this precise mould, sort of like Cinderella's slipper,' he laughed. 'And while many came close to owning it, none quite managed to fit in.'

'What was wrong, though?' I asked.

'You know Tara, people aren't inherently right or wrong, nor are the situations. It really comes down to what is right in relation to the other. It's specific to two individuals. That's why it's called a relationship. And each person relates differently to every other person they meet. It's a unique equation, an individual chemistry of two personalities. I may be everything you want in a man, yet, to another woman, I may be the most inadequate man she's ever met.

I'm not saying that marriage only works in complimentary situations, but that at a deeper level, your core values must be aligned. You must share a common underlying belief system.'

'What do you mean by that?' I asked.

'Tara, the world, for us, exists only in reference to the self. We don't inherently value an abstract person. What we really value is how they value that which matters the most to us. We admire the most about people, what we want the most for ourselves. Whether it's honesty or authenticity or independence or trust. It takes two to keep a whole intact.

I guess I'd grown up with two extremes. Beeja and dada on one hand and my parents on the other. The best possibilities of marriage and the very worst ones, the cherished joys and the intense sufferings, I had lived through both.

I knew if I ever married, it would neither be for the right time, nor for the right reason, but only and only for the right person. If she ever came along. If not, life's pretty good anyway. Why compromise?'

He made complete sense. I wish I'd had the wisdom to think about marriage and make my decisions with such maturity. Tej and I were clearly and entirely misaligned in our priorities and preferences. There was nothing we saw eye to eye on. Our belief systems were grossly incompatible.

And today, after listening to Dev, I finally understood why I was never valued in this marriage. Tej had always measured me against a benchmark that didn't reflect me, to begin with.

I suddenly felt better about myself, knowing lack isn't necessarily defined by what's missing, sometimes it's determined by what one is seeking.

As I wished Dev good night, the moon broke through patchy clouds.

I stood next to the car, washed in a new light.

Ten

'IT'S so good to see you here, Tara,' mom held me in a tight embrace. 'Welcome home. You made good time. Three and a half hours!'

'Yes. There was no traffic whatsoever. And we would've been here sooner, but for Seerat's tear-filled, heart-wrenching goodbye. She was so sad to see me go, even for two days. God knows what I'm going to do with this girl!'

'But you left at five this morning. Did she come that early?'

'She slept over last night to make sure she didn't miss saying goodbye to me. Well, I left her with plenty of homework. Hopefully, that will keep her occupied.'

Mom smiled. 'Looks like you're finally doing what you've pretended to do since you were a little girl. I can't believe you're teaching!'

'Isn't that true for life in general, though? Pretend long enough and it gradually becomes your reality. Maybe it's all a pretense, who knows what we really are?' I remarked casually.

'Sometimes your words go right over my head, and lately, you've been rather unpredictable,' mom shrugged, 'but more importantly, what time is your meeting? I'll get some breakfast made for you.'

'11 a.m. And I should get going,' I replied.

'By the way, Tara, it's quite nice of Dev to make all this effort to help you out.'

'Mom, you have no idea how helpful he is. And it's not just for me but everyone around him. He reminds me of dad—always kind, positive and so very respectful.'

'We could all use a little dose of positivity in our lives,' mom concurred.

'Now what about Tej? What if he finds out where you are?'

'He knows. I spoke to him a few days back.'

'You did? You never mentioned, Tara.'

'There was nothing worth mentioning. He's still his same obnoxious, arrogant self. He knew where I'd been all along. And he's still stuck in his comfortably numb cocoon, absolutely certain that I will return begging for him to take me back as soon as the tough reality of the daily grind and lack of comforts hits me.'

'And?'

'And, I've never felt better about myself.

You know, mom, so little of your life experience depends on the car you drive or the jewellery you wear, and so much depends on the people you're surrounded by, the laughter you share, the conversations you have. Sadly, he doesn't understand what real comfort in life is.

I breathe freely under the open sky. I think, I feel, I make decisions and I laugh, without the fear of someone lurking in the shadows, waiting to strike as soon as I falter. I'm neither insulted nor am I made to feel worthless at every instance. No one shouts. No one screams. No one throws things. I don't miss any part of that heavily compromised life. If at all that deserves to be called a life.

I just miss my Mehar and Sid. And no matter how far, they are with me through every step of this journey.'

'It's such a relief to hear that,' mom exhaled, resting a reassuring hand on her chest.

'But still, I have no capacity for any confrontation or drama. I suggest we leave for Kasauli right after the meeting,' I added.

'Good idea.'

'Tara,' mom called out as I headed for the shower.

'What, mom?'

'I must say I'm liking what I see,' she smiled tenderly.

'Me too!' I smiled back.

'Balwinder, could you drop me off right here, please?' I requested, staring anxiously at my watch. I fixed my hair, nervously tucking it behind my ears. I opened the file one more time to examine the presentation and notes. I felt a strange queasy feeling deep in the pit of my stomach—the same feeling I'd experienced right before my board exams. Like my life depended on the next few hours. My stomach churned, my lungs constricted and my heart pounded.

Just then, I heard a tap on the window. I looked up. Dev stood there smiling in his usual, calm repose.

'You look lovely, Tara. Haven't seen you in a saree before,' he remarked courteously as I stepped out of the car.

'I enjoy wearing sarees once in a while. Besides, I figured it was a little more "official", given we're meeting the Secretary of Education today.

Does it look too simple?' I asked plainly.

'Simple is always elegant. And a white cotton saree, nothing beats that.'

'How do you know so much about sarees?'

'I was often tortured into going saree shopping with Ma. She too loved everything traditional and everything cotton. I tell you, Tara, I still have nightmares about consuming bottle after bottle of campa cola, while watching handsome moustached men model around in pretty pink sarees.'

'That's funny,' I chuckled.

'Not exactly, but yes, now I can laugh about it. All right, time to go in. Ready?'

'You take the lead, Dev. I'm nervous. I don't have any experience talking to people in such important positions.'

'Relax, Tara. Don't think too much and don't place anyone on such a high pedestal. Talk to him like you would to any other person. You don't need to come across as the most intelligent or experienced person he's ever met. He just needs to see your point of view. And he only needs to hear a story that he can relate to. That's all.

Tell it as you feel it. Remember, behind every position, there's a person, who at the end of the day, is human.

And don't worry, I'll step in if you need me.

Although I doubt you'd need me,' he added, almost as a comforting afterthought.

'I'll try,' I said, still feeling grossly under-confident.

'Good morning, sir. Tara Grewal. It's a pleasure to meet you,' I extended my hand in greeting.

'Please, madam, take a seat,' Mr. Mehta, the Secretary of Education, politely offered.

'Dev, how are you? Long time! How did you remember us today?'

'Actually, Ms. Tara is on a social mission which she will talk about shortly. When she first mentioned it to me, I knew if there was anyone who could guide us, it had to be you.'

'Happy to help in any way I can. So, tell me, Ms. Tara, what can I do for you?'

My hands trembled as I took out the presentation and slid it along the table towards him.

'Take a look, sir. I've compiled some observations in here.'

He started flipping through the pages. 'Girls school, Tehsil Ajnala, few teachers, poor infrastructure, no facilities.'

'Sir,' I interjected. 'There's a girl named Seerat. A little girl who's been chasing a big dream. Time, effort and dedication—she's giving it her all. But the faster she runs, the further her dream slips away. With shackled ankles and wounded feet, she's struggling to run past the barriers of convention in the hope of entering a new world.

And there are hundreds like her that might keep running all their lives yet never reach that finish line.

In part because... as you know and I know, there is no finish line. And there never will be, unless we create one.'

He looked up from the presentation briefly.

'This is the answer I'm struggling to get. Are we truly capable of creating a finish line or must we remain silent bystanders watching them run aimlessly until their illusion bleeds away to non-existence? How can there be change without education? And how can there be education if the schools are nothing more than empty classrooms?' I continued.

He remained silent as he flipped through the deck.

And then he picked up the phone. 'Allocation? How many? This year? Okay.'

A moment of silence followed.

'Ms. Grewal, the budgets for the year are nearly exhausted, but as a special case, I will send an evaluation team to the school. We will get it qualified under Government of India's Smart School initiative. I will see to it that the infrastructure is restored and they have electricity, generator backup, adequate learning resources and the correct ratio of teachers to students.

However, factually speaking, what I have experienced in my life is that change does not come from handouts, it comes from owning the process.'

'That's exactly right,' I added.

'Not to worry. I will also put in a request for internet facility and a fully functional computer lab. If that is approved, consider your mission accomplished. Based on our learning from the "hole in the wall" experiment, to harness the power of organized self-learning is the key to success.

Perhaps, you could help craft a distance learning program to counteract any shortage of qualified teachers. Especially with subjects like English. We can put bodies out there, but it's challenging to find qualified resources. And in today's world, these kids just can't find jobs or compete based on an education in regional languages.

This is what I can offer to get you started here, but how far they run with it will depend on two factors—how well they learn English and how quickly they adopt technology. I leave that part for you to figure out.'

'Mr. Mehta, thank you. This is more than we expected out of this meeting. It's much appreciated,' said Dev, shaking his hand as we stood up to leave.

'Don't thank me, thank Ms. Tara. She's making our job easier. Initiatives are easy to implement, but it takes people like her to make them succeed.

Good luck Ms. Grewal. I will be following your journey. And good luck to the runners too. Hope they make it past the finish line in good time.'

'You did it, Tara!' Dev lauded as soon as we stepped out of the office.

'Did you see the impact your words had? He had no budget.

He created one, just for this school. Now you see how the power of sincerity goes much further than those facts and numbers you were so worried about.

Life lesson, Tara—right decisions may be made by the mind, but the best ones are made with the heart. It holds true for every person and every situation.'

'I don't know what to say, Dev. I couldn't have done this without you.'

'You just did, Tara. I hope you realize I didn't add a word. It was all you, and only you.

One more thing, learn to acknowledge your wins gracefully. Learn to own your success, however big or small.'

'I'm slowly learning. It's the unlearning that's taking time,' I replied.

'That too will happen,' Dev assured. 'All right, seems like you're headed to Kasauli now, I'll see you there tomorrow,' he added.

'Yes. See you there.'

I watched him disappear into the crowd, wondering if all this had actually transpired.

'Babyji, are we ready to go?' asked Balwinder, taking the files from my hand. 'Yes, we're ready,' I smiled to myself.

I stood at the gate, ringing the doorbell repeatedly, possessed by an impatience that was only exceeded by my excitement.

'Tara, what's wrong?' mom reluctantly opened the gate. 'I got worried. For a moment, I thought it was Tej ringing the bell in this manner,' she gasped, still a little unnerved.

'For a change, nothing's wrong, mama. Everything is right. Fabulously right! Hand me the phone, quick,' I demanded, humming a happy tune as I twirled my way past the lobby.

'Meeta, Mala, guess what?'

'What is it, Tara? You sound ecstatic!'

'And so I am! The school has been approved under the Smart School project scheme. The girls will finally have teachers and books and electricity, and if all goes well, they might even get internet and computers.'

'Wow! What an accomplishment! Calls for a toast. To this project and many more!' Mala cheered.

'Any excuse for a glass of wine,' chirped Meeta. 'But this one most certainly calls for a celebration. Our little sister is making us proud. Congratulations, Tara. This is a milestone, indeed.'

'Thank you,' I beamed. 'Mom and I are off to Kasauli now. We will call you from there.'

Mom and I chit-chatted our way up to Kasauli as I filled her in on Premo, Bittu, Darshi and Seerat. Her eyes were a mirror of a myriad emotions—widening with surprise, narrowing in concern, softening to delight and brimming with nostalgia. Two happy hours later, we stood in front of 'Drishti,' Ashok uncle's peaceful abode tucked far above the bustle of the valley.

'Welcome, bhenji. Welcome, Tara,' Ashok uncle greeted us as he opened the gate dressed in a white kurta pyjama layered with a gray sweater vest.

'I'll get the gate, saab,' Bahadur quickly followed behind uncle.

'You go call memsahib. Tell her, bhenji and Tara are here,' he indicated with a wave of his hand.

'Oh, aunty is here too. What a pleasant surprise!'

'Well, it hasn't been that pleasant around here lately, but come on in.'

'What did you say? I heard you,' aunty confirmed in a stern voice as she adjusted her saree and with admirable grace, transitioned her formidable frown seamlessly into a pleasant smile as she greeted us in.

'Oh I...I was only talking about the weather. It's been

uncomfortably warm... and muggy lately, hasn't it?' uncle attempted to explain in a heavily laboured voice.

'Okay, okay. No need to make things up. I know exactly what you meant. Now move aside, let me welcome bhenji and Tara.'

'So, Tara, you didn't want to come stay with us in Delhi? Ashu and I were looking forward to it.'

'I will come, aunty. Just been preoccupied with a few issues at the village. But as soon as they're sorted, I'll come visit you.'

We sat around the tea table overlooking the serene valley. The breeze picked up the fragrance of the blooms and birds began flocking to their trees. I shuttled distractedly between sipping tea and scanning my watch.

'Checking the time again and again will not make it go any faster,' Ashok uncle remarked. 'Another hour before the kids are ready to be picked up.'

I smiled. 'You always catch me, uncle. But to be honest, I am getting a little impatient. You all enjoy your tea. I'll get to the school early and wait there.'

'Have fun, beta. We will see you and the kids soon.'

I stood leaning against the car in the empty parking lot, my sight fixed at the top of the stone staircase. The mellow orange sun hung low in the sky and the green ivy crawling up the wall gradually took on a dull, drowsy appearance.

Against the dimming light of the setting sun, two silhouettes finally appeared, holding hands and descending carefully down the steps. It felt as though a sudden flash of light momentarily lit up the world again.

I ran up the steps to greet Mehar and Sid. And overcome with the various highs of the day, I spilled a few emotional tears.

'Mama, are you crying?'

'Of course not. It's just happiness overflowing. Happens when the cup is too full. Now hurry,' I smiled, quickly wiping my cheeks. 'So many wonderful things are waiting for you—nanima and treats and stories and feasts.'

'Let's go!' exclaimed Mehar and Sidak as they ran towards the car, dropping their backpacks behind.

No sooner than we arrived, the duo darted through the gates fighting over who got to claim nanima first. So much had changed between our childhood and theirs, yet the yearning for nani's embrace stood timelessly still.

'Ashok uncle and bade aunty,' they exclaimed joyfully, giving each one a special hug.

'Your bags are ready, right there,' uncle pointed towards the dining table. 'One for you, one for Mehar, and one for your mom.'

I smiled, nodding dismissively, 'I'm not even going to bother debating this one.'

'Good girl. Now don't waste any more time. Come on over. You need to help me win this. Your aunty and mom have been beating me at my own game,' uncle grumbled holding up his cards.

'That's what happens when women team up, men don't stand a chance,' said aunty, rubbing it in, as we all laughed.

The evening was spent playing rummy, watching movies and narrating extended bedtime stories.

A bright morning sun greeted us to a new day. I drew the curtains partially and found uncle, aunty and mom having their morning tea in the garden. I opened the window a crack and whispered, 'I'll be right down.'

Ashok uncle waved back at me.

I kissed my restfully asleep Mehar and Sid and pulled their blanket up, tucking them snug and warm.

'Tara, how come you never told me about any of this? I have a very close friend who heads the woman's cell in Chandigarh. One visit, and she would've put Tej firmly in his place. He would've never dared to raise his voice again,' aunty asserted, her frown lines deep and unforgiving beneath her fiery red bindi. 'These men! They deserve to be taught a good lesson. Shall I call her right now?'

'Not needed, aunty. I think I've managed to put that part of my life behind me.'

'One piece of advice, Tara. Thinking never defines a situation, a decision does. If you've really moved on, then waste no time. File for a divorce. Claim your rights.'

'I haven't taken it that far yet. I am still trying to understand if I am even capable of surviving alone and if at all he'd be willing to making amends. From what I've realized over the past few weeks, I'm stronger than I thought, and he's foolhardy as ever. My decisions are slowly emerging.'

'I also know some powerful women activists and lawyers. I'm happy to recommend one whom I know particularly well, and she herself survived this nightmare. Can you imagine, she was thrown out of her house in the middle of the night, with a paltry sum of Rs. 750 and nowhere to go. Poor thing, she had to resort to taking shelter at her maid's house for the night. But from there, this woman soared like a phoenix. She put herself through law school and eventually went on to become one of India's leading divorce lawyers. She fights for women's rights, not for her fees. And trust me, all the money in the world is not enough to buy her integrity.'

'Now stop it,' interrupted uncle. 'It's early in the morning, and you are ready to fight the world and wipe out the existence of men forever. Women cell, women activist, divorce attorney. Let us enjoy the birds and the sunrise and these beautiful flowers. Go find something else to do.'

'And you do nothing with your life but read poetry and drink tea all day long. Useless,' she muttered as she walked away to the kitchen and we shared a laugh.

'Bhai saab, stop quibbling now. You both have spent your life together,' mom urged.

'Bhenji, when do I quibble? I only put out the brush fires that keep erupting all day long. I'm a lover of peace and beauty. She is the fighter jet in this house, constantly bombarding my existence. What to do? Such is life!'

'So, Tara,' said uncle, turning towards me, 'Dev will be here soon. Your aunty and I have planned a picnic lunch. The kids will enjoy running around the open valley and splashing about in the streams. There's also a trekking trail that you, younger people, could explore if you want.'

'Sounds great, uncle. The kids will be thrilled. I'll help aunty pack the picnic basket.'

'Let her pack the basket. You go pack the wine and the music box, the good stuff. Paranthas and sandwiches, let her handle that.'

'On it!' I smiled.

Morning kisses from the kids, a house full of family, laughter and banter, and still much to look forward to in the day, what more could one ask of a blessed life?

Eleven

'ALL right! Everyone in the car now,' Ashok uncle directed. 'You too, if you're finished with your Mahila Mandal calls. It's 11 a.m. already.'

'Nothing to do in your own life and you have a problem with people who're doing something to bring about change in this world,' aunty moaned, twisting her face bitterly.

'If you could only change yourself, the world would be just fine…,' uncle mumbled to himself.

'You're the one who has hearing issues, not me. Don't think I didn't hear what you just said,' aunty retorted.

'Ignore him, bhenji. He's just joking,' mom intervened.

Suddenly Sid and Mehar dashed towards the door with an exuberant greeting, 'Hello uncle. How're you?'

Dev stood there smiling at them.

'I'm well, and how are you two doing?' he asked, wrapping his arm around Sidak's shoulder. 'Happy that mom is here?'

'Very! And nani is here too.'

'Nani,' Mehar called out. 'Come here and meet the delivery uncle who bought us gifts and letters from mama.'

'Dev uncle, please,' mom corrected Mehar as she walked out fixing her dupatta.

'It's quite all right, aunty!' Dev bent forward to touch mom's feet.

'God bless you, Dev. I'm grateful for everything you've done for my family.'

'Not at all. This is the least I could do.'

'Khush raho, beta. In fact, I've heard so much about you that it doesn't feel like we're meeting for the first time.'

'Nothing bad, I hope!' Dev wondered, casting a suspicious glance towards uncle.

'Not at all,' mom affirmed. 'Bhai saab and Tara are always talking highly of you, and now I can see why.'

'Final call. All aboard!' Ashok uncle announced, ushering everyone towards the cars as he waved his hands back and forth, setting the excitement in motion.

Mom, Ashok uncle, the kids and I drove in one car while aunty and Bahadur accompanied Dev in his SUV.

We drove up the winding hills and down the narrow dirt roads, arriving finally at Valley Park.

It was a crisp spring day. The mountains were wistful and tranquil, the grass abundant and lush and the sweet-smelling wildflowers, carefree as ever.

Mom and I spread out the picnic blanket while Bahadur and aunty got busy setting up the stove.

I laid out the sandwich platter on a red checkered blanket complimented with an assortment of sides. Chips and dips, fruit and lemonade and a freshly sliced loaf of banana bread. Moving the pitcher a little to the left and sliding the tray a little to the right, I stepped back and smiled at the perfectly aligned and rather picturesque spread.

Ashok uncle and Dev had wandered off to the stream with Mehar and Sidak.

I followed behind and stopped at a distance. Dev was teaching them how to skip rocks on water.

'Look for flat, round ones, they work best for skipping,' Dev explained while Mehar and Sid scrambled to find the perfectly shaped stones.

'This one, uncle?' Sid held up a stone.

'No, try this one. It seems to be better.'

I smiled. Mom placed a gentle hand on my shoulder and smiled with me.

'Nice to see them being kids, after all.'

'It is,' I added.

The sun shone bright in the clear blue skies. Flowers bloomed and the sound of the rushing creek added a pleasant melody to the breeze.

Lunch, banter and an hour-long trek had left us feeling both recharged and exhausted at the same time.

'Mama, why didn't we ever do this picnic thing before? It's so much fun,' exclaimed Mehar.

'Yes, we should do this more often,' I added, with little to contribute on family situations and interpersonal dynamics, which go into creating such experiences.

From a game of cards to dumb charades and from antakshari to hide and seek, the day was packed with laughter, fun and adventure.

Ashok uncle turned up the volume and hummed along with the radio, snapping his fingers to a happy tune as we got ready to drive back. The children giggled and joined him as well. Aunty smiled for a change.

It seemed like a great ending to a perfect day.

'Where are Mehar and Sidak?' I checked with mom after dinner.

'I was telling them a story in bed and they fell asleep just minutes into it. Seems like they're happily tired from the long day.

And it's about time for me to retire as well,' mom added.

'Good night, Dev.'

'Good night, aunty,' Dev responded politely.

Dev and I strolled along towards the far edge of Uncle's stepped garden.

'Watch out, Dev, there's a steep drop ahead,' I cautioned.

'I know! As a matter of fact, I can walk around this terrain with my eyes closed. I've been coming here since I was a little boy.'

'Here? What for?' I asked.

'Nothing much,' he extended his hand towards me. 'Two steps left and three down. And this is perfect.'

We sat on the little clearing overlooking the sweeping emptiness of the dark valley. And beyond that, hundreds of twinkling lights scattered about the majestic mountain like tiny fireflies.

'It's so quiet and peaceful here.'

'Isn't it? I would spend hours just staring into this emptiness, spinning world after world out of my imagination. This landscape was my happy bubble. It comforted me.

In fact, I loved this place so much that at seven, I'd already decided that someday I would build a house here.'

'Really?'

'Yes. Did you have a vision of something you really wanted in your life?' he asked, turning to me.

'I did, but it wasn't nearly as fascinating or ambitious,' I said, dismissing my own fanciful ideas.

'What was it?'

'Promise me. You won't laugh.'

'I promise I won't.'

I chuckled as I shook my head. 'It's rather silly. I grew up wanting to be this perfect wife who waits for her husband dressed in sarees and pearls, flipping impatiently through the pages of a housekeeping magazine, waiting for the clock to strike five. And then scurries about busily, arranging an elaborate set up of evening tea in the garden to welcome her husband home, amid blooming flowers and buzzing bees.

That was the ideal of a happy life for me. I never wanted much, really.'

'Not bad! So, you're one of those who belong to a different generation.'

'I don't know if I belong to a different generation, but I sure don't fit too well in this one. It's all too complicated for my liking. I like the ease and simplicity of life.'

'Do you see that light in the distance?' Dev questioned, pointing to the far left.

'Yes, I do.'

'I bought that lot many years ago. Finally, this year, I started the construction. It's a restful little place tucked far away from the turmoil and busyness of daily life.'

'That's incredible, Dev. So, you're one of those who don't give up on a dream,' I quipped.

'Well, I'm one of those who believe our dreams don't give up on us.

Speaking of busyness, who knows when this would've ever come to manifest? But as life would have it, two years ago, dad was diagnosed with last stage lung cancer. I returned from New York to be with him.

My entire life, I'd held a grudge against him. I somehow held him responsible for what ensued with Ma. But those few months with him taught me a lot. About understanding, forgiveness and accepting people for who they are—which might be quite contrary to what you make them out to be.

I'm glad I could find him before I lost him forever.'

'Why didn't you go back after that?'

'Tough to say. I guess I ended up liking it more here. Close to beeja, close to my childhood. There was a feeling of belonging and a strangely compelling pull, as though I had some unfinished business to take care of.'

'And, did you ever finish that "unfinished business"?'

'Things got busy. It took me a while to consolidate our lands. And then the orchard restoration happened and finally this building project.

And while I've secured many loose ends, I'm still searching for that undeniable reason. That one elusive thing which did not let me leave,' he smiled, looking towards me.

'Include me in the list of projects that needed your attention here,' I laughed, raising my hand. 'Maybe my situation and Seerat's dream conspired together to hold you back.'

'I don't know if you made me stay back, Tara,' said Dev, his tone no longer playful. 'But you definitely make me want to stay here. Right here,' he admitted, his eyes inescapably captivating.

I struggled to divert my gaze as I fumbled nervously, staring at my phone, 'We should get going. Ashok uncle must be getting worried.'

'He knows where to find me,' Dev said, offering his hand as I stood up.

'And just so you know Tara, no one has ever ventured into this space before. I always thought people could only take away from this experience, but you just proved me wrong. You enhanced what I thought was perfection. Thanks for sharing this evening with me.'

'Thanks, Dev. It will stay with me for a long time,' I responded, lowering my voice as my gaze fell to my feet.

We walked back in silence, the world around us seeped in the stillness of this pristine night.

Only hearts pounded, only longings murmured, only questionings whispered.

'There you two are,' yelled Ashok uncle raising his glass as we neared the house. 'And I've been sitting here in the company of these empty glasses all evening.'

'Tara, red or white?'

'Thank you, uncle, but I should go now. Need to check on the kids. You and Dev enjoy.'

'Good night, beta.'

Mehar and Sid were fast asleep. I lay next to them in bed with a million uncomfortable thoughts rushing through my mind. *'What if? Was I? Does he? Why? How?'*

I walked over to the window and stared at those lights in the distance. The night was still. The stars were shining. My kids were by my side. Everything was right, but for the tumultuous storm raging in my heart, that wouldn't let me fall asleep. Without turning on the light, I softly closed the door behind me and walked down the stairs into the kitchen.

I poured myself a glass of chilled water and opened the window a crack to let in some calming breeze.

'Tread carefully, Dev, this path can be treacherous,' I overheard Ashok uncle's voice.

'What makes you say that, uncle?'

'Beta, I've known you since you were a little boy. Why this sudden interest in my story? I thought you didn't believe in love,' uncle mused.

'Well, I'm still very skeptical of this "love". But today, I must admit, I had a strange realization that sparked a new curiosity.'

'Tell me, what did you experience?' I heard uncle prod him on.

'Perhaps, it could be called an unusual companionship.

As Tara and I sat beside each other staring into the vast

emptiness, I noticed there was a sense of ease in it. Like we understood each other without relying on words to communicate it. And the sheer joy and simplicity of a moment that hinged on absolutely nothing. Neither a relationship nor a bond, not even an outcome. Nothing had to change. Nothing more was needed.

That exact moment—so incomplete, yet so fulfilled.

For the first time, in that moment, I could relate to your feelings. Perhaps you must've felt something similar. Only much deeper, I assume, to be holding on it to this day.

What was it about her that you could never let her go?' Dev asked.

'Well, she came and never left. Neither was in my hands. It's simple as that.'

'What you don't understand, Dev,' uncle sighed, taking another sip of whiskey, 'is that I don't go looking for her, but still, I manage to find her everywhere. She climbs up this hill with the light of the rising sun and joins me for my morning tea. And then often, strolling along these empty roads, I unexpectedly bump into her. We hold hands and walk together for a little while and then she goes her way. Sometimes, when I fall asleep on this chair, she leans over and fixes my shawl while narrating fascinating stories. And in the evening, she sits by the window immersed in a book of poetry.

She's the only companion I've truly had. Just that I never had her and she doesn't know. Small problem. What did you just say about something so incomplete yet so fulfilled?'

'But what would it be like if she knew? Maybe she deserved the choice and that option in her life, to color her dreams, if not her reality. And it's not about the outcome. Maybe everything would have remained exactly as is, but perhaps her experience of life would have greatly transformed in knowing love had found her.

I believe it's only fair that she knew,' Dev argued.

'It's more complicated than that. What if she wasn't in love with me? What if she had children by the time I decided to tell her?' uncle debated.

'But that's my point. Why would any of that need to change? You, uncle, of all people, know that love isn't dependent on anything, least being possession.

If the only aim of love becomes attainment, then it's not even love anymore, it becomes a mere transaction.

The aim of love must only be love,' Dev insisted.

'So now you will teach me about love? The one who didn't believe in it until four hours ago.'

'I still don't, and I wouldn't dare go anywhere near it. I'm just an explorer. I like to discover and understand. Owning it is against my nature,' Dev laughed. 'And just for the record, I believe in a lot of other things—affection, adoration, caring, fondness, fancy, even worship, but love, it's just this abstract "love" that's too far beyond me. Never got it, never will. But I can appreciate what you feel. It must be quite special.'

I looked towards the stars and sent out a prayer for him.

The seas had finally calmed and I slept restfully, holding my children in the safety of my arms.

※

'Good morning, Tara beta,' Ashok uncle greeted me, as he sat buttering his toast at the breakfast table.

'How's it going with that school project?'

'I got an email from Mr. Mehta. The evaluation team will be there this week,' I responded, pulling out a stool as I joined him at the table.

'That's very good, beta.'

'Yes, we have some work on our hands, but I hope it all comes through. Once the lab is approved, trust me, with their persistence, these girls could land on the moon.'

'Stay positive. Good things will keep coming your way,' uncle added, taking a sip of orange juice from his glass.

'Is Dev coming?' aunty checked as she walked towards the table, holding a plate of eggs in her hand.

'Good reminder! Sorry Tara, I completely forgot. Dev called earlier today. He had to leave for Chandigarh due to some work. He wanted to know if you were planning to go back with him. In which case he would come back here, otherwise he would head straight to Amritsar tonight.

I did offer that my driver could bring you back in case Balwinder is unavailable. I hope that's all right with you.'

'Absolutely. He takes on too much responsibility for everything.'

'That's Dev's hallmark,' uncle admitted.

'He's so sorted. I wish Sonu was this mature. I still have to keep intervening in his day-to-day affairs so his life would stay on track, and even then, it barely does,' aunty remarked wearily.

'Unfortunately for Dev, he doesn't have that luxury called mother. And so, he doesn't have a choice but to manage his own affairs. Though, I wish he'd found someone to settle down with,' added uncle.

'That reminds me, what time are you dropping the kids back to school?' aunty inquired.

'They need to be at school by five,' I replied.

'Good, so we should plan to convene around six and discuss a few important things before you leave for Amritsar and bhenji returns to Chandigarh.'

'I have some thoughts I'd like to share. I suggest you, me, your uncle, your mom, Meeta and Mala discuss this matter together.'

'Leave the girl alone. She doesn't need any advice,' uncle protested.

'Everyone needs advice. Whether they take it or not is up to them. Our job as elders is to offer it to the best of our ability,' she snapped back.

'Tara beta,' Ashok uncle leaned over and whispered in my ear, 'the target has shifted. Tonight, you will be standing in the line of fire. Finally, an evening for me to enjoy my drinks in peace.'

'Hurry up, Mehar. Sid, are you packed?' I asked, my heart beginning to sink at the thought of their departure.

'Almost,' Mehar confirmed. 'But first, I need a promise.'

'Anything, my darling.'

'I want to spend time teaching with you in Amritsar,' Mehar demanded.

'I'd like to come too,' Sidak insisted. 'I can't teach, but I could play soccer with them.'

'Those are some feisty girls. They will beat you at your game.'

'Not with the tricks I've learned this year,' he countered.

'Shut up, Sid. I was talking first. Tell me, mom, 20–28th? Could we join you? Please?'

'As long as your dad is okay with it,' I hesitated.

'Why won't he be okay?' Mehar questioned, getting a little annoyed.

I sighed as I looked towards Ashok uncle.

'Let me see who stops you,' challenged aunty as she stepped forward and placed a protective arm around Mehar's shoulders.

'If your father has any questions, tell him to speak to Sarita aunty,' she directed.

'Yay! Aunty is the best,' they cried ecstatically.

'Now, make your plans, and if there is any problem, call me,' aunty instructed on a parting note.

Mehar inched up to kiss uncle and aunty goodbye, followed by big hugs from Sidak.

A tearful farewell ensued between nani and the two. And by the time my turn came, I had no choice but to be strong.

I smiled. 'I will let them know of your plans as soon as I get back. Prepare your lessons well, Mehar. And Sidak, practice your soccer skills. It's going to be showtime soon.'

'I will,' confirmed Mehar wiping tears off her cheeks. 'And I will too,' assured Sidak, trying to sound brave.

'I'll keep you updated about all the progress through letters and weekly calls. Now, study hard, look after each other, and be well, my babies.'

'I'm here, Tara. I will see them all the time. Don't worry,' assured Ashok uncle as he patted my back. 'Now go on, you're getting late.'

I dropped them off at school and watched them disappear past the empty steps once again.

The chatter of their conversations still floated around me like they weren't gone, they were somewhere around, just a little out of sight.

Twelve

AS I walked through the door, the room plunged into sudden silence and all eyes gravitated towards me.

Huddled around the dining table, uncle, aunty and mom bore a pensive expression as though struck by some great tragedy.

'Come, Tara, join us,' aunty somberly offered as I removed my shoes and placed my bag on the couch. 'Bahadur, bring Tara some water.'

'Everything all right?' I asked, sensing the palpable tension.

'Yes,' aunty confirmed, clearing her throat, 'We've been trying to evaluate the issue from multiple perspectives—you, the children, the family. It's not an easy place to be. However, tough situations call for tough choices and we'll need to make one today,' she stated, her gaze stern yet firmly contemplative.

'Everyone here would agree that this marriage has not served you well. And…'

'Before you continue firing,' uncle interjected, 'let me take a moment to explain things.

Tara beta, we all understand you didn't end up here by choice. And that you have exhausted all possible means to make this relationship work. You've compromised, yielded, accepted and endured. None of it helped.

And while you were hoping Tej will come through with redemption or a reconciliation effort, even that seems nowhere in sight.

So, where do you see yourself going from here? I mean, you cannot carry on indefinitely like this. At some point, you will have to stand up to your challenges and deal with them head-on.'

Uncle added, softening his tone, 'But don't feel we're coercing you to decide one way or another. If you miss your home and family, we will figure something out to make that work too. However, Tara, I urge you to consider your well-being before you consider any other parameters.'

The phone went off. 'Hello, Mala,' mom answered. 'I'm placing your call on speaker now. Is Meeta there too?'

'We're both here,' Mala confirmed.

I had been forced into the spotlight again, unarmed to deal with what was coming my way. I hadn't asked for any of it, not in my life, and not now. I drew in a deep breath.

'Thank you for your love, concern and time today,' I spoke as though addressing a gathering at my funeral.

'I would like to begin by telling you that when Mala and Meeta initially nudged me in this direction, I felt unprepared and unsure. But today, I am grateful to have experienced these few weeks that might suffice in themselves to speak of my entire life. This also gave me time to dwell on the rights and the wrongs. The blames and the games, the whos and the whys. I did not rush into this decision headlong.

Standing here today, I can see that by walking away from this marriage, I walk into the arms of freedom—a life without fears, a life spared of compromises.

And perhaps one could also argue, a life of no certainty, security, or social standing.

Well, I never had any of that to begin with.

Under these circumstances, the decision itself is rather self-dictating. But it's the experience of it that I'm ill-prepared for.'

Aunty leaped at that statement unambiguously, 'Let me warn you—it will be gut-wrenching and painful, but not any more than what you've already endured. You can handle it.'

I stared out the window for an unbearably long moment, gathering my thoughts and weighing my words, 'I will not go to court,' I stated. 'I will not create a mockery of my situation, nor will I give eager tongues a reason to wag on account of his follies. It will remain strictly between the two of us.

And I will neither demand nor beg. Whatever Tej offers, I will accept. If he offers nothing, besides a divorce, so be it.'

A wave of disappointment swept the room, followed by rising murmurs of disagreement.

'Don't be ridiculous, Tara. You've given 17 years of your life to this family. "Good girls don't go to court" is so passé. You can choose to keep it dignified, but there's no reason to be stupid,' Mala insisted.

'You know how it went the last time he offered to settle. It was a joke,' reminded Meeta.

'You have a life ahead of you, how do you propose to take care of that? Living costs, medical expenses, travel. Would you never buy anything for yourself or take your children on another holiday? Don't jump out of the frying pan into the fire. What you see as prudent is at best foolish.'

Having remained a quiet spectator through this argument, aunty finally spoke, 'Tara, what I hear beneath your words is your underlying desire to be selfless and self-righteous. Correct? Then be selfless! Be selfless for those women who don't have the education, the family backing or the financial standing to fight for their rights in court as you do. Do it for them. Do it for the rights of those women who are further discouraged each time a woman like you walks away from her rights because it's less painful. It's not what he chooses to give; it's what is rightfully yours, in the eyes of the law. Remember, it's not a matter of his generosity, but what he owes you for your standing in that family and the cost of practically your entire life.

And what petty compensation money is for a precious life wasted.

Look, Tara, this fight isn't so much about money or ego, but about what's acceptable and correct. If you have too much, donate it for all I care, but don't leave it unclaimed, so he can indulge the next woman, and the next, with what rightfully belongs to you.'

'Aunty is absolutely right, Tara,' Mala admitted.

'We agree with her,' concurred Meeta and mom.

'Beta, there's no right and no wrong, but there is a question of fairness,' uncle added. 'For a change, she's making sense.'

'Someday you will thank me for this, Tara. Money is not always an end to happiness, but many a times I've seen it become a means to fulfillment. Study, travel, start something. Do anything but walk away empty-handed. You need not pay the price for someone else's wrongdoing,' aunty insisted with empathetic practicality.

'I don't know what to say,' I sighed as I looked out again. 'All I know is that he will remain the only father to my children, and no matter what ensues, they shouldn't despise him. What if I'm not around tomorrow? The end of my relationship with him shouldn't lead to an end of theirs,' I deliberated in a resigned voice.

'They are children. They will be fine. And we will handle this with sensitivity and consideration. Let me deal with Varsha first, the lawyer I was talking about and then I'll arrange for the two of you to meet before filing,' aunty concluded.

'Also,' I added, 'I would like to inform him personally, not through a court notice, if that's fine.'

'Go ahead. First, he will try to talk you out of this decision by laughing at you, then by intimidating you and finally by threatening you with dire consequences—you will live on the streets, you won't get to see your children, etc. It's a well-structured process. Nothing new there, but try it anyway,' aunty forewarned, looking skeptically at her phone. 'And Varsha just texted. She would like to speak with you on Friday and file two weeks from now. Is that fine?'

'I guess so,' I added, reluctantly.

This moment, that I knew wasn't far, I had hoped somehow, would never come. It felt crippling. As though my heart was being repeatedly stabbed with each remark, with every decision, until the only dream it had ever harboured, one of harmonious family life, bled itself out of me.

'Good. So, my job here is done. We can all relax now,' concluded aunty as she stood up and headed towards the kitchen.

'Don't overthink it, beta,' said uncle, deciphering my expression as he placed a reassuring hand on my knee. 'Take it one breath, one step and one day at a time. Just think about what you can do to make today happy. We will deal with tomorrow when it comes.

Tara, you've already travelled a great distance. Hold my words true—the best is yet to come. It has to come,' he added, trying hard to uplift my spirits. But I knew better than to believe him.

I walked quietly up to my room. The weekend was over, the children gone, the agenda had been accomplished and my life stared at me again, emptier than ever before. I unzipped my bag and there, buried far beneath the books, I found the diary.

Welcoming, non-judgemental and entirely accepting, much like a good friend I'd ignored for too long.

I opened a blank page and began to write.

Dear Diary,

I must begin by uttering the same words again, why are some strangers, not strangers enough?

You seem familiar, even though we've hardly spoken.

We come to each other, empty in our own ways, standing at unknown crossroads at this decisive moment of my life.

A moment that lends itself to the beginning of a brand-new chapter.

A chapter we shall write together.

I do not know how it will begin, or for that matter, what the ending might be. I neither promise a thrill, nor much delight, but I will strive to ensure it delivers utmost honesty and absolute truth.

On my part, I promise to come to you with a bare soul and blind trust. And I hope you will come to me with wisdom, guidance and support.

I hope you will often read between the lines and help me see what I accidentally overlook. I also hope you will be better at predicting the next and reminding me of little things so easily forgotten.

For bringing me all that, I thank you already.

And remember, no matter where we go or what we discover, we will be in this story together.

You and I, my always known and newly found friend.

Yours,
Tara.

The phone beeped. It was a message from Dev, 'Hi, Tara.'

'Long life, Dev. I was just thinking about you.'

'What about me?'

'Well, I finally connected with the diary.'

'And how do you like its company?'

'Much more than my own, I suppose.'

'Then perhaps, I too should get to know it because I strongly doubt any company could be better than yours.'

I finally smiled, for the first time in many hours.

'Thank you. You're too generous with your words.'

'And you just don't give yourself enough credit.'

'Anyhow, a slight change of plans. The person I was scheduled to meet in Chandigarh missed his connection coming in. He didn't land until this evening. And since we just wrapped up the meeting, I'm going to stay back in Chandigarh tonight. Will leave for Amritsar around noon tomorrow.

What are your plans?'

'I'm planning to drive to Chandigarh with mom tomorrow morning and continue to Amritsar from there.'

'Why bother with two cars then? Once you're in Chandigarh, we could drive together from here. Besides, you'd also be helping the environment, if that's any motivation to bear my company.'

'What are you saying, Dev? I look forward to our conversations. Let me tie up the plans. I'll confirm shortly,' I added.

'Tara,' Ashok uncle called out as I walked into the lobby. 'Dev texted me a little while ago.'

'Oh, he texted me as well,' I responded.

'I think what he's suggesting will work well. You should be in Chandigarh by 11 a.m. Plan to drive together from there.'

Uncle turned towards mom, 'Bhenji, this will also give her time to discuss her decision with a peer. Sometimes, children open up differently to friends than family. And his advice is always worth its weight in gold. Dev is a sensible boy,' uncle confirmed.

Mom, aunty and I stood by the car, bidding goodbye to uncle. The three of us, though departing together, were headed on different journeys—mom for her home in Chandigarh, aunty for her 3 p.m. flight to Delhi and me, back to Amritsar.

'And you finally have your freedom back,' I whispered as I gave Ashok uncle a goodbye hug. He winked at me, extending his hand just far enough for me to see the cigarette he held in it.

'Eat your medicines on time,' said aunty in a forbidding voice as she stepped into the car. 'And don't drink too much, and this better be the last cigarette to celebrate my departure. No need to get back to this lousy addiction,' she instructed, closing the door shut.

'How do you always know?'

'I have eyes at the back of my head. Remember that,' she said in a reprimanding voice.

We laughed as we drove off, past these winding narrow roads, on to a busy congested highway, weaving dexterously between overcrowded Himachal roadways buses and impatient tourist taxis.

Slowly, the congestion eased into an orderly flow. I observed troops of monkeys huddled around the bends grooming their little ones, while chewing leisurely on stolen fruit and scattered peanuts under the crisp mountain sunshine.

We talked for a little while and then aunty fell asleep. Mom took a Dramamine and rested her head back. I plugged in my airpods and tuned into the music. As I opened the window just a crack, a burst of cold air hit my face, leaving my neatly tied hair playfully ruffled.

The sun was bright, the day was new and I was once again enjoying the company of music.

I was reconnecting with that pleasant aspect of travel, which creates lasting memories, long after the journey is over. I observed the mountains and the rushing streams. I thought about people returning home with logs of wood on their heads. About that bird which sang, pining for its love.

And I thought about Seerat. Just how excited she would be when I break the news to her. I imagined all the ways in which I could tell her.

I was also realizing that I liked 'happy'. Happy thoughts, happy people, happy surroundings.

I had lived with despair for so long that it had grown into my default state of being. Wherever I went, its dark shadows cast themselves before me. I was trapped in this prison of melancholy with pain, tears, resentment and anger for its inmates. I wanted nothing to do with any of it anymore.

Yet again, the overbearing sentence had been imposed on me.

The mere mention of filing for divorce had spun me far into the blues. But I knew the only way out was through. And the sooner, the better.

Dev picked me up at noon and we set off for Amritsar.

'How's beeja doing?' I asked.

'She's well. It's Sunday. She must be busy stirring up a storm in the kitchen. Brunch menu and dinner plans. She's done this all her life. After a while, it becomes second nature.'

'I know a thing or two about second nature,' I contributed in a small, dreary voice, followed by a long contemplative silence.

'What is it, Tara?'

'We are moving forward with divorce filing next week.'

'Are you ready for it?' Dev asked, his easygoing manner suddenly replaced with thoughtful concern.

'I'd rather not think of myself as an escapist, but the truth is I'm not ready. Nor will I ever be. I neither want to go back, nor do I want this marriage to end. But again, only if we had these choices in life. The choice to not choose.'

'What's preventing you from moving forward?'

'The fact that no matter how far I go, Tej and I will remain connected by these 17 years and two children. The pain, the trauma, the fight seems unbearable. It's like telling a defeated soldier that the war is just beginning. I don't have it in me. Neither the strength nor the will to fight. I'd rather lay there like a wounded warrior waiting for my end to come to me than go valiantly looking for it.'

'What if someone tells you that you've already won the war. This fight is only the closing battle. Would you give your life another chance, knowing this will soon be over and you get to go home free?'

'But the war has already destroyed my home. There is no home left anymore. There's no one waiting for me there. I have no home,' I replied as the haunting pain of my own words was reflected in my eyes.

'And your children? They'd still be waiting. With or without the home. Maybe for them?'

'Yes, my children. I still have them...yes,' I mumbled.

'And while we are at it, let me also ask you why you wouldn't go back?'

'For one, because he hasn't asked me back.

Dev, do you think it really makes no difference to his life that I'm gone? He has my number. He knows where I am. He hasn't even tried.'

'Tara, what can I say? This man neither knew what he had nor does he know what he is losing. Until one day, when he suddenly wakes up and lives to regret it for the rest of his life.

Will you have any regrets about this decision, Tara? Reach deep into your heart and say whatever you feel. No matter how absurd or irrational it might be. Let it come out.'

I remained silent for a while, regurgitating the same thoughts, the same feeling as tears welled up in my eyes.

'Tara?'

'Dev, I didn't kill it, but I couldn't save it either,' I cried. 'I couldn't save it. I tried, Dev. I tried very hard. I gave it my all. But it died. It just died,' I wept inconsolably. The stream of warm tears against my cold cheeks felt involuntary and unrestrained.

I was finally coming face to face with this eventuality. Everything was over. I was finally getting a divorce.

Dev pulled the car over onto the rough pavement. He reached inside his pocket and offered me a handkerchief.

'I'll give you a few minutes,' he said, as he stepped out of the car.

Unguarded, my tears flowed, fiercely ravaging my heart, until the tempest was finally over, and my eyes were empty, cold and dry.

I reconciled with the inevitable. I finally owned my loss. A loss that had found a permanent resting place in my heart. Its thick stench and gaping void, I was to carry forward with me for the rest of my life.

Dev finally knocked on the window, offering me a glass of sugarcane juice. Maybe a few minutes had gone by, or a few hours, I couldn't tell.

'Don't worry. I had him wash the glass. Thrice. With bottled water,' Dev confirmed with a smile.

'Strange that the crushing of sugarcane could yield something so sweet,' he remarked as we resumed our journey.

We did not talk much thereafter.

I quietly mourned the death of my marriage, and Dev gave me ample space for it.

Thirteen

I looked at the red digital display flashing 5:20 a.m. Reaching for my robe and slippers, I made my way to the bathroom. I was suddenly struck by a faint chatter buried within the distant sounds of morning Gurbaani. I leaned in closer, putting my ear to the door before I pulled it open.

Sitting by the doorstep in the dim light of a low-voltage bulb suspended from the overhang, I found Seerat and Premo engaged in a hushed conversation.

'You're awake, bhenji,' said Premo, pleasantly relieved as she stood up and ushered Seerat towards me. 'There you go. This girl has been here since 4 a.m. I told her how late you had slept last night, but she wouldn't budge.'

'Aunty!' Seerat cried as she flung into my arms. 'You were gone too long.'

'Kamli,' Premo shook her head dismissively. 'It was three days!'

Seerat's eyes suddenly lit up as she held out a piece of paper. 'I wrote this for you, in English.'

You are a fairy. Sweet and nice.
Never go again.
Smile and be happy.

Beneath that, she had scribbled my portrait in pencil. Adorned with a crown, I held a book in one hand and chocolate in the other. Floral showers, flying birds and colourful rainbows completed her depiction of 'Tara aunty'.

'Thank you, Seerat. This made my day,' I smiled, touched by this heartfelt expression of pure love.

'And, in return, I have something that will make yours.'

'What is it, aunty?' Seerat jumped with curiosity.

'Not quite yet. Patience makes all things sweeter.'

'It's chocolate,' she speculated.

'That too,' I laughed, reaching inside my bag as I handed her a bar of Cadbury's.

'But you said I must wait.'

'There's a sweeter surprise awaiting. I promise. No lessons for today. Be here at 7. We will go to school together. And bring your mother along.'

'What could it be? What could it be?' Seerat scratched her chin, unable to contain her excitement.

'I don't know,' she said, throwing her hands up in the air. 'I'll be back with Mother,' she giggled as she ran off into the breaking daylight, leaving the patter of happy feet and a ton of goodness behind.

I looked at the sketch again and smiled to myself. Suddenly, everything seemed worthwhile.

🍂

'Seerat, assemble all the students while I have a quick word with the Headmaster,' I instructed.

After pacing the corridor and checking on us casually a few times, Seerat finally knocked on the door, 'Aunty, the girls are waiting.'

'Ah, yes. We will be right out.'

Disconcerted by the rather profound and emotionally complex expression on Masterji's face, Seerat quietly slipped back into the noisy gathering that awaited the announcement.

'Children,' Master ji addressed the assembly. 'This day marks an important milestone in the history of our school. Tara beeba ji has finally stepped into her grandfather's vacant shoes to take his great legacy forward. I once heard that legacy is not what you leave behind for others, it is what you leave behind *in* others. He would be proud of her today, just as we all are.'

His voice choked as he took off his glasses and wiped a stray tear. Premo and Darshi stood among the silent audience.

'I am happy to announce that our school has been elected to become a Smart School.

Finally, we will have funding for additional classrooms, playgrounds, books and meals. They plan to deploy 12 new teachers, and if all goes well,' he paused, looking up for a brief moment, 'you might even get to work on computers. This is not merely the fulfillment of a dream, know that this is the beginning of a thousand dreams. Your lives will never be the same.'

A wave of cheer washed over the barren grounds, as the girls broke out into a rapturous celebration. Some spun around in circles doing the kikli, while others ran amok in spontaneous merriment.

Premo and Darshi wiped their tears as each came forward to place a silent hand over my head.

'Beeba ji,' Masterji bowed with humbly folded hands, 'The future will remain indebted to you.'

'I didn't do anything,' I firmly maintained. 'It was their dreams, your vision, these mothers' prayers and Waheguru's grace, which made this possible. And along the way, some incredibly kind people held the doors open. I couldn't have come this far alone.

But now we have work ahead of us and not enough time.'

'Whatever you tell us, beeba ji. We are here,' Masterji confirmed. 'Watch out…'

Before I had a chance to react, I found myself suspended mid-air as Bittu swooped me to his shoulder, breaking into celebratory bhangra moves. 'O, balle! Smart School for our village!' he sang.

'Fitteh muh!' Premo cursed him.

'Let her go. Right now. So grown-up, but your brains are no bigger than that of a bird's. Who lifts a woman like that?' Premo lashed out.

Regaining his composure, Bittu quickly apologized and planted my feet back on the ground.

I laughed, shaking my head, 'It's okay, Premo! He's like a younger brother.'

'Now, don't worry about it. Come on, everyone, back to work.'

'So, Tara beeba ji, what do we need to do?'

'First and foremost, I need a worksheet filled out before the evaluation. This will list our requirements item by item, along with an estimate of the costs involved. They will assess our current situation and stated needs against their budget to determine the gap and the tranche schedule. Essentially, what projects get priority allocation and what percentage of our requirements get funded will depend on this.

More importantly, I would like this to be a project that the entire village becomes engaged with, to some degree. Think of this as a collective avenue for overall village progress. Bittu, Premo and Darshi—you will arrange meetings with local men and women to get the word out. Gurduwara, mandi, bazaar, panchayat, wherever you can spread the word.

We need to promote this opportunity as a channel for organic, sustainable growth for the entire village. We will try to give out work contracts to locals wherever possible.

For this, we need them to gain a clear understanding of the requirements, so they can determine what they can contribute to.

Directly or indirectly. Electrical, plumbing, construction, whatever. Perhaps, this could be an opportunity for some to find a source of livelihood, while securing a commitment to the success of this project.

And soon, they will begin to see for themselves where this change can take us.'

'Beeba ji, you're right. We need to rally all the support we can manage.'

'I have an idea, bhenji,' Bittu proposed, revving with excitement once again.

'Why don't we have a village-wide panchayat meeting here? In the school itself. We can explain all the job details and handhold them through the entire process. And as you know, momentum sustains itself. There is great power in collective action. They will be encouraged by looking at one another, and the bidding will also become competitive.'

'Great idea, Bittu. Maybe you're brighter than what everyone here gives you credit for.'

'I've known it all along, bhenji. People just take time recognizing my genius,' he remarked, adjusting his collar.

'Beeba ji, I will make sure everything is arranged at my end,' Masterji assured.

'Darshi, Premo and Bittu, 10 a.m. tomorrow,' I confirmed.

Just then, doctor saab walked in with a pile of colourful boxes stacked one on top of the other. Leaning sideways, he stuck his head out and announced, 'No celebration is complete without laddoos.'

I rushed to help him with the tilting, precariously balanced pile.

'So many boxes!' I exclaimed, lending a hand.

'Why not? This is the real occasion, the birth of a new future. After years of stagnation, this village will once again take a significant leap forward. Thanks to your effort, Tara. You have revived my own will to bring about change. Tell me what job you have for me.'

'Thank you, doctor saab. As a matter of fact, I do need your help. As one of the most respected citizens of this village, if possible, I would like you to address tomorrow's gathering to harness a unified community-wide vision. I want people to believe they own a part of this success.

Also, down the line, perhaps, you could help us in setting up a distance learning program for Biology.'

'Bittu's girlfriend Preeti is studying medicine. She already has access to all the latest material and technology. Bittu, why don't you ask her to help with this part?' doctor saab suggested.

'Daddy, why do you want to turn this school into the field of Kurukshetra? It will be the next maha yudh between mummy ji and Preeti.'

'Oh, she can't do much more than crib and complain. She will eventually get tired and stop on her own. She always does. Besides, this is not about me, you, or your mummy ji, it's about our daughters and their future,' doctor saab proclaimed.

The next day started with a festive feeling. A palpable jubilation filled the air.

Girls arrived dressed in their best clothes. Premo and Darshi showed up early to sweep the premises, and Master ji brought in colourful streamers that crisscrossed above the rubble path from the link road to the main building.

'And this is it!' he affirmed, pinning up the last string to the office entrance as he wiped his brow and fixed his turban.

We stood ready to receive the village well before the scheduled time—the girls, Masterji, Darshi, Premo, Bittu and I.

I looked at my watch. It was 10 past 10.

We stood there waiting. Neither a soul appeared in sight, nor a leaf stirred on campus. Hundreds of eager eyes remained silently glued to the deserted road.

I looked towards Master ji. He shook his head in tacit assurance.

A 'Good luck' notification from Dev popped up on my phone.

I also had two missed calls from mom.

I drew in a deep sigh, as a sudden bout of anxiety began to take deeper roots. It was 10:30 a.m. now.

A few tense minutes later, I heard a faint sound in the distance. The sound of a beating drum. It grew consistently louder and visibly closer until, to my horror and extreme embarrassment, I realized this wasn't a drum at all, but the good old Punjabi dhol. The grand procession being led by none other than our much-revered doctor saab.

My face turned a deep shade of crimson as I observed the huge crowd dancing their way towards the school.

The girls applauded and rejoiced.

I panicked. 'What is this? Why are they celebrating already? We're not even through the first stage yet. It's not a done deal.'

'Welcome to Punjab,' impressed doctor saab as he walked up and placed a hand on my shoulder. 'One of our traditions. We dance before we have reasons to celebrate. Mostly because people are too drunk by the time real celebrations roll around,' he laughed.

'It's all in the spirit. Euphoria, they call it.

I discovered this quite early on, that in us humans, the "feeling" of happiness is much stronger than "understanding" of the events that call for happiness. You wanted me to get them involved, right? There you go. They're celebrating our success, much a part of it, and I didn't have to say a word.'

'Tara,' doctor saab explained, 'after a while, people will forget what you said, but what they will never forget is how they felt. This collective celebration will change everything. You watch.'

I looked towards doctor saab, surprised at his unconventional wisdom.

'Don't look at me like that. Join the party. And take the girls with you,' he offered, extending his arm.

Tea, sweets, dancing and garlands finally gave way to projects, plans, needs and goals.

The unanimous decision was that the estimates would be significantly lower than expected because the village community will pitch in with their services free of charge. All enhancement would come to the school 'at cost.'

The days of the week progressed. The evaluation team came and left. And finally, I received the much-awaited phone call.

'Tara, this is Mr. Mehta. Good news, the budget has been fully approved. We will release it in three tranches, subject to the successful completion of each stage. I must tell you, whatever you did, your estimates were by far the most competitive we've ever seen. The decision on the approval of the computer lab is still pending. I will know better by next week.'

'Thank you, Mr. Mehta. I am grateful for all you've done.'

'It's been my pleasure. Good luck.'

I hung up and stared at the phone for a long while. Did we just accomplish this? It felt surreal. I neither had the expertise, nor a plan. Then how did this happen so effortlessly? Like somehow, all this was pre-ordained, and I just coasted right through, connecting the dots and unlocking secret doorways.

Dad always believed in this kind of synchronous orchestration of the universe. 'There are no coincidences in life and no accidents either. It's all a part of the greater flow,' he would often repeat.

Surprisingly for me, I neither felt a sense of giddying elation nor an uncontainable rush of joy as I'd expected. Instead, there was a humble grounding and a deep reverence for that greater power, which made me appear like a minuscule speck in the overall scheme of life.

And no, I did not want to call mom, Mala, Meeta, or for that matter, even Dev. I did not want to share this with Master ji or the village folks yet. All I wanted was to go somewhere, sit still and allow this feeling to settle within me.

I wanted this strange new reality of accomplishment to sink in.

I collected my diary and walked out into the warm sunlight, not knowing where this trail would lead me. I kept walking—through the quiet fields, past the open pastures. I walked further along until my sight fell upon the old kikkar tree and the familiar train tracks beside it. Spinney shrubs of beri still flanked its sides. This landscape seemed uninterrupted since an afternoon from many decades ago.

Those hazy winter days of idle pursuits, plucking fruit from the shrubs and waving at passersby all afternoon long. In a world with no cellphones, handheld gadgets, or streaming content, we were often forced to create our own entertainment. Counting the wagons, timing the train, or simply devising narratives around where these people were travelling, or why.

I rested my back against the coarse trunk of the tree and stretched my legs out on the pale, dry grass. A native, balmy breeze caressed my face as though welcoming me back.

I opened my diary and began to write.

Dear Diary,

The past few weeks have been rather tumultuous. A lot has happened—both good and bad.

Well, more good than bad, I should say, but still, change is change, always unsettling.

And you might somewhat understand my extreme aversion to it. In any situation, on any given day, I have preferred the predictable, mundane and ordinary. I like life in status-quo. For someone who wouldn't even change what they ate for breakfast day after day, year after year, the magnitude of this transition has been disconcerting.

Oh, by the way, did you hear the school will finally get its due? And the girls might realize their dreams after all.

It all came together and I'm grateful for that.

But the greatest realization that has come from this change is that the further I walk away, the clearer I begin to see what I've left behind. And the closer I approach the new destination, the louder I begin to hear that distant song which had been humming in my ears all my life. I feel closer to home. Whatever that home might look like.

Until next time,
Tara.

I closed the diary and took out my phone, slowly making my way back.

'Dev, we did it! The budget stands fully approved. Mr. Mehta said it was the most competitive bid they'd ever received.'

'That's fantastic. Congratulations, Tara.'

'Thank you. The village truly came together to make this possible. Now fingers crossed, hope the lab goes through as well.'

'It will. Don't worry,' Dev reassured me.

'So, when do we get to see you again? And unlike last time, you have plenty of commitments and a packed schedule. Now you tell us what works for you, ma'am.'

'It's nothing like that,' I laughed, 'I've been wanting to see beeja myself. I have to share all the updates with her. Later today or tomorrow, whatever works for you.'

'All right, so let's meet today at 5 p.m. while we also have a big reason to celebrate.'

'Sounds like a plan. Hey Dev, aunty is calling me on the other line.'

'Sure, go ahead. We will talk later,' he signed off.

'Hello, aunty. How're you doing?

'I'm fine, Tara. I was calling to inform you that your uncle spoke with Varsha and explained to her how busy you've been with the school project. So instead of having you come to Chandigarh, she mailed the Vakalatnama and some other documents to you a few days back. You can sign these and courier them to her. You will only need to come in person for the actual filing and final arguments.

Simplify your life where and when you can, Tara. It's a difficult pill to swallow, but it must be taken in order to get better. I hope you understand.'

'Yes, aunty. I'll do the needful.'

I entered my room and turned on the fan. A brown package rested on top of the pile of neatly ironed clothes.

'Bhenji, a courier came for you. I put it upstairs, in your bedroom,' yelled Premo from the courtyard.

'I have it, Premo,' I confirmed.

I opened the package, scanned through the documents and quietly returned them to the envelope.

The room felt unusually stuffy. I loosened my scarf and opened the window to let in some fresh air. A sweet melody came riding on the breeze.

I leaned over to the ledge and looked out the window. There

Darshi was, rocking back and forth on the swing, singing with joyful abandon while the women clustered around her appeared completely spellbound.

All I remembered was that Darshi could sing, how well, I'd never realized. Her voice was ethereal.

I waved to the women who indicated for me to join them.

'Tomorrow,' I confirmed as I waved back with an approving smile.

I lay down on the bed to catch a little rest.

The song lingered on, mingling playfully with the balmy breeze.

Fourteen

DEV stood at the door holding a bunch of fragrant white liliums.

'You know these are my absolute favourite, right?' I smiled, opening the door.

'Why am I not surprised?' Dev laughed.

As I held the flowers, my thoughts drifted back to Tej. His slighting comparison of the cheap liliums that I'd wanted, against the expensive orchids he'd ordered.

Perhaps, in the end, it's not the offering in itself that matters, but what the receiver draws from it—beauty, fragrance, joy, inspiration or mere comparison.

'Preoccupied?' Dev prompted.

'No, pleasantly surprised. Thank you, these are absolutely splendid.'

'Bhenji, I'll place these in your bedroom,' Premo offered, taking the flowers from my hand.

On our way, I eagerly shared details of the progress we'd made so far. From Master ji's vision to doctor saab's contribution and the unprecedented outpouring of support from the community.

'Mr. Mehta said he'd never seen anything like this in his entire career,' I told Dev with great pride.

'That's remarkable, Tara. Now, this calls for a real treat. Did you ever eat golas when you were growing up?' Dev questioned abruptly, with a mischievous glint descending in his eyes as he pulled over in front of Kishan Mishthan Bhandar.

'Gola? Kala Khatta? Of course,' I laughed. 'Ah! It brings back so many memories. We lived on it all summer long. That was the highlight of our summer holidays in Amritsar, besides flying kites. Gola or guddi, was often at the core of our existential debate when it wasn't "smoking" Phantom cigarettes or twirling to the "washing powder Nirma" jingle.' I laughed, reminiscing about old times.

'Perfect then, I've brought you to just the right place. This place sells the best golas you can find on the face of this earth. And trust me, you can't imagine the places I've experimented at to arrive at my verdict.'

Dev dashed out of the car and returned a few minutes later, carrying two colourful, chunky snow cones mounted on slender wooden sticks.

'It's delicious,' I said, licking the drippings off the gola's edge, careful to keep my white suit from staining. 'Back home in Chandigarh, we often experimented with our own version of snow cones, laced with roohafza and khus syrup. It was mostly a miserable failure,' I chirped, finally feeling the high of all we'd accomplished and all that I was reconnecting with.

'And that went quick!' said Dev, beeping the horn as we arrived at the gate. 'Beeja has probably been keeping an exact tally of the number of minutes and seconds since I left. She couldn't wait to see you tonight,' Dev remarked, turning towards me.

'I'm happy to be here,' I smiled back.

'My darling Tara!' beeja greeted me with her contagious smile. 'How I missed you!' she held me in a tight embrace.

'I'm back, beeja, and with a lot of updates, but first, my patase.'

Beeja joyfully undid the knot on the edge of her dupatta.

'Three for you and two for Dev. Now quickly come inside and tell me everything.'

Over a cup of perfectly brewed ginger tea, I explained to beeja all about the meeting with Mr. Mehta, our Kasauli trip, the village collaboration and the most recent budget approval.

'Very good! That's my girl. Calls for a toast. Go, Dev, bring a bottle of champagne. I have the chiller well-stocked today.'

Beeja raised a toast, 'To the adventure that is just beginning and to a blossoming friendship. May it last forever,' she pronounced with a heartwarming smile.

Dev looked into my eyes.

'Salud!' he raised his glass.

We sat on the stone patio overlooking the gardens as crickets chirped, and Ghulam Ali played in the background.

Soon the overcast sky came to greet the parched earth in a torrential downpour.

'What a beautiful evening!' I remarked, 'And that smell of wet soil, what's the word for it?'

'Petrichor,' Dev completed my sentence.

'Thank you. Don't you just love it?' I remarked, soaking in the moment.

Between the three of us, we finished a bottle, enjoying the rain and the soulful music, chattering aimlessly and staring silently into the hazy evening.

'I miss him sometimes, his dada. Ghulam Ali was his favourite. We would sit for hours on end staring into the night, just like this, as ghazals played on and fireflies danced. I think we discovered this about us during our African safari. We had all day to each other, and after a while, we would run out of conversations. And that is when music would fill the silence between us,' beeja shared, swept by the nostalgic parallel.

'I too love ghazals. Qawwali parties and ghazal nights were quite the staple in our household. Dad imbued in us a keen sense for fine arts and culture. Things that were, in his opinion, integral to a harmonious life.'

'He did a fine job I can see,' said beeja, looking fondly upon me.

'You miss him, don't you?' she asked.

'Every day,' I answered reluctantly as I took another sip from my glass.

'And what else is on your mind, Tara? I recognize a faint distraction like you're here, but not all of yourself. Something is gnawing away at your heart. What is it?'

'Nothing, beeja. Everything is fine,' I said, forcing a smile.

'You shouldn't confine things to your heart. It can become toxic. Learn to speak your mind and pour out your heart. Let people think what they will. You will sleep better, I promise.'

I exhaled deeply before reaching into my bag. I took out the brown envelope and placed it on the table in front of us.

'Divorce petition. Aunty wants me to sign it.'

'And you?' questioned beeja in a flat, point-blank tone.

'I mean, as a basic courtesy, I wanted to inform him personally before I sign,' I answered.

'And I took out the papers a few times but...' I stuttered, 'but my hands are failing me with such a crucial decision.'

'Do you want to sign it?' beeja questioned.

I hesitated for a moment.

'Tell me, do you want to sign it?' beeja repeated, leaning in.

I closed my eyes and reached within my heart. The answer was there—loud, clear, categorical.

'Yes. Yes, I do,' I blurted.

'Oye, Dev, she said "I do," get two bottles of champagne. One for the divorce and second for her new life.'

'Beeja, relax,' Dev tried to dissuade her, gauging the sensitivity of the situation by the bewildered look on my face.

'You relax! This is important. Stop meddling in it. I know how the biggest decisions in life are made, without thinking too much and without too much drama. One has to be brave and trusting. Everyone does it with all the rona dhona involved.

Tara, you must celebrate it. You have one life, and it's coming back to you. Finally, it will be yours. You will own it again! What could be better than that?

Now Tara, finish your glass, sign this paper and seal the deal.'

'Beeja, not like this. Not here and now.'

'Yes, like this, here and now. Come on,' she insisted, sliding the papers towards me and handing me a pen.

'Beeja, let her take her time,' Dev insisted.

'Seventeen years is all the time she needed. Now she must do it without overthinking or second-guessing,' beeja maintained her stance, inching the paper closer.

Dev deterred me, 'Tara, there's no pressure. Do it when you're ready. I don't want you to regret this. Beeja, this is not child's play. Do you understand her entire life will change forever based on this decision?' he protested, his voice growing impatient and apprehensive.

'Well, think about what you just said—her life will change forever. This pen is the key to her prison door. Do you want her to rethink if she wants to remain confined to misery, or do you want her to walk free? You're not helping here, Dev. Remain quiet,' beeja insisted.

'Take a deep breath, Tara, remember Waheguru, take a sip of champagne and sign it,' she instructed precisely.

I picked up the pen with trembling fingers.

'Wait,' beeja interrupted. I paused to look up.

'I want to document this moment of your second birth. Today as you sign this, you will embrace another life. This Tara that I just captured will be gone with this signature, and a new Tara will remain sitting in her place. The one who is only answerable to herself. The one who will soar like a free bird in the open skies. Tara, who will finally mingle with the stars, the place where she rightfully belongs.

Go ahead. You may sign it now. Worst case, if you regret it, you can always remarry him.'

'Remarry him? Beeja, not in my worst nightmare,' I laughed, struggling to shake off my jitters.

I closed my eyes, transporting myself momentarily to the Gurudwara.

A gust of wind roared, followed by bolts of lightning, resounding thunder and heavy downpour.

'Well, life just decided a little drama was in order,' I concluded as we shared a laugh.

Soon, my fears were overcome by a strange tranquility. I found myself suddenly approaching this moment with light steps and a trusting heart. Maybe this was the best way to walk towards it, anyway.

Finishing the last sip, I signed across the petition, 'Tara Grewal.'

Another bottle of champagne popped open.

'The first step into a new life.'

'Cheers.'

'And now, the second step. Hit the ground running,' insisted beeja.

'What second step, beeja?'

'Call him. What else?'

'Now? It's 9 p.m.'

'Yes, now and I'm certain he's not sleeping at this time. Don't look for excuses to put this off.'

'Beeja, I promise I'll do it once I've had a moment to think this conversation through,' I pressed.

'Beeja, let Tara decide her comfort zone. Some things in life are personal. We should respect her need for space and privacy,' Dev contended.

'More than her need for support and strength?' beeja questioned.

'This is as comfortable as she'll ever be. Trust me, it's a lot harder to do this alone. There's no place in this for tears and self-pity.

Tara, no need to get into details, apologies or regrets. Don't let him intimidate you. Just state the facts and that if he has any questions, he should contact your lawyer. I'm standing right next to you. You put him in his place once and for all. And don't get angry or emotional. Remain indifferent. That is what hurts the most.'

'Shall I do it?' I asked, turning towards Dev, a little buzzed from all the champagne.

'Your call, Tara. I do not like telling people what to do. You must make your choice. But once you do, I'm with you. 100 per cent'

'Hell beeja, oops bad word. I never use bad words, but today I'm letting go. I'm letting everything go. Let's do it, beeja. Give me the phone. I'm not afraid of anything!'

Beeja laughed.

'Tara, are you all right? Are you sure you want to call him sounding like this?' Dev confirmed.

'Like what? You think I'm drunk?'

'No, I didn't say that, but perhaps, you're not entirely sober either.'

'Dev, I'm letting it go. Didn't I just say that? In fact, just for making that statement, pour me another glass.'

'Listen to the lady, Dev,' beeja instructed.

'You two are driving me crazy. I'm getting out of here. See you both in a few.'

'Go. You're no help anyway,' beeja admitted.

'Send Chotu instead, at least he will bring us something good to eat,' she laughed.

'Go ahead, Tara. Think your biji is with you.'

'I love you, beeja,' I gave her a hug and wiped my tears as my words began to develop a slur.

'I love you too, my child,' she said, kissing my forehead.

I dialed Tej's number.

'Oh hello! So, reality finally kicked in. Yeah? Enough of being a Masterani?' Tej scorned.

'Enough of you and this nonsense you gave me all these years.'

'What? Are you out of your senses?' Tej questioned, clearly flabbergasted.

'No. I'm finally coming to my senses.'

'Do you know who you're talking to?' he demanded, raising his voice, unable to digest I had dared to speak up to him.

'I don't, Tej. I honestly DO NOT. You're not the man I married. Nor are you the man I'd hoped I would marry. Too bad it didn't work out. Actually, too bad for you it didn't work out. You will get divorce papers in the mail. See you in court.'

'What nonsense? Where are you? Who are you with?'

'None of your business anymore. Good night and goodbye!'

My eyes widened with disbelief and horror as I hung up and slapped my mouth shut, 'Beeja. Did I just do it?'

'That's my girl!' beeja clapped. 'He would not know what just came and hit him. Now turn off your phone and enjoy the evening. Dinner will soon be ready.'

Dev walked back a few moments later, 'Did you?'

'I did. I did it, and I'm not regretting it. The only thing I am regretting is why I didn't meet you both sooner. I wasted so much of my life. But I love you both. Better late than never,' I said, now a little delirious.

Dev smiled, shaking his head.

'Beeja, what did you do to her?'

'Don't ask her, talk to me,' I demanded. 'She liberated me. She gave me wings and pointed to the sky. I did the rest. I flew away.'

'Dev get me a glass of water, please. No more drinks. Done. Everything is done. Everything. DONE,' I repeated.

'I only hope she doesn't regret this tomorrow morning,' Dev mumbled.

'Oye chup kar, you pessimistic killjoy! Crossing the threshold is the hardest thing in life. Once you're on the other side, life's flow carries you.'

'Right, beeja,' I added.

'The great flow. Dad talked about it too. Beeja, did I just tell you I love you?'

'Oh, my sweetheart Tara, all panj patase for you today.

Now drink some water and eat some food. It's all behind you. Dev will take you home soon.'

After dinner, on the way back, I rolled down the car window and smiled at the stars above, 'The great flow. You know that, Dev? *The future's not ours to see, Que sera sera. What will be, will be,*' I hummed.

It was a sultry afternoon at school. I sat at the desk as warm breeze filtered through the mesh windows bringing with it the smell of dry mud. The fan above rotated slowly, a little off kilter, making a consistent, creaking sound. I put my glass of water aside as I scribbled the contact number for a distance learning provider.

'Beeba ji,' Master ji walked through the door, 'the funds have been deposited. We can begin our sourcing and construction soon.'

'That's good news!'

'I also received the confirmation that all 12 teachers will be joining on the first of next month,' he added.

'That's a week from now,' I said, looking at my phone.

'That's right.'

'So, developing the curriculum and purchasing books should be the highest priority.'

'That's right.'

Just then, my phone rang. It was an unknown number.

'Excuse me, Master ji. I need to take this call,' I said, stepping outside.

'Hello. Tara Grewal,' I answered.

'Hello, Tara. This is Varsha. I received your papers today.

Glad that you're moving forward with the petition. Now, as previously decided, we will file on Friday but remain prepared, they might come at you in multiple ways—offers of settlement, coercion, pressure—direct and indirect. All you need to know is that they can cause no harm and you are not under any pressure to accept what you're uncomfortable with. Any questions?'

'No questions, but I do have a request. I would like to refrain from dwelling too much on the reasons for this divorce. We should try to keep it as amicable as possible.'

'I'll keep that in mind. Good luck.'

Almost a little panic-stricken, I texted Dev, 'Just spoke

with Varsha. Wondering if I could've done anything differently. Looking hard for answers in my own mirror, but too much dirt has accumulated over the years.'

'The dirt is not a fault of the mirror but that of its surroundings. Don't blame yourself for someone else's negligence.'

'Thanks, Dev, for helping me get through this.'

'Don't credit me for what you owe to yourself. And never let go of your brilliance. By the way, I'm headed to Chandigarh now, but I left a package for you. The driver will drop it off later today.'

'What package?'

'Just a small token that deserves you.'

'Deserves me? Dev, I'm not sure I understand. And I would be uncomfortable accepting anything like that.'

'It's just a piece of work that's very close to my heart.'

I remained uncomfortably silent.

'As an old Punjabi tradition,' he explained, 'mothers and grandmothers often started embroidering baghs and phulkaris from the moment a girl was born. They made one for my nani, too—a khaddar phulkari, which she handed down to Ma. Ma wore it on every occasion she could. It held sentimental value for me, so I didn't allow beeja to give it away. But over the years, the charms with which it was woven and worn have been withering away in the darkness of my closet. Sending it to you. I trust you can bring back its sunshine.'

'It will be an honour, Dev. I know what it takes to part with something so precious.'

'Be well, Tara. I'll see you soon.'

The weekday mornings went by in planning, sourcing and overseeing construction. Languid afternoons were spent singing with Darshi, reading my books, or doing small projects with the girls. And occasionally big lunches were followed by long, lazy afternoon siestas.

And soon it was Friday. I stood at the packed Chandigarh courthouse, waiting anxiously for Varsha to arrive. Aunty and mom accompanied me as well.

From a distance, along the paan stained corridor, I noticed Tej storming towards me. His dark menacing eyes shot out like daggers, nearly shattering my new-found confidence.

'Step aside. I need to talk to you. Alone,' he demanded, gripping me harshly by my arm.

Aunty agreed with a vague nod as though permitting me to wander just far enough to test the waters.

'You remember one thing,' he fumed, holding a firm finger in front of his bloodshot eyes. 'If you think you will get anything by going to the court, you're mistaken. With the money I have, I will buy every judge and every lawyer out there to make sure you end up penniless on the streets and never get to see the faces of your children again.'

'You don't have that right, Tej. The children will always remain mine.'

'Watch out. I will fabricate any story I need to. Whether I have to shred your character to bits or prove you mentally unstable, I will not hesitate. And don't forget you live in India. It takes money and connections to win anything. Good luck with that,' he snapped, spitting in the corner as he walked away.

Aunty and mom hurried towards me. 'What did he say? Did he threaten you?'

'I was prepared,' I replied, drawing in a deep breath.

Just then, I heard a cheerful voice, 'Hello, my lovely ladies,' I turned around to find a stunning woman with a dazzling smile walking towards us, holding a Starbucks cup in her hand.

'Varsha Khanna,' she introduced herself.

Her long, black court gown was paired with sporty white sneakers and her hair was pulled together in a sleek ponytail. Oversized Prada sunglasses, a sleek Chanel handbag and sizable solitaires studded in her ears, added to her unique charm. I gasped. Was that really my attorney?

The world around her fell into a visible pause as she walked through the aisles of modest Chandigarh lower court. Steps halted, heads turned, eyes widened and jaws dropped. She appeared nothing less than a spectacle here.

'Sorry, my flight from Mumbai was slightly delayed.'

'No problem, Varsha. I'm glad you're here. This is Tara. Thanks for taking her under your wing. Now, I can finally sit back and relax,' sighed Aunty, looking visibly relieved.

'Tara, Varsha is very selective in her cases. You're lucky that she agreed to handle this personally.'

'Good to meet you, ma'am' I added, feeling reassured in her confident persona.

'Tara, we got this! The minute I heard your story from aunty, I knew I had to do this. I believe in reasons of the heart. I make my decisions emotionally, on a whim. If something resonates with me, I'm in, or else I'm out. Simple.'

'What's the courtroom number?' She checked, glancing at her watch. 'We should go now.'

The case filing went as expected. Tej stood there with his entourage of lawyers and assistants, observing the situation closely.

Varsha smiled with her usual charm, disarming their threats as she casually walked up to Tej and introduced herself, 'Varsha Khanna, pleasure to meet you. Seems like we'll be seeing a lot of each other moving forward.'

He responded with a stiff, awkward, 'Hello', retreating soon to the hallway, as his crew followed behind.

Leaning into her ear, aunty spoke in a muffled voice, 'While you're at it, Varsha, press for the children to spend a week with Tara in Amritsar.'

'That's no problem, aunty. Tara, jot down the dates you want and consider it done,' she smiled.

I instantly felt better. Like the looming perpetual gray clouds were finally giving way to a flicker of sunshine. Maybe life too wanted this and was, therefore, sending just the right people in perfect time to salvage each aspect of my broken life. I had much to learn from it.

The day I'd feared the most had come and gone. As I drove back that afternoon, I dedicated a page in my dairy to fear, closing my thoughts with,

Isn't it true that often, the fear of an outcome is more painful than the outcome itself!

Fifteen

'BETA, the filing went smoothly, we have much to be grateful for. I think you should visit the Golden Temple when you have a chance,' mom suggested.

'It's been on my mind as well. You're right, I should do it sooner, rather than later. Okay, mom, I'm getting late for school now, we will talk later.'

'Take care, beta.'

It was a rather quiet morning at school when I heard Bittu's voice in the corridor.

'Don't be shy, Preeti, come on over.'

He walked through the door with a dainty five-foot-two figure trailing behind tentatively.

'Now, why are you frozen there? Come forward and take Tara bhenji's blessings,' Bittu motioned towards my feet.

'Oh no, Preeti, not at all. Take me as an older sister or a friend, whatever you prefer, but this is absolutely not required,' I insisted, reaching out to greet her.

She blushed in acknowledgment, her face reflecting the colour of the red cotton suit she wore.

She appeared young, very young. Her black, waist-length hair was parted in the middle and pulled back neatly by clips on either side. Her flawless honey and milk complexion enhanced her round face, tiny eyes, button nose and a near-perfect smile.

'She's adorable, Bittu. You better take good care of her.'

'Bhenji, no worry, and no problem. You can ask her, we've already split our jobs—she will wash the clothes, and I will iron them, she will make dinner, and I will eat it. Sorry, I meant I'll do the dishes,' he laughed. 'If she's going to be my better half, then everything will be 50-50.'

I laughed, 'You trained him well, Preeti.'

'He came well trained. I didn't have to do much other than agree with him,' she chuckled, finally lifting her eyes.

'Bhenji, Preeti is one of the toppers in her college. She's already started compiling all the teaching material. As soon as we have internet and computers, she will begin taking online lessons from Amritsar. She will also try to come on weekends to work with the girls on practicals.'

'Thank you, Preeti. That will go a long way for girls who are aspiring to become doctors.'

'I will do my best, didi,' she assured me in her sweet-tempered, silky voice.

'Okay, bhenji, we will take your leave now,' said Bittu, 'otherwise, Preeti will get late for her classes. I just wanted to make the introduction.'

'You two came all the way here, now have a cup of tea at least,' I offered, escorting them down the hallway.

'I personally believe it's a sin to refuse tea. But I must keep my promise to Preeti. Better sorry than late. I meant better safe than sorry,' Bittu joked as he kickstarted his bullet and put on his black aviators.

'Okay, bhenji, I will see you soon,' he waved.

After a rich meal of sarson da saag and makki di roti topped with dollops of freshly churned butter and a full-sized glass of sweetened lassi, I felt rather sluggish on this unusually warm afternoon.

I drew the curtains and decided to curl up with a book.

Soon I fell into a restful nap, interrupted shortly by a phone call.

'Hi, mom,' I answered in a drowsy voice.

'Hi, beta. How was your day at school?'

'I met Bittu's girlfriend today. Quite a charming girl. Now we finally have someone to lead our sciences stream remotely, which I'm quite thrilled about.'

'You sound tired, though,' mom remarked.

'It's called food coma, mom. My eyes are becoming bigger than my stomach.'

'A little indulgence is good once in a while,' mom granted.

'Anyway, I was calling because Manjeet aunty, Tej's aunt, called to appraise me of some new developments.'

'What kind of developments?' I asked.

'Well, when you left initially, the family was in comfortable denial. Convinced of your absolute dependence on Tej, they did not think you had what it takes to leave someone. However, the sudden news of court filing caught them off guard. They're gripped with utter confusion, shock and disbelief. You see, what happened with your filing is that you had a chance to deliberate the decision, but they did not see it coming at all.'

'Perhaps, more than the shock of filing, it's his ego which can't come to terms with the fact that he was not the one who let me go, rather I was the one who left him,' I surmised.

'Yes, possibly. But at this time, his entire family has flocked to his side. They are busy fanning the flames of his already distorted version of reality. And he's conveniently emerging as the ultimate victim in this whole situation.'

'Oh, please, mom, everyone knows him. The only reason he's garnering this pity and self-victimization is to compensate for his emotions of humiliation and powerlessness.'

'You're possibly right, Tara. But long story short, she said there is rage, bitterness and absolute vindictiveness surrounding this situation.

Overnight, assets have been transferred to holding companies, lockers have been emptied and credit cards have been frozen. And they are actively fabricating negative evidence to weaken your plea and prevent you from obtaining any custody rights. This seems to be their trump card.

Manjeet aunty, however, was very appreciative of how patiently you have shielded his shortcomings all these years. Having gone through a similar ordeal with her own daughter, she wanted you to know that even though she's related to him by blood, she will not hesitate to stand by you in court and state what she knows of you.

Beta, it may not be an easy fight.'

'I did not expect it to be, mom,' I responded, strangely unperturbed.

'And while I cannot prevent them from doing any of this, I refuse to give up my belief in a judicial system that is capable of filtering through such lies. I have nothing to prove, fight for, or defend besides my truth. And that truth is sufficient unto itself.'

'It always is! May His grace be with you,' she added. 'Take care.'

I spent the rest of the evening immersed in books, hoping to keep my mind anchored down, albeit unsuccessfully. A vague feeling of unease kept surging within me, rendering me restless. I remembered the bottle of wine Dev had sent back with me the other day.

Refreshed from a cold shower, I changed into my white kurta, lit up a candle, turned on some music and poured myself a glass of Malbec.

It turned out to be a good bottle, smooth and bold with a lasting finish. I began browsing through my photo library, enjoying Mehar and Sid and our travels together. Before long, I had wandered into a more relaxed and happier frame of mind.

It was just a little past 9:30 that evening when Ashok uncle called.

'Hello, uncle.'

'Hi, Tara beta. How's my trooper holding up?'

'Fighting fit, uncle. How've you been?'

'As usual, living my life somewhere between reality and illusion. It's the ultimate bliss!'

'Keep at it, uncle!' I cheered.

'Do you have a few minutes, beta? This is somewhat sensitive.'

'Sure, uncle, go on. I have all the time in the world.'

'Dev was in Chandigarh today. We met for lunch. Now, I treat you both equally as my children. It would pain me to see either one of you getting hurt,' he went on.

I listened quietly, fearing I knew where this conversation was leading.

'Tara, Dev was born in these arms. I could tell what he wanted long before he learnt to express it. Which means I understand his words, but I also understand his silence.

I'm afraid he has developed feelings for you, which run deeper than just friendship. Beta, he is in love with you.'

I stood stunned and speechless, consumed with an overriding guilt of ways in which I might have contributed to this situation.

'I know, Tara, this is neither the right time nor the right place to talk about this, but I wanted to handle it personally while I have the chance. I don't want you to find yourself in an uncomfortable spot.

Dev is a very direct person. He is bound to express his

unfiltered feelings sooner or later. Maybe he was waiting for you to file, or he might wait until the divorce is finalized, but one day he will be honest about expressing his feelings to you.

And that is why I need to know. Depending on how you feel about him, I will handle it before it goes too far.

So, what do you think about it?'

I stuttered, 'I mean, how's it even possible? He knows I have kids and I've never seen him in this light, nor have I led him to believe in the remotest possibility of such an outcome. I mean, I like him and respect him as a person. He's a great friend and an even better human being, but I can never be in love.

You know me, uncle, I didn't fall in love when I was 16. And now? At 38 and with two kids, I wouldn't even dare to dream of it.'

'Beta, when love comes, it tramples past all barriers. And dreams! You know well, they neither shy from daring nor abide by any limitations you impose on them. When love knocks, they throw open every door to welcome it in.

But that's beside the point,' he added, pulling himself back from his musings. 'My only question to you is this. Do you feel anything for Dev? Don't be afraid to admit.'

I sighed deeply, feeling a little disappointed. 'I do not feel anything for him. I can't. Besides, what he's mistaking for love is nothing more than a lot of sympathy, some level of pity and a degree of redemption. He feels the need to end my suffering and prevent a repeat of his mother's story. That's all. There is no real basis for anything else. He will soon realize it.'

'I wouldn't go that far,' uncle jumped in Dev's defense. 'Emotions don't need a reason or rationale, but very well, beta, if that's what you want. I know how to handle it from here. You don't have to worry about a thing.'

'Uncle, wait a minute.'

'Yes, Tara?'

'I also want you to know if we'd met in another life or at another stage, I would not have asked for anything more.'

'This, beta, is a very potent statement,' he concluded after a contemplative pause. 'Will talk about it another time. But for now, relax and stay happy. I will see to it that you don't have to deal with any embarrassment on this account.'

I stared blankly at the phone for a while before dialing Meeta's number.

'Meeta, I'm dumbfounded. How could he harbour such feelings for me? It's wrong. I've never ever led him on. Yes, he helped me and all that. And we're good friends, but this! It's taking it too far. I'm no poor soul he's feeling so sorry for. I did not go soliciting his kindness or sympathy. He knows my situation well and he knows me. And yet? It's just not right.'

'Tara,' Meeta spoke after a brief pause. 'Do you hear yourself? You're blaming a man who might genuinely be in love with you. It's no crime. He's single and he has the right to feel anything he wants, for anyone he wants.'

'Not me. He cannot feel for me.'

'Okay, Tara, now you're getting me concerned with your overreaction. It almost feels like you're in denial of your own feeling towards him. You're afraid you like him too. Nothing else explains this angry outburst and this mindless rambling. Get a grip.'

'Look, Meeta. I'm exhausted. I have no capacity left to deal with any more emotionally disconcerting situations. I don't need love or, for that matter, anything else. All I want in life is some peace of mind. I'll take a dull, uneventful, boring existence any day. A life that is steady and uncomplicated. I want to teach, read books, snuggle with my children and sleep well. Is it too much to ask? Can I just be left alone as I am, where I am?'

'You asked me, Tara, so I offered my view. But let me ask you something, has he ever expressed any such thing to you? Or hinted at it in a roundabout manner?'

'No, he's been very respectful towards this friendship and towards me. The fact that he understood his boundaries well is what allowed me to feel so comfortable in the first place.'

'In that case, what if Ashok uncle, being his colourful, romantic self, is reading into his words? I mean, it's not entirely unexpected. He imagines love stories everywhere around him. What if he got bored of his own and decided to invent a new one?' proposed Meeta, breaking into a burst of spontaneous laughter.

'At Dev's expense,' she chuckled again.

'Listen to me, Tara, if I were you,' she said, composing herself, 'I would forget this entire conversation and shove it off of my plate for now. It's already overloaded. Go back to life as usual. Let time unfold the rest. If he does, at any point, say something from his own mouth, in his own words, we'll deal with it then. I mean, no point stressing over speculation.'

'You're right, Meeta. I agree with your hypothesis. It's entirely possible that Ashok uncle might just be indulging in another fantasy. He did start the conversation by saying he's living his life somewhere between reality and illusion. There you go. He explained himself.'

'Perfect. Chapter closed,' confirmed Meeta. 'Now, step outside to clear your mind. Listen to chirping crickets and gaze at twinkling stars. All is well.'

'I love you, Meeta. Good night. Kisses and hugs!'

'Ditto!'

'Bhenji, your tea,' offered Premo, handing me a steel tumbler as I headed towards the taxi.

It was 4 a.m. and the morning sky appeared pitch dark. There was neither a movement nor a stir in a world that seemed immersed in a restful slumber.

Slowly, the sky began to lighten up. Trucks, scooters and motorbikes streamed evenly towards the city. Dogs barked, shutters opened and men could be seen doing their morning ablutions by the roadside dressed in white vests and colorful lungis.

'Madam ji, I'll have to drop you right here,' the driver informed me as we came down the flyover. 'This is as far as they allow cars to go now.'

'Thank you. I will call you once I'm ready to return,' I replied.

As I navigated my way through the recently constructed heritage walk, I felt like a stranger in his own town, who had forgotten his way home.

The newly erected structures did not exude the least bit of familiarity. My eyes longed for a sight, any sight that faintly resembled my memories, but it had all changed. Everything was different.

With souvenir shops, apparel stores and towering Roman Colosseum-like architecture, this updated spectacle boasted of everything spectacular, but traces of its own originality.

Like me, it had come far but, in the process, forgotten who it truly was.

It was everything, yet nothing. Beautiful, yet soulless.

I deposited my footwear and stood in line among the jostling crowds to catch that first glimpse of that precious golden reflection. The rays broke through, the sun gently ascended and a peace emanating Gurbani washed over my being.

The reflection of the Golden Temple stirred lightly on the

ripples, still untouched. I sat by the edge of the sarovar, on the cool marble walkway as I closed my eyes and remembered our quaint 4 a.m. trips. Back then, this place was neither as elaborate nor as grand, but it was intimate. Handful of people quietly engaged in a sincere offering—sweeping, washing, preparing tea and even praying. I felt a pang of separation. Like I'd lost something that I'd preserved so dearly intact over the years.

I sought blessings and left like an empty-handed visitor amid an array of selfies and videos bombarding social media this very hour, hash-tagged spirituality.

I returned home, a little satisfied and a lot thirsty.

I opened my diary and poured this deep yearning of my heart.

Views have changed tremendously, yet the golden reflection remains the same. Perhaps because it isn't a 'thing' that can be modified or improved and maybe progress isn't always about creating a lot of new, sometimes it is about preserving a lot of old.

As I sat by the chulha awaiting my next parantha, the phone beeped.

'Congratulations, Tara. Permission granted. Children would be spending the week with you in Amritsar—Varsha.'

'Where is Seerat?' I rushed to Premo.

'I am not sure, bhenji. Probably in school. What happened? You seem happy.'

'Premo, Mehar and Sidak will be here with us next week,' I answered, barely able to contain my excitement.

'Badhaiyaan, bhenji. I can't wait to see the children. Kho-Kho, stapu, gidda, we will organize so many activities that they would never want to leave their nanka,' she exclaimed.

Next, I dialed mom. 'We did it, mom. Mehar and Sid will spend their holidays with me. We have nothing to fear now.'

'Oh, Tara, didn't I tell you? There is great power in prayer,' she affirmed.

'You did, mom. You never stopped believing. Thank you.'

As I walked into the school premises, I noticed Master ji sitting on a chair fanning himself with his handkerchief, overlooking the busy construction site in sweltering heat.

He stood up and slowly made his way towards his office in an unsteady stance—shoulders drooping, sight lowered and voice barely audible.

'Are you feeling all right, Master ji?' I asked, following him into the office.

He did not answer. He quietly handed me a letter and returned to fanning himself with the handkerchief again.

'What? The lab did not get approved?'

'Beeba ji, they do not have any more funds to spare,' he remarked, resting his hand on his forehead.

After reading the letter a few times over, I placed it back in the drawer and walked out into the yard.

'Lab project shelved for lack of funding,' I reluctantly texted Dev.

'Illusions,' I reminded myself, observing the distant mirage which appeared to be dousing the blazing tar.

A reply popped up on my screen. 'Nothing in life is final. Hold tight. We might need to readjust the path, but not the goal. I had anticipated this. Don't worry. I have a backup plan. Will stop by in a few hours.'

'What back up plan?'

'Will discuss shortly.'

'You mean we could still have the lab somehow?'

'Yes.'

'But how?'

'I'll be there soon. Until then, stop questioning and take a few pictures of the school.'

'Pictures? Why?'

'Again? Relax, Tara. Have I ever let you down?'

Still a little uncomfortable given last night's conversation with Ashok uncle, I hesitated.

'Now, the sooner you do it, the faster we'd be on our way,' he confirmed.

'Master ji,' I turned around,' 'it appears there still might be a way for us to have the lab. The friend who had introduced our case to Secretary of Education thinks he has a solution for us.'

It was a little past 1 p.m. The sun was high and a busy gloom appeared to have descended on the school.

Soon, Dev's car pulled up through the dirt road.

The three of us sat at the desk in this unusually oppressive afternoon heat. Neither the fan nor the windows made much of a difference today.

Doctor saab and Bittu knocked on the door and joined us in the office.

After a brief introduction, I asked impatiently, 'So Dev, what's the plan?'

'If I have permission, I would like to address the girls and get them involved in this process as well. This will form a part of their greater learning experience,' he explained.

'Dev, they will be very disheartened to hear that our request for a computer lab has been rejected. We should only tell them once we've exhausted all means,' I protested.

'Shielding them isn't necessarily protecting them, Tara. In our capacity as their true well-wishers, we must make them aware of challenges and disappointments, which are bound to be a part of their journey. But what this experience will teach them is that we can either give up along the way, or we can forge a way forward, regardless.'

'Oye balle, bhaji! I am a fan of this dialogue. Please repeat,' said Bittu, standing up from his chair.

'Sit down. This is serious,' doctor saab admonished him as we shared a much-needed, lighthearted moment.

Master ji smiled in approval, '100 takke di gal kiti, Dev saab. I will assemble the girls.'

Hundreds of inquisitive eyes followed Dev and Master ji's hasty footsteps to the makeshift podium.

'Children, today we have with us, the man who made the Smart School project possible,' Master ji made the introduction as Dev stepped up.

'I will begin by asking you one simple question. Does life always go as planned?' Dev asked.

'No,' came the unanimous response.

'What can we do when our plans fail? Yes, we can always cry and complain and we can always give up, but what else can we do?'

Seerat raised her hand.

'Yes?'

'Remember our dreams.'

'Very good. And what would that do?'

'It will give us a new plan.'

'Exactly right. A new plan.'

'I have two lessons for you today—one, the power of forging a path where none exists, and two, the power of technology to connect people with their dreams.

We received a rejection letter today. The government does not have funds to support our computer lab.'

A wave of appalling dejection swept across the faces as distressed murmurs began to rise to the surface.

'But that does not mean we can't have one,' Dev clarified.

An arresting silence followed the swift movement of Dev's hands as he opened his computer.

'This, right here,' Dev said, pointing to his laptop, 'is the key that will help us reach millions of people who will partake in our dream and help us realize it.'

The girls looked on in fascination, wonder and intrigue.

With a few clicks on his keyboard, Dev created an account, ToFundMe.

'And now we are ready to reach the world.'

He then uploaded some pictures and tagged them—the school, the students and the classrooms.

'And now they know who we are and what we look like,' Dev remarked.

'Tara, do you have an estimate for the lab?'

'Yes, between computers, generator, air conditioner, etc. about 18 lakhs,' I confirmed.

'Now they know how much we need,' he stated as he keyed in the amount.

'And now, we will record a small video. Tell me what you aspire to become and why.'

Dev walked down the stuffy hallway holding his cellphone as eager voices echoed their message.

'Doctor, I want to help people.'

'IAS officer, I want to change everything for women.'

'Pilot, I want to fly an airplane.'

And so it went.

Dev uploaded the video with the caption, 'Using technology to gain technology, so someday these don't remain empty dreams.'

'And now, with the last click, we will go live.

'Master ji, please do the honours,' he requested. With one

click, a ticker appeared on the screen. We were live.

'Here,' he pointed to the rapidly changing numbers on the screen, 'we will be able to track our goal versus the collections. Watch how strangers who believe in our dreams continue to support them.

Remember, the means will be found as long as dreams lead the way.'

Everyone converged around the laptop, buzzing with curiosity. Premo and Darshi, who had also joined in, appeared enchanted. The word got out and soon, the village community started streaming in.

'One computer,' we counted together. 'Two.'

Between the counts, nothing stirred. They were in a state of hypnosis, as though witnessing some kind of magic. Some brought in biscuits for tea, while others brought in matthis. All eyes remained steady on the laptop.

'Dev, how are we getting such large contributions, and so quickly?' I asked, curious about the pace of funding.

'I sent this as a personal link to my colleagues in New York. Don't worry, most of them own yachts, expensive enough to fund the entire district for such projects. They're always looking for good causes to support.'

'What did you do in New York? Sorry, I never asked.'

'I ran a hedge fund,' he replied casually.

It was nearing 9 p.m. and we were still going strong.

Soon Dev announced, 'One more to go…

And YES! We are fully funded.'

A roar of cheer and jubilation swept across as the village broke out in festivities, congratulating one another.

I looked towards Dev a little in awe, a little in gratitude.

By the time he closed the fund, we were 140% overfunded.

'I guess New York is just waking up,' he smiled.

Sixteen

Six months later

'Congratulations, Tara. This was one of the strongest judgement orders I've seen in a long time. You should be very pleased. From what I'm told, and expectedly so, they plan to challenge the order in High Court. Perhaps, the fight is not quite over yet.

But look at it this way, we have not only built a strong foundation but also made a significant head start. The judge granted a settlement suitable enough to sustain you comfortably. Now you have no worries on account of your day-to-day dependencies.

You did well, my girl! Welcome to an independent existence.'

'Thank you, ma'am. Personally, the most important thing this order secured is that my children will continue to have both of us in their lives.'

'Tara, what are you even made of? After all that Tej did to malign your character, you're still thinking about him. I guess that's what differentiates you from the rest. Well, what goes around, comes around. Good luck. Once they move courts, we will take it up again.'

Construction at the school had finished, the computer lab was functional and an in-house distance learning program had been successfully instituted. The addition of teachers and a committed community had significantly accelerated our growth trajectory.

Preeti had stepped into the project in a big way. The community had come to develop great admiration for her sincerity, intelligence and charm. By now, she was a fond household name and Bittu's mother had transitioned from her stubborn disapproval to proudly introducing her as 'would-be daughter-in-law'.

As for me, I had finally allowed myself some time off in Kasauli to recover from these tumultuous eight months.

'Tara beta,' Ashok uncle called for me as he held out the phone. 'Here, your aunty wants to speak with you.'

'Tara, welcome to a new life. School commitments are over and the case is resting in a strong place. Come see us in Delhi now.'

'I will aunty, hopefully soon, now that this whirlwind is finally showing signs of slowing down. I really want to thank you for nudging me in this direction and for introducing me to Varsha. I can't imagine where I'd be without each one of you being exactly where you were.'

'Beta, such is life. It gives us what we need when we need it, as long as we keep moving forward with fearlessness and belief. God bless you. See you soon.'

I sat by the edge of the garden, looking into the wide-open valley carpeted in lush grass and peppered with blooming carefree wildflowers. Soon the misty clouds drew closer, descending upon the garden in a thick haze.

I held the cup of tea in my hand and drew in a steaming sip, thinking about what life had in store for me next.

'Dev?' I wondered, hearing that familiar voice.

I got up and walked over towards the veranda. And there he stood at the door, animatedly discussing something with uncle.

I looked at them. They both paused and began speaking in tandem, eventually breaking off in laughter.

'You disclose the news,' said uncle extending his hand towards Dev.

'Great. Happy to do the honours.'

'Well, I got a call from Mr. Mehta. India Times wants to run a story on you.'

'On me? About what?'

'About how you took a dying institution and not only revived it into a state-of-the-art smart school, but garnered community support, sparked organic village growth and implemented a successful in-house distance learning program.

They want to promote this model as a template, so this kind of success can be replicated in other schools that the government is investing in.'

'But I hardly did anything. It was others who made it happen. How can I claim the credit for it?'

'Tara, no one creates this level of success alone, but there is always someone who starts it. They say it takes a village to raise a child, but you've raised an entire village—what does that take?

Remember what I told you, learn to own your success gracefully.

The interview is scheduled in Delhi early next week,' Dev confirmed.

'And that will make your aunty happy too. There you go, killing two birds with one stone,' added uncle, sounding totally agreeable.

'But Dev, uncle…'

'No more debating this. Come on, Tara, you're going to be famous,' uncle said in jest.

Aunty came to receive me at the airport, and I spent two happy days with Ashu and Sonu. We bonded once again over our childhood memories around late-night ice-cream trips to India Gate, shopping for video cassette at Palika Bazaar, scouting for posters in Sadar Bazaar and countless pizza trips to Nirula's in Connaught Place. It was truly refreshing to walk down memory lane once again.

Ashu had planned a packed next day for us. Brunch at Smoke House, shopping at Hauz Khas, massage at the Imperial Spa, followed by an early dinner at The Spice Route. It was a perfect day, well-earned and well spent, in Ashu's words.

'Good night aunty, good night Ashu and Sonu. I have to be up early for the interview tomorrow.'

'What? Don't be a bore,' Ashu persisted. 'I just got back from the hospital. Come on, you have your entire life to sleep. Ice cream at India Gate is a must-do for old time's sake, and the paan too. Come on, get in the car!' Ashu pulled me off the couch.

We drove through the lush streets of central Delhi, enjoying the balmy breeze, Sufi music, midnight tea and aimless banter. We returned home at 3 a.m. sneaking in on tiptoes, only to be caught and reprimanded by aunty for very 'irresponsible and immature' behaviour on our part.

Giggles, guffaws and a restful night ended this short but beautiful trip.

'Okay, aunty, I'll catch a flight back to Amritsar after the interview. Thank you for everything. Let Sonu and Ashu sleep. I'll speak to them soon.'

'Goodbye, Tara. Hope to see you back here again,' said aunty as she saw me off at the gate.

Back at the pind, I had just returned from my morning Gurudwara visit when I noticed a bunch of missed calls from mom.

'Mom, what's the matter?' I asked, nearly panicking.

'Tara, my phone has been ringing continuously since morning. India Times did a front-page story on you. It also has your picture on it!'

'Really? They told me they were rather constricted on space

and didn't think it would be out until next week's publication.'

'Well, it's here. I'm sharing a picture of it. But figure out a way to get an actual copy. It's something else when you're holding it physically in your hands,' exclaimed mom, ecstatic beyond words.

'Will do, mom.'

Beeja called as soon as mom hung up. 'Tara. Didn't I say you belonged among the stars? Look at you! You made it in record time. Come tonight. As usual, our champagne awaits.'

I let out a laugh. 'I will, beeja, but first, I must figure out a way to get my own copy so I can share it with my girls. The interview speaks about how their dreams ignited mine. In reality, it's a tribute to their persistence and efforts.'

'Don't worry. The driver will be there with 25 copies soon. Take them all to school. Let me hang up now. I'm sure you have a beeline of callers waiting to speak to you. Come tonight, okay?'

'See you then, beeja,' I beamed.

The morning went by answering calls from Meeta, Mala, jiju, Dev, Ashu, Sonu, uncle and aunty. Dr Meghadri called from the US as well, delighted to hear about all the progress.

Also, Mehar and Sidak got special permission to call after mom informed the school.

The next few hours were spent sharing the impact of this article with our community, discussions led further by Master ji, Bittu, doctor saab and Preeti.

For the first time in life, a viable sense of self-worth began to make its presence felt within me.

Later in the afternoon, as Premo and I sat chit-chatting under the tree, my phone rang again.

'Bhenji, you're very much in demand today,' Premo chirped.

'Uh, yeah... I'll be back, Premo,' I said, hurrying upstairs to my bedroom.

It was Tej calling.

'Hello,' I answered tentatively.

'Hi, Tara,' he said in an uncharacteristically mellow voice.

'Varsha told me,' I responded, 'I want you to know I will never come in the way of you spending time with our children…'

'Tara,' he cut me off abruptly. 'That's not what I was calling about.'

'Tej, what's the matter?'

'I… I saw your picture in the paper. I deliberated for a long time about calling you. I couldn't tell for sure if it was my own feeling of recessed pride in your achievements, but I felt like congratulating you.

Good or bad, perhaps 17 years is a long period of time to spend with someone.'

I remained quiet.

'I'm happy you're doing big things and going places. Maybe, I could've been more supportive all along.'

'What's the point discussing this, Tej? It's too late to change anything now, but I want you to know that your calling me today means a lot.'

'Tara, I also decided that I will not be contesting the court's verdict. I hope you find your happiness.'

A long awkward silence filled this bitter distance of eight months and 150 miles.

'We could never be friends when we were together, and I doubt my actions in the past have left any room for that going forward. But I hope that down the line, whenever we meet, we can face each other without any regrets or shame.'

'Tej, I respect your sentiment, and this is the best thing we can do for each other and for our children.'

'I know you might be wondering what brought about this

sudden change or if this is yet another pretense. To be honest, Tara, what your tears and pain could not trigger in me all these years, your self-sufficiency and independence did. The fact that you didn't need me anymore shattered me. And that not only were you gone, but you were better off without me, came as the real awakening. Sometimes, it takes our losses to remind us of the treasures we once possessed.'

I swallowed a lump in my throat, 'Tej, I appreciate you reaching out to me with such honesty.'

'A broken man has nothing left to preserve.

You won, Tara. You truly did,' he said, his voice, for the first time sounding weary and defeated.

'Tej, I...'

'Don't say another word. You don't have to explain.

Come next weekend if you're free. The children would be home. Maybe we could all have lunch together. Would you come, Tara?' he asked, a deep pain and uncertainty shrouding his question.

'Yes, Tej. I'll come.'

'I'll wait, Tara. And the kids would be waiting too. Goodbye.'

I held the phone next to my heart. My face flushed with a warm surge of blood, my heart palpitated and my lungs felt ablaze. Soon it was replaced by a dull, grinding pain, crushing my battered heart just a little more. Warm tears streamed down my cheeks.

Now? After all these years of longing to hear this. This was all it would've taken. It could have all been this easy.

But now! It had to come now, when our paths had parted and I had walked so far out that even the longing had left me.

Maybe it would have been easier to live with the regret that it never came, than with the regret that it came too late.

'Why are you so quiet, Tara? I expected you to be over the

moon today,' prodded beeja with a mischievous smile.

'Beeja, today it feels like I have attained all that I'd wished for. Some came without asking, and some left me asking why it came at all.'

'I don't know what you're questioning, Tara, but make the best of whatever comes to you,' said beeja pulling out a smooth black velvet pouch.

'And this comes with my love. Keep soaring higher.'

'No, beeja, no presents needed. Your love is the biggest present of all.'

'Love takes on many forms. This is one of them. Oye Dev, bring out the gramophone and play some Nusrat, please.'

'Look, Tara, take a look at what's inside the pouch.'

Inside the pouch, wrapped in red silk square, was a gold coin strung in a black thread.

'Beeja, what is this?'

'Mohar, it's a traditional piece of the heritage jewellery worn in older days.

The reason I picked this over any kangan or pajeb is so this sone di mohar ensures absolute abundance in your life and the black thread will protect you from maadi nazar. Stay happy, my Tara,' she said, kissing me on my forehead as she placed a hand filled with pure blessings on my head. 'Jug jug jeyo.'

'It's very thoughtful, beeja. Thank you. I will treasure this.'

'You know, Tara,' said tayaji stepping onto the patio as he drew in a puff from his pipe. 'These coins used to be imported mostly from Bukhara or St. Petersburg. They were much appreciated by our traders even though the coins weren't officially a part of our currency. And they would be proudly displayed and talked about for days, once circulated. You're actually holding a piece of history in your hand.

Think about the distance this coin travelled, the hands it changed and the years it waited to be here with you in this celebratory moment.'

'That's a beautiful perspective, tayaji. Makes it even more precious.'

'Enjoy darling! Come over anytime you're in a mood to discuss history.'

After spending a lovely evening with beeja, Dev and tayaji, I returned home. A little exhausted from the day's excitement.

Friday came, and as per my promise, I left for Chandigarh. Mehar and Sid were coming to spend the weekend with Tej.

I had prepared my lessons ahead of time. And the day's English class was to be taught by a volunteer from Preeti's college.

Midway through the journey, I received a text from Tej.

'Hello, Tara. The kids and I will wait to see you in the morning.'

'I will be there by 11,' I confirmed.

I spent a quiet evening by the lake, in solitude shared only with my diary. The water was calm. Families boated, vendors hawked, joggers ran along the walkway and the silent hills continued to carry many secrets buried deep within their hearts.

Later that evening, I dragged out the photo box from underneath mom's bed, browsing through the pictures from my childhood. I wanted to revisit our summers at nani's home. It was exactly the same and I still saw my home in it.

I was already beginning to miss it.

I couldn't get much sleep knowing the kids were so close and yet we weren't together.

'I'll see you in the evening. Bye, mom,' I said, rushing out the door the next morning.

'Finish your tea, at least.'

'Nah, the kids would be waiting. I can't be late.'

It was just nearing 11 a.m. I stood at the gate, ringing the doorbell to the unfamiliar place I once called home. It welcomed me like a reluctant host greeting a visitor with an uneasy smile, conscious that what remained of it today were only some neglected walls where cobwebs of broken relationships hung and haunting memories wandered through empty corridors.

'Mama!' Mehar and Sidak rushed barefoot to the gate, clinging to me like little monkeys.

'It's hot, where are your slippers?' I rebuked.

Tej walked behind them with visibly softer eyes and a heavily burdened smile. These eight months seemed to have aged him. He had put on weight and lost some hair.

'Welcome home, Tara,' He greeted me in a gentle voice.

'Thank you, Tej,' I responded awkwardly as kids led me in.

I spent the morning organizing Sid's Legos and cleaning out Mehar's closet. We talked about their school and mine. About plans, practices and exam preparations. The hours flew by.

As we sat around the dining table at lunchtime, Malti, our cook, spoke, 'Bhabi, as a special request, bhaiya had me cook kadhi for you. He knew you always liked it.'

I looked towards Tej with questioning eyes as he smiled and looked away. 'Yes, I just happened to remember how you always wanted to go to your mom's house when she made kadhi.'

'And those flowers in the lobby, those liliums, did you get those as well, Tej?' I questioned.

He looked up from his plate and smiled, 'Not soon enough, but yes, I did.'

We both went back to eating quietly as questions, memories and regrets hung thick in the air.

'The kids look happy today,' I said, taking a sip of tea later that evening. 'Thank you for making this afternoon possible.'

'You made it possible, Tara. I didn't think you would come.'

That uneasy silence surfaced again, reminding us of the gaping chasm that stood between us, one that could never be bridged again, no matter how hard we tried.

'All right, Tej, I should head back now,' I said, looking at my watch.

'Stay for dinner.'

'Mom is expecting me today, but I'll be back again.'

'You know mama, papa is taking us out for ice cream tonight. He will also take us shopping tomorrow before dropping us back to school.'

'Have fun, Sid, and send me pictures.'

'Mama, won't you come with us?'

'Beta, nani is alone tonight. I'll spend some time with her.'

'Okay, mama, I love you. See you in Kasauli soon,' he said, planting a kiss on my cheek.

As I walked down the hallway, I noticed an old picture of the four of us in one frame. I picked it up and instinctively wiped it down with my scarf.

Tej stood there, observing me quietly.

'It had collected dust,' I muttered, stifling my tears as I walked back to the car.

※

'Tara beta, this came for you a few days back. I totally forgot to mention,' said mom handing me an envelope.

'What is it, mom?' I asked, taking the letter from her hand.

'I don't know. It was addressed to you, so I didn't open it.

What is it, Tara?' asked mom noticing my puzzled expression.

I kept reading the letter over and over, digging my eyes deeper into it.

'What, Tara?' she repeated, approaching me closer. 'What is it?'

I handed her the letter and sank into the chair.

'Based on the two-page pre-interview write up I'd shared with them, the editors at India Times have offered me a weekly column in their paper.'

'Since when did you start writing, Tara?'

'Since Dev gifted me the dairy,' I answered.

Seventeen

Two years later

The sun shone brightly on this crisp April day. Flowers bloomed and a sweet fragrance permeated the air. We waited eagerly in the stalls for the annual function to begin.

'Tara, you're looking lovely in this blue saree. You should wear colours more often,' aunty observed walking towards us. 'I only see you in white or black all the time.'

I laughed, 'Aunty, those are easy colours, they don't stand out as much. And this is mom's old saree that I decided to wear today.'

'Oh, that is why! Old things are evergreen,' aunty remarked with discernable pride.

'Good to see you, bhenji and bhaisaab,' mom greeted Ashok uncle and aunty.

'Hi, Dev,' I added as he reached for mom's feet.

'Hello, Tara. Hope we're not late!'

'Not at all. Your timing is perfect. The program is just about to start,' I replied.

'Mehar is leading the marching band today. And Sid decided to keep his performance a surprise,' I laughed, adjusting the camera lens. 'Be on the lookout.'

Seated in the audience across from us, I noticed Tej. I gestured a cordial greeting, and he waved back in acknowledgment.

'Is he alone? Didn't his parents join him for the children's annual day?' mom questioned with a hint of disapproval.

'I don't know mom, but after the function, we should go to meet him. The kids would be happy to see that.'

'Do whatever you please. I'm not too keen,' mom added reluctantly.

'So, Dev, now that the construction is finally over, when is the housewarming?' I asked.

'Whenever you come,' he replied, looking into my eyes.

'Shh, they're starting,' aunty interrupted.

Soon, a perfectly synchronized parade marched on to the grounds. I leaned over to capture some close-up shots. Mehar noticed us cheering in the crowd and smiled as we waved out to her. The parade was followed by regional dances, music ensemble, and Sid's theatre performance where he played the Duke in *Twelfth Night*.

Then, the Headmistress stepped up to deliver the keynote speech.

'And today,' she announced before her closing remarks, 'we have amongst us a well-known social activist and author of two books, whose most recent work *The Catalyst* has sparked several education development initiatives and remains on the bestseller list. Please join me in welcoming her and presenting the honorary community award. For spreading the love of learning—Ms. Tara Grewal. Please.'

'This is your moment, Tara. Your children must be so proud,' Dev remarked as he stood up, making way for me to pass through the stalls.

I stepped into this surreal moment amid cheer and applause, taken completely by surprise. 'Please share a few words of advice with our students.'

'Thank you. I'm rather unprepared for this,' I admitted, clearing my throat. 'I don't have any profound words of wisdom or advice to share.'

'But there's one thing I'd like you children to know about life,' I added, reflecting on beeja's words. 'It gives you only what you expect from it. I wouldn't say life is unfair, but it is certainly biased towards those who demand of it. Never settle for what it brings you.

Have the courage to ask life to deliver what you want.

And, this courage is not so much about bravery or fearlessness, as it is about trust. A trust that tells you that no matter which way life takes you, or however much it tests you, it will not let you down.

So, keep on expecting, trusting and moving forward with dreams in your eyes and love in your heart. Remember, obstacles turn into stepping stones and with ashes we can colour our rainbows, if we so chose to believe.

Shine on!'

I walked back amid applause, feeling humbled and deeply blessed.

A few parents requested me to sign copies of my book.

'And one more, please!' I heard Tej's voice. I looked up. He stood there, holding a pen and an open page of my book. With him was a pleasant-looking woman, dressed in jeans and a floral top.

'Simar, meet Tara, Mehar and Sidak's mom.'

'Hello, Simar,' I greeted with a pleasant smile.

'Tara,' Tej hesitated, 'Simar and I might be getting engaged next month.'

'That's great news, Tej. I'm truly happy for you. Simar, congratulations to you as well.'

'And congratulations on becoming a bestselling author, Tara. This is an inspiration for many,' she smiled through her deep-set kohl-lined eyes.

Uncle beeped the horn. Aunty waved her hand calling for me as everyone waited in the car, ready to head back.

'Unfortunately, I need to go now but it was nice meeting you, Simar,' I added as I signed across Tej's copy and handed it back to him. 'Enjoy the rest of your trip.'

In the dwindling daylight, we sat gathered around the backyard.

'These garden lights seem to be a new addition, uncle. I love how they're projecting onto the flowerbeds.'

'Glad someone appreciates it. Your aunty has been giving me sleepless nights over this project. Only a person with an aesthetic sense and romance can understand it.'

'In that case, no one can appreciate it more than you for sure,' Dev added with a laugh.

'Worry not, my boy. You are not too far behind,' uncle responded with a wink.

Crickets chirped, lights shone on the mountains and a pleasant breeze blew, carrying with it, distant notes of pine and cedar.

Mehar and Sidak played in the garden to mom's 'be careful' note, uttered intermittently, more from habit than worry.

Aunty walked towards the garden holding uncle's phone in her hand. 'There, first you left the invitation on the kitchen counter, and now your phone. Vinod has been texting you non-stop. Your Sunaina has finally resurfaced after all these years. She's attending the 50th reunion. Why did you refuse to attend?'

'Not your problem. I don't feel like going!'

'What do you mean you don't feel like going?' said aunty, pulling up a chair.

'First, you waste my life because you can't get over your love for her. Then you spend decades posting letters to old addresses and searching for her on Facebook. And now that you can finally meet her in person, after 50 years, you don't want to go! What logic does that hold? Anyway, it's your love, your romance, your reunion and your friends. What do I care?' She said, 'Let me check how long it will be to dinner.'

'What? Aunty knew about it all?' I asked, astounded at her nonchalance.

'What to do, Tara beta, she always catches me at everything. I don't even have the freedom to dream as I choose.'

'But really, is Sunaina the same woman? So then why aren't you going to the reunion?' Dev questioned curiously.

'Yes, she is,' uncle admitted, shaking his head pensively as his gaze drifted towards the valley. 'And now that I've finally found what I'd searched the whole world for, I'm afraid I don't want this 50-year-long fantasy to be shattered by a reality I don't recognize. Sometimes the longing itself becomes sweeter than attainment. Doesn't it?'

From lively dinner, desserts and a game of cards, the house gradually began to quiet down as the lights turned off one by one. Everyone was now asleep, except for uncle, who sat in the living room listening to Shiv Kumar Batalvi and drinking scotch.

Dev and I walked over to his spot, taking our glasses of wine with us.

'Two steps left and three down,' he held out his hand again.

'I remember,' I smiled.

We sat in the clearing once again, overlooking the million scattered lights greeting the mystical night sky.

'Tara, remember the first time we sat here when I told you I'd been looking for that compelling reason which made me stay back.'

'Yes, I remember,' I answered.

'You happen to be that reason, Tara.'

I was a little startled at this sudden admission but not entirely surprised.

'All my life, I denied the existence of love. I was certain love had abandoned me. And on the rebound, I had convinced myself that there was no room for it to return.

Yes, finding compatibility and settling down was one thing, but being in love was unfathomable. Being vulnerable again was unimaginable. And then you came along. As though I suddenly stood face to face with a familiar dream knocking on my heart, albeit a little vaguely. Slowly, over the days and months, the haze lifted and that dream emerged clearer than ever.

My dada used to say that we witness three kinds of dreams in our life—dreams that we see with our eyes wide open. They are our practical dreams, dreams of our conscious mind. Then there are dreams that we create unknowingly. Dreams that silently watch over our deepest desires and express back to us, that what is most meaningful to our existence in our waking lives. These are dreams of our own longing that we do not recognize—the dreams of the subconscious mind.

And then there are the third kind of dreams. Dreams that come floating to us out of nowhere—random, uninvited and unexplained—these are the dreams of our heart speaking to our soul. These are the dreams that leave us with a thirst. A longing for that which we do not know, but which alone can quench it. These are the dreams that we set out to realize upon waking and spend a lifetime hankering after.

You are that third kind of dream, Tara. It was this dream that could never resonate with another heart.'

I sat pondering quietly over his words. After a long pause, and with great difficulty, I began to articulate my thoughts.

'Look Dev, I like you too, but you're single, and I'm divorced with two kids. I have nothing left to give you.'

'Tara, the question is not what someone is capable of giving. The question is what another is capable of receiving. The sun is only concerned with being itself. It doesn't give. It simply allows itself to be. Yet, each day, we receive so much from its presence—light, warmth, life and our very existence.

I don't need anything from you, just be yourself. That's all. I'll draw my joy and my inspiration from it. Tara, I will neither put you on the spot about making any choices nor do I expect my love to be reciprocated. It will neither demand a name, nor a commitment. You're free to explore your own dreams, follow your own longings. What you want, how you want and as long as you want it.

But if your longings ever happen to lead you this way in life, know the doors of my heart and home will be wide open. And if not, I will continue to find my happiness in yours. And that's my problem to deal with, not yours.'

'It's easier said than done, Dev. It's easy to find love but very difficult to lose it.'

'Only when a person is not afraid of losing does he become capable of loving, Tara. Don't worry about me.'

'Thank you, Dev. Thank you for this honour and for all that you've done for me.'

'Tara, a guiding star lends both direction and purpose. Only if you had the slightest idea of what you've done for me, you wouldn't be thanking me.'

We sat together for a long time staring into the empty night—enjoying the comfort, the silence and this strange togetherness.

Slowly, we walked back towards the house.

'May I?' he asked, leaning forward.

I closed my eyes, and he planted a gentle kiss on my forehead.

'Be well, Tara,' he said, placing a hand over my head.

I lay awake for a long time reminiscing his gaze, his touch and his deep love. And this time, I felt loved, without a doubt, without a question.

It was a busy house around the breakfast table.

'Good morning, beta. Perfect timing. Sit, your aunty is making gobi paranthas today.'

'Wow, uncle, that's a real treat!'

'Come,' he offered, pulling out a chair next to him.

'Mehar and Sid, at the table now,' I called.

'We already ate, mom. We want to play outside.'

'Let them play,' said uncle as he turned to me.

'Tara beta, Dev is a good boy,' uncle began speaking. 'And he likes you a lot. Yesterday, you saw that Tej has found someone. He's moved on, why don't you also think about settling down again? Besides, the kids are quite attached to Dev.'

'Uncle, marriage is not for me. And this "love" of yours and I have maintained a very distant relationship. I'd rather not get into something I don't understand.

Besides, Dev's friendship is much too important in my life to lose to something as frivolous as love. And all those feelings and emotions we have no control over.

I mean, my life has just settled. Finally, I've found my stability, my peace of mind and a dependable friend. And finally, I feel somewhat in control. Why would I give all this up?

I have my kids. I have Seerat, my village and my writing. I work hard and I sleep well. I don't want to complicate anything.'

'I can't argue with your reason, beta. No one has won that battle. It's your life, your choices,' uncle concluded with an exasperated sigh.

'Thank you, uncle,' I said as I walked up behind him and held him in a tight embrace.

'You can thank me, or you can thank your heart for being dormant. Never forget, it's like a volcano, Tara. One day it will erupt without notice and all your reason will melt away like smoldering lava that will dictate its own path. You will be helpless.'

'Hmmm… very poetic!' I laughed.

'I'll leave a little early here. Will stop by at Dev's place after dropping the children off to school. I bought him a housewarming gift. I'm sure he'll like it.'

'What did you buy him?' mom asked.

'A set of lanterns and candles. Perhaps, each time he lights it, it will serve as a little reminder of what he's been in my life. It was so dark when he came and how he kindled a warm flame of love and hope.'

'Bhenji,' said Ashok uncle, turning to mom. 'I don't understand your daughter. She cares for Dev so much. They talk all day long. They've taken every step together in the last two years, yet she refuses to accept his love.'

'Just a humble clarification, it's still more understandable than your love, uncle. To my point, it's complicated and unnecessary.'

'I can't win the argument of words with a bestselling author. Do as you please,' he answered, throwing his hands up in the air.

Mom and I dropped the kids off to school.

My phone rang.

'Everything all right?' I asked, speaking into the phone as my heart raced.

'Don't worry, Preeti. I'm on my way. Listen, take care and stay calm. I'll be over soon.'

'What happened, Tara?' mom asked, bearing a worried tone.

'Bittu met with an accident. He's out of danger but still under watch,' I said, growing pale with worry.

'Balwinder, we won't be going to Dev's place anymore. Let's drop mom home and head straight to Amritsar.'

'Rab bhala kare, bhenji,' Balwinder prayed.

I stormed into the emergency room. 'Bittu, doctor saab's son?'

'Madam, he's been moved out of emergency into ward number 3.'

I rushed through the corridors and found everyone gathered around his bed.

Preeti flung into my arms. 'How many times I've asked him to sell this wretched Bullet,' she cried.

'But how did this happen?' I asked.

'He was riding the Bullet, wearing aviators at night. He couldn't see the cow standing in the middle of the road.'

'Oye balle, bhenji, you made it back. Don't listen to their stories. I could very well see the cow. I kept honking, but the cow refused to listen. It was a minor miscommunication.'

I closed my eyes and let out a prayer.

'Don't bother praying here. I'm fine. Sukh naal, we will all go to Darbar Sahib soon.'

'I will offer Rs. 101 in parshaad,' said aunty, 'and get you two to exchange rings right there and then.'

'Oye balle, mummy ji, in that case, this accident should've happened sooner. I wasted so much time for no reason.'

'Fitteh Muh,' aunty chided, as we all shared a laugh.

I spent the later part of the evening with Seerat. She was beginning to write fluently and speak in broken but conversational sentences.

Following a light dinner, I sat on the veranda, looking forward to some quiet time. I walked to the almirah in biji's room and took out a patasa as I looked towards the stars, munching on it.

'Wherever you are, biji and beeja, hope you're watching over us and smiling.'

Walking past the peti, I suddenly remembered the briefcase. It was still in my bedroom closet. I decided it was time to return it to its resting place. As I walked down the steps juggling a glass and my phone in one hand, and the briefcase in the other, my phone went off. The briefcase dropped and papers flew about everywhere.

'Call you later, Dev,' I texted as I rushed to collect the papers scattered about the yard.

As I walked out of biji's room after restoring the briefcase, Premo called out for me. 'Bhenji, you left this piece of paper behind. Not sure if it is of any use,' she suggested looking quizzically at it.

'Oh, let me see,' I extended my hand, taking the paper from Premo.

It was a hand copied Kalaam of Bulleh Shah which read,

O' Bulleh Shah
(Oh Bulleh Shah),
Zeher vekh ke peeta te ki peeta
(What is the point of drinking poison after examining and evaluating it?)
Ishq soch ke keeta te ki keeta
(What good is falling in love after deliberating and dwelling on it?)
Dil de kar dil lain di aas rakhi ve Bulleya
(If you give your heart in the hope of begetting one in return, oh Bulleya)
Pyar eho jeha keeta, te ki keeta
(If such is your love, then have you really loved?)

I read and re-read the Kalaam wondering what Bulleh Shah knew about love to write something so profound. Was this the kind of unconditional love Dev felt too?

With the single piece of paper and a thousand questions resting on my chest, I closed my eyes and drifted off to sleep.

'One day, you too will open your eyes and come looking for me, the way I know, I've been looking for you,' he whispered, disappearing into the darkness.

'Dev, where are you?' I said, looking frantically for him. There was no answer.

'Dev, please come back. Dev, where are you?' Not even an echo of silence returned.

'Dev, why don't you answer me?' I questioned as I stood helplessly among the vastness of open fields.

'He cannot hear you,' said an old man sitting by the edge of a trail.

His white turban, long flowing beard and khaddar shawl wrapped around his shoulders, conveyed age-old wisdom.

'Why not?' I questioned reluctantly.

'Because you call him with your words, not with your heart.'

'But my heart does not speak,' I lamented.

'Then no one can help you,' he said as he stood up and walked away, driving his cattle into the breaking daylight.

'Wait,' I urged as I ran behind him.

'Every heart speaks. Close your eyes and listen. Listen, as it calls a name… A name, it calls…every heart calls a name!'

He began to recite another kalaam as he kept walking away into the morning mist.

> *'Nahin langda vaqt vichore da*
> (The time of separation doesn't seem to pass)
> *Bin yaar guzara kaun kare*
> (Who is capable of spending a lifetime without the beloved?)
> *Duniya to kinara ho sakda,*
> (One can do away with the world and its precious belongings)
> *Yaran to kinara kaun kare*

(But who can ever walk away from their beloved)
Ik din hove te lang javey Bulleya,
(If it was merely the matter of one day, perhaps I could've borne the pain of separation, oh Bulleya)
Sari umar guzara kaun kare'
(Who has the capacity to bear a lifetime without love?)

'Dev,' my heart finally uttered.

The old man was gone, and Dev stood in front of me, leaning closer and closer until his lips brushed tenderly against mine.

I woke up with a jolt and sat upright drenched in sweat, waiting for my breathing to normalize. I took a sip of water and switched on the light. I looked at the silent piece of paper resting by my bedside and prayed to Waheguru until the morning light broke through.

As we sat in the school canteen, sipping tea and catching up over trivial events, a strange pull of my heart seemed to draw me elsewhere. I suddenly felt strangely incomplete and uncomfortably out of place.

The haunting words from the dream pierced my heart like a sharp arrow. 'One day, you too will open your eyes and come looking for me, the way I know, I've been looking for you.'

I tried hard to suppress this echo, but it followed me endlessly from one class to the next. I shut my ears, but what help was that to be? Once I'd heard my heart speak, there was no way to keep myself from listening, just as there was no way to keep it from beating.

'*Duniya to kinara ho sakda, Yaran to kinara kaun kare,*' it repeated.

I rushed out, preoccupied with my thoughts.

'Beeba ji, where are you going so suddenly? Is everything all right?' inquired Master ji as he chased behind me.

'Yes,' I answered as I continued walking faster. 'I'll be back soon.'

Sitting in the taxi, I dialed Mala's number.

'Mala,' I began speaking, 'all along, I have liked Dev because of how I felt when I was with him. But today, after all this while, I suddenly realized that even though I'm not with him, he still continues to be with me. He has become me.

All my life, I kept hiding from love, but love found me after all. Even here, it found me. Love found me, Mala—finally. Even if imperfectly. Even if now. I could reason with myself, but I couldn't argue with my dreams. And my heart—it knew this all along. It had been telling me for years, that which I finally just heard.

I finally heard it—the name that it calls.

Maybe, Ashok uncle was right when he said that loving someone is a choice we have but being in love is not.

I'm on my way to Kasauli.'

'Tara, you finally recognized what we knew all along. Good luck, my little one.'

The sun was mellowing, and the birds fluttered anxiously about, waiting to return to the safety of their nests.

And there Dev was, busy planting his garden, wearing his grandfather's fine yet understated Patek Philippe watch.

'Only you, Dev! Only you could pull these together, the timely and the timeless, the past and the present, the luxury and the grounding…the letting go and the silent pulling.'

He looked up towards me and smiled, 'Hey Tara, you finally made it.'

'Finally, Dev. I made it.'

We walked through the garden into the family room. It was a cozy space with floor to ceiling wrap-around windows and a stunning fireplace centered amid fine leather furniture and earthy galeecha rugs.

'It's beautiful, Dev,' I said, looking around me.

'Some tea?'

'How about a tour of the house first?'

'How about a tour of the only place that will matter the most to you? The library. It's been waiting.'

He led me into a room with an oak ceiling and a winding staircase mounted against the double story bookshelf. A desk, leather chair and a chaise lounge stood in the middle of the room with my shawl hanging over its edge.

I looked towards Dev as he shrugged his shoulders. 'Well, you left it at beeja's, and I decided to keep it as a present for myself.'

'Look at all these books, Dev. This place is heaven. This one is my favourite,' I said, pulling a book off the shelf. 'And this has been on my reading list forever, and this too, and this one.'

Suddenly I stopped. 'Were you keeping a note of all the books I ever mentioned?'

'Of course, I wanted to be ready in case you ever changed your mind.'

Two empty chairs overlooked the wildflower valley with a firepit blazing in front of it. Streams of Edison bulbs crisscrossed overhead, lending a spectacular canopy to the quaint evening.

I looked at the bulbs, and I looked at our wine glasses, reflecting the light as I smiled at how far I'd come.

'Cheers, Dev.'

'Cheers, Tara.'

'I knew you would eventually come. I'm only glad you came much sooner than Sunaina did!' Dev remarked as we laughed our way into the setting sun.

The carefree wildflowers swayed to the pleasant breeze,

surrendering to its flow, blooming cheerfully to their own song, colouring the world in their own joy.

These wildflowers, that exist only to be who they are.

Glossary

100 takke di gal kiti	what you said is 100 per cent correct
aam papad	mango leather
aloo	potato
antakshari	popular singing game
Babaji	God
Badhaiyaan	Congratulations
baghs and phulkaris	folk embroidery of Punjab worn as a traditional attire
baheda	large deciduous tree found throughout India
baithak	lounge
bala tali	calamity averted
bare bhenji	older sister
bas	that's it
beeba munda	good boy
beri	a type of fruit
beta	child
bhabi	sister-in law
bhai saab	brother
bhangra	Punjabi folk dance
bhenji	sister
bhog	concluding prayers

bhutta	corn
bibi ji	madam
biji	grandmother
bindi	a colored mark worn traditionally on the forehead by Indian women
bun-tikkis	potato patty burger
buri nazar	evil eye
chaat masala	tangy spice powder mix
charkha	spinning wheel
chole	chickpeas
chulha	stove
churan	spice candy
darji	grandfather
dharna	peaceful demonstration
dhol	double-sided regional variant of drum
dolus	metal canisters
Ekonkaar	insignia, phrase in Sikhism that denotes one supreme reality
Fitteh muh!	An expression of exasperation and disbelief
gajra	hair accessory made from fresh flowers
galeecha rugs	knotted wool rugs
ghar-ghar	children's game, involves playing 'house'
gidda	a traditional folk dance of women in the Punjab region
gobi paranthas	cauliflower stuffed flatbread
gola	shaved ice

guddi	kites
gulab jamuns	milk-solid-based Indian sweet
Gurbani	Sikh prayer
hai	exclamation of horror, shock, grief, surprise, etc.
Hai Waheguru, tera lakh shukrana	Oh lord, a million thanks to you
hatti	local shop
jalebis	spiral shaped, deep fried Indian sweet
Janam Din Mubarak ho	happy birthday to you
jiju	brother-in-law
Jug jug jeyo	may you live long
juttis	slippers
kadah	holy offering
kadha	metal bracelet
kadhi	savoury yogurt preparation
Kala Khatta	spicy-tangy flavour used in ice popsicles
kamli	silly
kangan	bracelet
karta dharta	benefactor
khaddar	homespun cotton
khes	traditionally woven cotton coverlet
kikkar tree	a thorny tree of the region
kikli	holding criss-crossed hands and twirling with a partner
kinnow	orange varietal

kirana	small, family-owned grocery store
kitthe	where
kurta pyjama	Indian outfit consisting of top tunic, kurta, and bottoms, pyjama
Kush raho	Stay happy
ladoo	sphere shaped Indian sweet
lassi	buttermilk
lungis	cotton cloth wrapped around the waist, worn by men in Punjab
maadi nazar	evil eye
maali	gardener
maasi	maternal aunt
maha yudh	great war
Mahila Mandal	women's group
makki di roti	maize flour flatbread
mama	maternal uncle
manja	cot
Masterani	slighting expression for a teacher
matthis	flaky, deep fried snack
mitti	soil
mogra	Arabian jasmine
morchas	organized march or rally
muklawa	ceremony when a husband comes to take his bride back from her parents' place
mynah	Asian starling that typically has a distinct, loud call

nahar	river
nani	maternal grandmother
nanka	maternal home
O balle!	Hurray!
Oye chup kar!	oh, keep quiet!
paan	betel leaf preparation
paathis	cow-dung cake fuel
pajeb	anklet
panj	five
parantha	fried, and often stuffed, flatbread
parna	turban like head covering
parshaad	holy offering
patase	sugar drop candy
Pathani suit	regional attire
Phantom cigarettes	cigarette shaped candy
pidhi	foot stool
pind	village
Pippal tree	sacred fig, a species of fig native to the subcontinent
pulao	rice preparation
puri	deep fried, round flatbread
puttar	child
Rab bhala/mehar kare!	God bless you
rajais	blankets
rona dhona	crying and mourning
roohafza	a rose flavoured summer drink

roshandaans	combined skylight and ventilating windows, a feature of many traditional homes in North India
rotis	bread
Sadke isde	I sacrifice myself to its wellbeing
sardari	chieftaincy
sarovar	pool
sarson da saag	mustard greens
saunf	fennel seeds
sehra	wedding headdress
shagans	ceremonial gifts
sone di mohar	gold coin
stapu	hopscotch
sukh naal	by His grace
tandoor	clay oven
tayaji	father's elder brother
teen Deviyaan	three Goddesses
thekas	liquor stores
Vakalatnama	letter of legal engagement
Waheguru	term used in Sikhism to refer to God
Waheguru Mehar Kare	May God keep you in his grace